Enrollment Form

☐ *Yes!* I WANT TO BE A *Privileged Woman*.
Enclosed is one *PAGES & PRIVILEGES™* Proof of
Purchase from any Harlequin or Silhouette book currently for
sale in stores (Proofs of Purchase are found on the back pages
of books) and the store cash register receipt. Please enroll me
in *PAGES & PRIVILEGES™*. Send my Welcome Kit and FREE
Gifts -- and activate my FREE benefits -- immediately.

More great gifts and benefits to come.

_____
NAME (please print)

_____
ADDRESS   APT. NO

_____
CITY   STATE   ZIP/POSTAL CODE

PROOF OF PURCHASE ONLY

NO CLUB!
NO COMMITMENT!
*Just one purchase brings
you great Free Gifts and
Benefits!*

Please allow 6-8 weeks for delivery. Quantities are limited. We reserve the right to
substitute items. Enroll before October 31, 1995 and receive one full year of benefits.

Name of store where this book was purchased_____

Date of purchase_____

Type of store:

    ☐ Bookstore   ☐ Supermarket   ☐ Drugstore

    ☐ Dept. or discount store (e.g. K-Mart or Walmart)

    ☐ Other (specify)_____

Which Harlequin or Silhouette series do you usually read?

_____

Complete and mail with one Proof of Purchase and store receipt to:
U.S.: *PAGES & PRIVILEGES™*, P.O. Box 1960, Danbury, CT 06813-1960
Canada: *PAGES & PRIVILEGES™*, 49-6A The Donway West, P.O. 813,
        North York, ON M3C 2E8

"Haven't you ever thought of me?"

Guy asked.

His arrogance infuriated her. "What I've thought about you couldn't be printed."

A muscle moved in his cheek. "I couldn't forget you, either."

"Don't flatter yourself," she said silkily. "My memory of you is like a scar I got climbing over a barbed-wire fence as a kid. I use it to remind myself what happens when I do something really stupid."

"Is that how you remember that night? A stupid mistake?" The moment he looked up at her again, she forgot about everything else. Those eyes took no prisoners. "I remember how your skin felt against mine. What your kisses did to me. How soft and innocently eager you were."

"Then maybe it's true what they say about men like you. You only remember the ones who got away."

"Did you get away, Michaela?"

Dear Reader,

We've got six more exciting books for you this month, so I won't waste any time before telling you all about them. First off, we've got *Caitlin's Guardian Angel*. This book represents a real milestone; it's the *fiftieth* Silhouette title by one of your favorite authors: Marie Ferrarella. It's also our Heartbreaker title for the month, and hero Graham Redhawk certainly lives up to his billing. You'll find yourself rooting for him in his custody battle for the adopted son he adores—and in his love for Caitlin Cassidy, the one woman he's never forgotten.

By now you know that our Spellbound titles are always a little bit different, and Lee Karr's *A Twist in Time* is no exception. Join forces with the hero and heroine as they journey into the past to investigate a murder whose solution is the only way to guarantee their own future. Laura Parker begins a new miniseries, Rogues' Gallery, with *Tiger in the Rain*. Years ago, Michaela Bellegarde brought Guy Matherson the best luck of his life. Now he's forced to turn to her once again—but this time, danger is on his trail. Leann Harris returns with *Trouble in Texas*, the story of a woman doctor "stranded" in a small Texas town. Love with the local sheriff is definitely the cure for what ails her, but, as so often happens, the road to recovery is not an easy one. Historical author Jessica Douglass makes her contemporary debut with *Montana Rogue*, a story of kidnapping, rescue—and romance. Don't miss it! Finally, welcome new author Amelia Autin. In *Gideon's Bride* she tells the story of a mail-order marriage threatened by the bride's deep, dark secret.

So sit back and enjoy all six of this month's Intimate Moments titles, then come back next month, when we bring you six more compellingly romantic books by some of the best writers in the business.

Yours,

Leslie Wainger
Senior Editor and Editorial Coordinator

Please address questions and book requests to:
Silhouette Reader Service
U.S.: 3010 Walden Ave., P.O. Box 1325, Buffalo, NY 14269
Canadian: P.O. Box 609, Fort Erie, Ont. L2A 5X3

TIGER IN THE RAIN

LAURA PARKER

Silhouette®
INTIMATE™MOMENTS®
Published by Silhouette Books
America's Publisher of Contemporary Romance

 **SILHOUETTE BOOKS**

ISBN 0-373-07663-0

TIGER IN THE RAIN

Copyright © 1995 by Laura Castoro

This edition published by arrangement with Harlequin Books S.A.

® and TM are trademarks of Harlequin Books S.A., used under license.
Trademarks indicated with ® are registered in the United States Patent
and Trademark Office, the Canadian Trade Marks Office and in other
countries.

Printed in U.S.A.

Books by Laura Parker

Silhouette Intimate Moments

Stranger in Town #562
*Tiger in the Rain #663

Silhouette Special Edition

The Perfect Choice #137
Dangerous Company #203

*Rogues' Gallery

LAURA PARKER

A Texas native, Laura recently made a "major" relocation. Her office is now on the third floor of a turn-of-the-century Colonial house in northern New Jersey, where she lives with her husband and three children. Laura is often told that she must have the best career around. "After all, my hours are my own. I don't have to get up, dress and commute to work. I'm available if my children need me. I can even play hooky when the mood strikes. Best of all, I get to live in my imagination—where anything is possible."

Chapter 1

Baton Rouge, Louisiana

"So much for our state's illustrious history as a hotbed of pork-barreling and nepotism!" Michaela Bellegarde muttered as she rose from a leather chair in the office of the senior partner in the law firm of Bellegarde, Girod, and Camp.

Laughing at his niece's outrageous words, Leon Bellegarde sat behind the beautifully carved mahogany desk that anchored the generous space of his office. "If you want a career practicing law, you'll have to put your ethics ahead of your ambition."

"Easy for you to say, Uncle Leon." Michaela pointedly eyed the dark wood and cordovan leather furnishings, brass lamps, Turkish carpets and custom-made bookshelves where hundreds of leather-bound volumes stood behind beveled glass doors. "But what good are ethics when I'm broke?"

This time her uncle merely lifted an eyebrow in response.

"Sorry. Guess I'm more on edge than I realized." Michaela subsided back into her chair and impatiently brushed back the curly length of her mahogany-black ponytail that had swung forward across her shoulder. She crossed her denim-clad legs and the eleven slender silver bracelets that cuffed her right wrist tingled faintly as she moved. Her uncle's after-hours summons hadn't given her time to dress properly. Not that she should have bothered. He had just informed her that she'd have to wait a few more weeks before beginning work at the family firm. There were good and practical reasons for the delay. Unfortunately that didn't solve her financial crisis.

Leon Bellegarde rested his laced fingers on the tabletop. "This little demonstration of the Bellegarde temperament wouldn't have anything to do with last weekend's announcement of Daniel Larroquette's impending marriage, would it?"

"What Daniel does hasn't been my business for nine months." Despite her level tone, Michaela blushed. She only wished she had been warned. The announcement of the impending marriage of the state's leading candidate for attorney general had been major media news. The happy couple had been the top local story for all weekend.

"Don't suppose you enjoyed seeing old footage of you and Larroquette on TV. Makes the man seem fickle, to my mind."

"Maybe he has political enemies in the media who hoped to embarrass him," she tossed off casually. She was a very private person. Daniel craved the spotlight. Photo ops were his life while she would do almost anything to remain out of the camera's eye. Part of the reasons behind their breakup had been about just such personal differences.

"Or maybe it was Larroquette's idea," her uncle said censoriously. "The Bellegarde name carries political cache in this state. At least the news said you broke off the engagement." He winked at her. "Former fiancées aren't often portrayed as having good sense and better taste."

As he chuckled, Michaela found herself admiring the senior-most male member of the Bellegarde family. Possessing the sleek and pampered look of a successful man of fifty-five, Leon Bellegarde was seventy-plus years. His silver-white hair threw into stark relief the natural deep tan of his exotic good looks. Bellegardes had settled along this stretch of the Mississippi long before the Louisiana Purchase, absorbing the succession of Creole, Cajun, Bayou Indian, West Indies African, and indentured Irish that came up the river in the following decades. They were a proud and gregarious family and fiercely protective of their own.

Michaela knew her family hadn't liked Daniel though they never directly said so. The quiet smiles that greeted her announcement of the canceled engagement had been the only sign of their feelings on the subject. Yet that subtle persuasion had contributed to her own misgivings.

"I regret the inconvenience our business policies are causing you," Leon Bellegarde continued in his sonorous Southern accent. "Yet, I assure you, the difficulties are momentary."

"I'm not angry, Uncle Leon, just disappointed." In order to avoid accusations of favoritism, her uncle had informed her that he would be interviewing other applicants for the job he promised was hers. "It's simply a matter of timing. I've been unemployed for four solid months. Of course, I spent the summer studying for the bar—"

"Commendable, considering your score," he replied.

"Thank you. But I can't afford to go another month without an income. Even without rent I have expenses. I may have to apply for a cashier's job at the Piggly Wiggly."

"If money is a real concern, I suppose I could advance—"

"No!" Michaela leaned forward with a hand raised in protest as he reached for his wallet. "I don't need charity. I'll manage somehow. Grand-mère won't mind my company a little longer."

A new and tender warmth filled her uncle's face at the mention of the lady. "How is Tante Delphine?" In his gorgeous voice the family's French-influenced name for the Bellegardes' legendary matriarch sounded as elegant as the lady herself. "Corrine and I have been meaning to get out to Belle Isle." He shook his head slightly. "I don't know how the time gets away."

"Grand-mère is fine. You can see for yourself a week from Saturday. At her hundredth birthday party?" Michaela prompted.

"Saturday?" He reached to flip through his daily calendar and then smiled. "Ah yes, it's right here. We'll be there."

His gaze shifted to his phone as a light began blinking. Frowning, he looked up at her. "I'm expecting this call. If you don't mind waiting a moment in the outer office, I'd like to talk with you about a little matter concerning Tante Delphine."

Michaela stood up quickly, certain she knew what the little matter was and wanting to avoid it. "I'd like to, Uncle Leon, but really I can't." She glanced at her watch. It was a little after five-thirty. "If I hurry, I may just be able to convince Yancy to ferry me out to Belle Isle before dark."

She turned briskly away. "See you Saturday a week."

The late October sunshine splintered in glassy slivers that danced on the asphalt as Michaela stepped out into the sultry heat of the afternoon. Despite that heat, a chilling unease settled over her.

"Grand-mère must be working one of her *mo jos*," Michaela murmured, making light of her great-grandmother's reputation as a mystic and healer. The very idea had both enthralled and embarrassed her ever since she had been old enough to understand what that meant. Stranger still was the fact that many people believed in Tante Delphine's supposed powers.

The soon to be hundred-year-old Bellegarde matriarch, known to all the locals as Tante Delphine, had been born in a time and place when doctors were rare. As a folk healer, she had relied on herbal cures learned from her own grandmother to help neighbors. When more conventional medicine came in to replace folk healing, Tante Delphine had retired. Yet many people continued to seek her out for special remedies and potions. Some believed she could cast spells and see into the future. The modern Bellegarde generation thought it was all superstitious nonsense. But no one dared say so.

Michaela had tried to explain away her great-grandmother's incredible intuitive powers as the accumulated wisdom of a shrewd observant soul. Still, there were many instances which mere powers of observation could not explain. So, Michaela found herself sitting on the fence, looking at examples but unwilling to believe in the inexplicable.

She smiled when she spotted the small group of male admirers that always seemed to gather whenever she took her great-grandmother's museum quality 1948 maroon Buick out for a drive.

"Yours?" inquired a young man in an expensive suit.

Smiling, Michaela nodded.

"Don't supposed you'd consider selling her?" asked the man who'd been inspecting the vintage whitewalls.

"No."

She ignored the male glances turned her way as she unlocked the door and slid in. She knew that she, too, had inherited the Bellegarde sultry good looks. Dark-eyed and caramel-skinned with long thick black hair pulled tightly back to reveal her high round forehead, she remained thoroughly feminine even when dressed in jeans and a mantailored silk shirt. A natural reserve kept her from using to advantage her attractiveness.

The man in the suit rapped lightly on her window. When she rolled it down he handed her a business card. "In case you change your mind." He smiled encouragingly. "Or anything."

She accepted it without a word. The fact that she turned down most of the invitations that came her way led many men to believe she was snobbish. What she was was shy.

Within minutes she had gingerly maneuvered the car into the rush-hour traffic. She rotated her shoulders, trying to relax. Most often she enjoyed driving the great old car but as she hit the sun-baked blacktop of Interstate 10 heading upriver, she wished she was driving her dull little compact equipped with air-conditioning. Sadly, her car had dumped its transmission at a stoplight a week earlier.

Michaela sighed. She wasn't going to have the sixteen hundred dollars needed to retrieve it from the mechanic for some time. So far, the only good to come out of her delayed employment was that she'd be living a little longer with Grand-mère at Belle Isle.

The river island, an hour's drive north of Baton Rouge, had been in the family over two hundred years. Now it belonged to Grand-mère Delphine who lived there alone. Yet she couldn't live forever. What would happen to her great-grandmother's beloved island afterward worried Michaela.

She suspected Uncle Leon's little chat would have been an effort to put forward yet again the family's position. Many thought Belle Isle should be sold after Grand-mère died. They weren't the only ones to see the financial possibilities of the property.

Two weeks ago a representative for an international chain of casinos out of New Orleans had appeared uninvited on Belle Isle with plans for an upscale resort that his company wanted to build. Luckily, she had been there to run interference. Afterward, she'd given Yancy strict orders that no strangers be allowed to disturb Grand-mère in the future.

Yet she knew she couldn't hold off reality forever. There was nothing wrong with Belle Isle that a quick infusion of money couldn't cure but she might as well be counting on winning a lottery to get it.

Thoughts of easy money triggered a memory of her one disastrous attempt to make a fast buck. It had ended up being the most humiliating experience of her life. She had been nineteen and full of herself, wanting to show her independence. She'd begged her parents to allow her to change from a state college to a private one but the cost difference was more than they could afford. So, she'd decided to earn the money and surprise them. Two college friends who had spent the previous summer working in Las Vegas had convinced her it was an easy way to make a lot of money fast. So she'd applied and been hired as a blackjack dealer. She could still remember her stunned disbelief when she had discovered the nearly ten thousand dollars she had saved had been stolen by her roommate.

Grand-mère Delphine had always said that when one is lost in the jungle, one should appeal to the tiger for protection. Taking that advice to heart she'd hatched a desperate plot: she would hire a gambler to help her recoup her loss. Not just any gambler, Guy Matherson. Guy Matherson was a tiger in Vegas. Unfortunately, she had forgotten that tigers are carnivores.

Michaela pressed the pedal and the speedometer needle edged up toward seventy. The acutely embarrassing memory refused to go away.

She'd chosen Guy Matherson for the most obvious of reasons, because he was young, successful, and gorgeous. Her private response to him had been elemental—pure female adoration in the face of a rogue male. He was tall with the taut sinewy strength of a street fighter and amazing aquamarine eyes that smoldered beneath a prominent ridge of jet black brows. Dressed in a tux, he looked like a throwback to another era when men looked tough and acted tougher. Yet their isolation hinted at a vulnerability that attracted women by the bushel. Garfield, Cagney, Bogey; images from the late show of quiet men packing equal amounts of malice and charm—that's how she'd thought of Guy. The reality had been traumatic. He'd not only refused to help her, he'd used his hustler's charm and malice to chew her up and spit her out without even working up a sweat.

A blinding slat of late afternoon sunlight sliced in around the edge of Michaela's sunglasses, jolting her out of her reverie. Strange, she hadn't thought of Guy Matherson in years. If his image still held a corner of her adolescent psyche hostage it was only because it was so much better than the reality of the man.

A stranger could easily have missed the turn off the highway onto a narrow farm road which led through cane fields to the river. Michaela barely braked as she swung the heavy maroon car onto the shoulder and then sent it scooting smoothly through the ripening cane break.

By the time the ferry reached Belle Isle the sun had slid below the horizon, turning the sky just above it the ripe red color of a watermelon slice.

"Thanks, Yancy! See you in couple of days!" Michaela waved through her window to the ferryman and then gunned the engine of the car to climb the incline from the ferry dock up onto the bank.

As she crossed the sandbar that made up the western edge of the island, the sharp cranking of cicadas vied with the bass croaking of frogs for dominance. The air was warm and heavily perfumed with the pungent odors of the dying day. Belle Isle was a haven, a place apart from the real world, out of sync with life on either shore. She felt the tug of its sultry allure with every indrawn breath but it didn't calm her edginess.

Fireflies drifted along either side of the dirt road as she drove through the cedar swamp that separated the sand from the fertile grounds of the estate. The tiny flashes seemed to light her way with their green-gold glow. Of course, it was impossible to get lost. The island's only road led to the house.

The old two-story Louisiana plantation-style house was nestled in a semicircle of equally ancient oaks so that a visitor was usually upon it before realizing it. But tonight surprise was impossible. Electricity had been run out to the island by the state of Louisiana half a century earlier though Grand-mère seldom used it, preferring oil lamps and candlelight. Yet the wattage filtering through the trees tonight was extraordinary. Her apprehension increased.

As she reached the edge of the circular drive, her scalp began to tingle. She flicked on her brights and caught the mirror shine of a very expensive late-model car in her beams. In the glare she saw printed along the metallic strip surrounding the license plates the words New Orleans.

"Damn!" She braked hard, sending turf and dust flying out in her wake. She had been right to worry. Yancy had assured her that Belle Isle had had no visitors today but he had been drinking when she stopped by his house to ask to be ferried over. Perhaps he was so drunk he didn't remember. Yancy had a fondness of whiskey that any spare change kept fed. If some unscrupulous agent had bribed Yancy in order to press Grand-mère to sell her property, she would not be responsible for her actions. She slid out from behind the wheel, steeled for a fight.

As she hurried across the dark yard at a near trot, she could hear the voices of the two silhouetted figures sitting on the front gallery. One was Grand-mère Delphine's. The other was a man's, low and well modulated. A stranger's.

Her hands clenched into fists. She couldn't guess how long he had had to plead his case, but she was going to give him the heave-ho before he got in another word.

When she reached the porch she marched up to the pair of peacock-back Victorian wicker chairs that stood in deep shadow and burst into speech. "It's all right, Grand-mère. I'll handle this." She swung around to the man who'd risen to his feet. "I don't know who sent you and I don't care! I want you off this island." She jerked a thumb toward his car. "Now!"

"Why Michaela Françoise Bellegarde," exclaimed Tante Delphine with the slightest inflection of foreign influence in her voice. "Is this any way to greet my guest?"

Michaela turned to the tiny silver-haired woman dressed in a flowing saffron caftan and turban. "I'm sorry, Grand-mère, but I thought I had taken care of this. I don't care what he's told you, you don't have to do anything you don't want to. You didn't sign any papers, did you?"

Tante Delphine rose slowly from her chair to her full height, which was considerably less than five feet, and rested a frail hand on Michaela's arm. "For shame, 'Tite. Will you not behave more graciously to the handsome young man I have been entertaining especially for you?"

"For me?" Thrown off-guard by this, Michaela turned back to the man who stood silently regarding her.

He was a stranger. He wore an expensive suit and tie, and looked for all the world like a yuppie corporate lawyer.

"If you're here about plans for Belle Isle you can forget it," Michaela said ungraciously.

"I'm here to see you, Ms. Bellegarde." He smiled and extended his hand as if she had greeted him most charmingly.

"Why?" Michaela let the word convey her suspicion as she left his hand dangling in the air. She did a rapid mental regrouping. If he wasn't here about Belle Isle then he could be a reporter looking for dirt about Daniel Larroquette. Same song, different verse: he wasn't welcome.

"Are you the same young woman who seven years ago worked as a dealer in Las Vegas under the professional name Kiki?"

Michaela's gaze slipped sideways toward her great-grandmother. No one knew about her summer debacle in Vegas. She'd been too ashamed to tell them. Yet someone had found out about it. Who was it, and why? "Why do you ask?"

The stranger's smile didn't falter as he lowered his arm. "All I need is a confirmation. I have something for you." He turned away and picked up the briefcase that stood by his chair. "If you will open this, I believe it will clear up the mystery of my presence."

Michaela gave the briefcase a considering glance but she didn't take it from him. "What is it?"

"See for yourself, Ms. Bellegarde."

"Very well, if you insist on being mysterious." Michaela took it, surprised by its weight, which dragged her arm down to her side.

"Allow me." The man took it back and set the expensive alligator-skin case on the nearby wicker table and opened the locks. He stepped back and gestured to it. "Please, open it."

With a strange feeling of trepidation, she slowly lifted the lid, half expecting some sort of prank. What she saw was surprise enough. "My Lord!"

"What is it, 'Tite?" Her great-grandmother approached and peeked over the lid of the case. *"Bon Dieu!"*

"It's $100 thousand in cash," the stranger pronounced as cheerfully as a game-show announcer.

Michaela stepped away from the money, wiping her palms along the seams of her jeans. Something was wrong, so terribly wrong she felt her palms pricking with premonition of disaster. "If this is some sort of bribery attempt—"

"It's quite legal, I assure you."

Michaela's gaze swung to meet his. "Don't assure me, Mr...."

"Wilson. Beau Wilson, of the New Orleans firm of Lafayette, Burnes, and Gerard."

"Well, Mr. Wilson of New Orleans, I happen to be an attorney myself, of the Baton Rouge firm Bellegarde, Girod, and Camp." She saw his eyes widen in recognition of the name. "So you may begin by telling me just who you represent."

Beau Wilson seemed incapable of an awkward moment. "I'm glad you asked that question, Ms. Bellegarde. My client was very specific that I mention his name only if you asked for it."

"I believe I've done just that," she said impatiently. "Who is he?"

"Guy Matherson."

The name caught her as unprepared as a slap in the face. "I don't like practical jokes, Mr. Wilson, if that's who you are."

He reached into his pocket for a card. "I can prove it, if you'll just call this number."

Michaela took and studied it. It was a card for the New Orleans firm with Beau Wilson listed as a junior partner. She pocketed it. "I'll admit this much. I once met a man in Las Vegas who called himself Guy Matherson. We had one fifteen-minute conversation. End of story."

"Then the money is yours."

Michaela noticed that her great-grandmother had faded back into the deep shadows of the porch, as if she were trying to remove herself from the proceedings. Did she feel it, too, this ominous sensation like the too still air just before a thunderstorm? "Why would a man offer a near stranger, whom he hasn't seen in seven years, what amounts to a fortune?"

This time Beau Wilson made a point of looking away from her. "Truly, Ms. Bellegarde, I can't say."

"Can't or won't?" He shrugged. "Then answer this. Where is Mr. Matherson?"

His gaze came reluctantly back to meet hers. "I suppose, strictly speaking, he didn't ask me to conceal his whereabouts." Still he hesitated before saying, "He's in St. Jude's Hospital in New Orleans."

This was not what she expected. "Is he ill?"

"Not exactly." To her surprise the unflappable Mr. Wilson seemed decidedly uncomfortable. "I have a short document for you to sign, stating that you received and accepted Mr. Matherson's gift."

"No. I don't accept."

"But, Ms. Belle—"

"If you think you can just foist money from heaven-only-knows where on me without an explanation, you're sadly mistaken. I want an explanation, Mr. Wilson."

"Very well." The young attorney closed his Mont Blanc pen. "Mr. Matherson said I could tell you that the money is your share of the bet you asked him place in a poker game seven years ago."

"But he didn't—" Michaela paused in midsentence. She'd asked Matherson to gamble for her but he had refused. Something more was at the bottom of this. "And?"

Beau Wilson smiled again and this time it was as charming as a Delta breeze on the sultry night. "And Mr. Matherson said he needed to square his last debt."

Suspicion nudged her. "Why is he in the hospital?"

His smile dissolved as he again avoided eye contact. "I'm not at liberty to say."

"Why not?"

"Ms. Bellegarde, that need not concern you in any way. I've come here to deliver your money. I assure you, there are no strings attached."

"No strings?" Michaela took a step toward him. "No strings? This doesn't make sense. I want to speak with Mr. Matherson myself."

"He doesn't expect that." He looked genuinely distressed for the first time. "In fact, I'm certain he wouldn't want that."

"Well that's just too bad," Michaela replied. "Nobody tries to buy my good will without first explaining what it is he thinks he's getting in return."

"This is right." Tante Delphine stepped from the shadows. The light of the night instantly gathered in her jet eyes until they gleamed like those of a creature of the night. "The signs are strong, 'Tite. There is something waiting for you in New Orleans, something good but also dangerous. You know what you got to do?"

Michaela nodded though she did not consider her sense of urgency as an omen of supernatural origin. "I'm sorry about all this, Grand-mère, but I really must go. I'll just pack and few things and then—" She paused. Her car was in the shop.

"You take the Buick, 'Tite. It's a good car. It won't fail you."

"I've plans to spend the night in town but I'd be happy to take you with me back to New Orleans in the morning, Ms. Bellegarde," Mr. Wilson offered.

"No, thank you. I intend to find out what I want to know tonight." Michaela walked over to the briefcase and shut and locked it. "In the meantime you should keep this." She shoved the closed case at him. "At least until I'm satisfied that I deserve it."

"You don't want it?" His slack-jawed gape of wonder was at odds with his sophisticated gloss. "You're a rare person, Ms. Bellegarde. No wonder Mr. Matherson thinks so highly of you."

She jerked in surprise. "Did he say that?"

The young attorney smiled. "He's offering you $100 thousand, isn't he?"

Dr. Ramey scanned the chart he'd opened. "Given the trajectory of the bullet, he shouldn't be alive. The shot from a 9 mm semiautomatic entered just under his ribs, grazed a lung and just missed his heart."

The doctor looked up sharply from the chart at the sound of a gasp. "I'm sorry. Did I upset you, Ms. Bellegarde? You look a little wobbly."

"No, no." Michaela reached casually for the corner of the nurses' station counter. She'd never in her life done anything as silly as faint. Still, she was glad for the counter's support. "It's just that I didn't know, exactly, what was wrong."

The physician recoiled in surprise. "I beg your pardon. I simply assumed that, as the next of kin, you'd been informed by the police. Mr. Matherson was shot."

Shot. The word ricocheted through Michaela's mind. Guy Matherson shot? "Who shot him? Was he—did it involve anything illegal?"

Dr. Ramey's professional mask slipped back into place. "I really couldn't say, Ms. Bellegarde. You'll have to ask the detective in charge of the case. I can only comment on Mr. Matherson's medical condition."

"I see." Michaela clamped down on the tremors of apprehension running just beneath her skin. "Go on, doctor."

He gave her another sharp look before continuing. "Mr. Matherson lost a lot of blood before the paramedics could get to him. Still, he's doing remarkably well. Owing strictly to a bit of luck, he missed serious internal damage."

Michaela nodded but the explanation of Guy Matherson's condition didn't connect with anything in her experience. The words didn't touch her compassion or her fear, but they made her very, very nervous.

She didn't know people who had been shot. The patients she had visited in hospitals were there for events like the birth of a child or for some disorder requiring surgery or treatment. None of those illnesses had violent origins. Her apprehension redoubled. "So, will he survive this?"

The doctor smiled but his eyes remained grave. "I wouldn't want to understate the seriousness of Mr. Matherson's condition. He came out of ICU only twenty-four hours ago. While the indications are that he should recover completely there's always the chance for complications. You may want to speak with Mr. Matherson's physician, Dr. Gallager, in the morning. Still, I'm sure it will lift Mr. Matherson's spirits to see a member of his family tonight. I see by his chart he hasn't listed any next of kin. You may go in for five minutes but don't tax his strength."

"I won't," Michaela assured the doctor and shook the hand he offered her. "Thank you."

She moved down the corridor of the hospital slowly, as if the sound of her heels might attract undue attention. She had made the drive to New Orleans in a little over three hours. It was midnight, well past visiting hours. After being refused entry, she had snagged the arm of a doctor who, out of compassion, decided to talk to her after she lied and told him she was a member of Guy Matherson's family. She didn't know why she had done that. She could as easily have waited until morning, like any normal person, and saved the need for deceit. But she was compelled by an urgency that would not be denied. Grand-mère would say a devil was riding her. She decided that this particular devil's name must be curiosity.

She knocked softly at the door bearing Guy's name. When she didn't hear a reply, she pushed it open. She simply wanted to look at him to verify that this was the man she remembered. Perhaps it would be better if he was asleep.

The hospital room was dim. A curtain was pulled halfway around the bed to shield it from the door. She stepped past it and looked at the figure on the bed.

The single narrow beam of light above the bed seemed blindingly bright. For a moment his face was obscured by its halo. She moved closer, blinking against her fuzzy vision and then paused to stare.

She recognized that face, the features broadly chiseled into equal parts of beauty and brutality. Oh Lord! she thought, a little panicky. It didn't seem possible. How was it possible? Of all people . . . She felt the blood drain from her face and then return with a force that made her cheeks sting. It was *Guy Matherson.*

He hadn't changed, at least not in ways the passing of seven years should have changed a person. Even asleep he still looked lean and hungry, a man who had yet to be satisfied by any taste that life had offered him. His thin upper lip was slightly lifted in a sneer. Yet the soft fullness of the lower forced on her memories of long, slow, wet kisses that had lingered in her emotional register for months afterward. Malice and charm, Guy Matherson still packed that lethal combination.

The last time she'd seen him he'd been dressed in evening wear. Tonight he wore a wrinkled hospital gown open at the neck and a sheet pulled up to his waist. His curly black hair, cut shorter on the sides than she remembered, formed damp half-moons at his brow. He was in need of a shave. There were damp patches on his gown front, as though he had been sweating. No, that must be wrong. Guy Matherson never sweated. He wasn't like other men. He didn't worry, or fear, or hurt... or give a moment's thought for anyone else.

His eyes fluttered. Michaela didn't move but suddenly she wished she'd stood closer to the door. Then Guy Matherson was looking at her with those extraordinary eyes, twin flashes of aquamarine between black lashes. He didn't even look surprised.

"Hello, Michaela." His voice was the same, a rough low-pitched purr. His hand moved on the sheet, the IV in the crook of his arm making his movements awkward as he lifted his hand toward her.

Michaela thought she saw uncertainty enter his expression when she did not immediately respond. She rejected the idea as only a projection of her own wariness. But she was no longer nineteen. He couldn't best her by intimidation. She put out her hand.

As his warm fingers closed a little too tightly over hers he said without irony, "It's been a long time."

Chapter 2

"Have a seat."

"Thank you," Michaela said, relieved by his polite suggestion. She wanted a few minutes alone with this man who was watching her with unnerving interest. Yet as she looked around for a chair she realized he hadn't let go of her hand. She felt his fingers play over her silver bracelets and turned back to him with a questioning glance.

"You look upset, Michaela. Or should I say Kiki?" His voice moved across her thoughts like a bow on violin strings. Every nerve in her body vibrated. Again his long forefinger stroked her bracelets. "I suspected you lied about your name. Still..."

He paused and frowned. He reached up and flattened his left hand against his side. She wondered how much discomfort he was in and if he had been a victim of random violence—or had he earned that pain? Guy Matherson was a dangerous man. She had always known that. Guy Matherson was a gambler. He lived a dangerous life. She knew that, too. But to have been shot...

The moment he looked up at her again, she forgot about everything else. Those eyes took no prisoners. "I thought you were more real than the others."

She didn't have to ask what *others*. She knew he was referring to the many women who'd paraded through in his life that summer seven years ago. But she wasn't one of those. She'd run away in time. "I'm quite real, Mr. Matherson, I just wanted to make certain you are."

"You can see for yourself." His fingers tightened on hers. Did he think she would flee or was he just trying to unnerve her with a display of male dominance? "I'm real enough."

"Right." Michaela tossed her handbag onto the chair she couldn't reach and then turned to face him, her interrogating lawyer's expression in place. "A Mr. Wilson came to see me tonight carrying enough cash to choke a full-grown gator. He said you sent it to me. I want to know why."

"Didn't he tell you?" This time his voice sounded weaker, less certain of its register. He didn't resist when she twisted her wrist free of his slackened grasp. "We have unfinished business, you and I. A history."

She folded her arms across her chest, the action lifting, into more prominence, the shapely breasts she knew he had been casually perusing since the moment she had entered the room. "We don't have a history," she said shortly, drawing his gaze a reluctant eight inches higher to her face. "We had a run-in. Check your rap sheet. It'll be listed under misdemeanors."

He laughed, a coarse hollow sound cut off almost instantly by a grunt of pain as he clutched his side.

She moved closer, a frown ridging her brow. "Are you all right?"

When he met her gaze his eyes were dark with pain. "Why don't you check and see?"

Michaela cautiously bent closer as he lowered the white sheet to his hips with his left hand and then pulled up his hospital gown. Ignoring the fact that he obviously wasn't wearing underwear, she concentrated her gaze higher. The

large square dressing taped to the lower left half of his chest
was pink with seepage but not bloody. "The bandage needs
changing," she said as casually as possible. She shouldn't be
sharing intimate moments with a dangerous stranger who
had taken a bullet.

She moved away from the bed. "Now, are you going to
answer my question? What's the money for?"

"Haven't you ever thought of me?" he replied, again ignoring her question.

His arrogance infuriated her. "What I've thought about
you couldn't be printed."

A muscle moved in his cheek. "I couldn't forget you, either."

"Don't flatter yourself," she said silkily. "Your memory
is like a scar I got climbing over a barbed wire fence as a kid.
I use it to remind myself what happens when I do something really stupid."

"Is that how you remember that night? A stupid mistake?" His voice was pitched so low she took a step closer
in spite of her reservation. He closed his eyes, as if too weary
to speak again but he did. "I remember how your skin felt
against mine. What your kisses did to me. How soft and innocently eager you were."

She stared at his smug expression, wishing she had an ar-
senal of withering retorts at the ready. "Then maybe it's true
what they say about men like you. You only remember the
ones who got away."

"Did you get away?" What might have been a smile
softened his features though his eyes remained closed.

Michaela never knew what she might have replied. The
words went right out of her head as the door opened. She
turned toward it in relief, hoping that it was the night nurse
coming to toss her out.

The first thing she saw edge past the door was a short rod
like the end of a mop handle. And then she saw a hand.
Even as she shook her head in disbelief her brain was telling her that it was *not* a mop handle but a *gun barrel* and

that the hand she saw was wrapped around the butt and trigger.

She screamed, screamed louder and longer than she had thought possible. The sound echoed around the room even as she dove for the floor. She hit her chin painfully on the metal edge of the bed, her movements made awkward by muscles locked by fear. And then the door swung shut.

"What the hell!"

She looked up from the floor the see Guy sitting up in bed, one arm tucked protectively to his damaged side while the other grasped the bed rail as he glared down at her.

"I saw—" Michaela took a deep breath. "There was someone at the door with a gun!"

"I've told you repeatedly what I saw." Michaela sat in the hospital lounge flanked by two detectives. "A hand, a gun barrel, that's all."

The man on her right tapped his pencil impatiently against his pad. "You're certain?"

"Of course I'm certain!" Michaela surged to her feet, spilling a little of the coffee someone had pressed into her hands during the past half hour. She concentrated on the brown drops which marred the shiny white floor. "I know what I saw. I'm not the hysterical type. I don't start at shadows. The man had a gun. I screamed and he ran."

"How do you know it was a man?" asked the detective on her left. He wore a brown plaid blazer while his partner wore blue serge.

Michaela sat down and shut her eyes and began massaging her brow with her free hand. How did she know? "I saw a shoe tip, a man's shoe, inside the doorway."

"You're doing fine, Ms. Bellegarde," said Blue Serge. "We got a better description of the intruder from one of the desk nurses. We just need your impressions to confirm it."

Michaela lifted her head from her hand. "Confirm what?"

"That Mr. Matherson's attacker isn't finished with him yet," answered Brown Plaid. "Would you mind explaining why you were here visiting at this hour?"

"Certainly not. I'd just come in from out of town, that's all, and thought I'd drop by to see a sick friend."

"At midnight, Ms. Bellegarde?" Brown Plaid was smiling at her in a way that made her very unhappy. "I understand you're not related to the patient. Why did you say you were?"

"I lied," Michaela said contritely and wished she hadn't stooped to the petty deceit. "It was past visiting hours and I wanted to see Mr. Matherson because I was in town only for the night. I didn't even know about an attempt on his life until Dr. Ramey told me he'd been shot."

She pulled one of her uncle's business cards from her purse and turned the full power of her stare on Brown Plaid as she handed it to him. "I'm an attorney. You may place a call to my uncle, Leon Bellegarde, if you think it's necessary."

Brown Plaid took the card and smirked as he read it. "I don't think that'll be necessary." He passed it on to his partner with a lifted eyebrow. "Is your relationship with Mr. Matherson professional?"

"I think you'd better ask him that question," Michaela replied, hoping to avoid what were certain to be more difficult questions about her relationship with the man who'd been the target of a bullet twice in as many days.

"I don't think that will be necessary," said Blue Serge.

Feeling that she'd gotten back control of the situation, Michaela decided to ask a few questions of her own. "I'm curious. Why would anyone want to kill Mr. Matherson?"

Brown Plaid smirked. "You'd better ask your friend. And then you can tell us."

Michaela frowned. "I don't understand."

"Mr. Matherson has been what you might call uncooperative," Blue Serge supplied in answer. "He says he doesn't know who would want to kill him or why."

"I see." Michaela suddenly wished she had stayed up-river, had minded her own business, had sent Beau Wilson packing before he'd been able to get a word out. People who were shot had not been engaging in what she would call ordinary events. People were shot in crimes of violence, because someone wanted them out of the way—dead.

It didn't take much imagination to dream up reasons why someone might want to shoot a gambler. None of them made her feel any more at ease. What they did was frighten her half to death. Someone had risked coming into the hospital to shoot a man who had already been shot. That someone wanted Guy Matherson dead. That, in turn, made her want to be as far away from him as possible. "Is there any chance the man will try again?"

"There's no need to worry," Blue Serge replied. "We've ordered around-the-clock police protection for Mr. Matherson."

"That is, unless you have reason to think you're in danger as well," Brown Plaid added with what seemed undue relish. "Do you?"

Michaela shook her head then spied Dr. Ramey striding toward her. "Mr. Matherson would like to see you," he said when he reached her.

Michaela stood and backed away even as she spoke. "I don't think so. I'm really tired. I've had enough."

"I understand your concern, Ms. Bellegarde, but he's not being what I'd call a model patient. It might help get his pulse rate down if you'd just show him you're okay."

But I'm not okay, Michaela wanted to shout. *I could have been killed tonight!*

"I suppose I could stick my head in the door," she heard herself say against her own better judgment. As her feet carried her toward the room a second time, she couldn't believe she was doing the opposite of what every impulse for self-preservation urged her to do.

This time his room was a blaze of lights. The things she had missed before—the monitors, IVs, the catheter bag, and the slightly gray cast of Guy Matherson's skin—couldn't be ignored. The man was gravely ill, had nearly died. Yet when he saw her, the pallor left his face and the daze disappeared from his eyes.

"You saved my life." He said the words slowly, carefully.

"I don't know about that." Michaela tried but failed to find the courage to approach him. Earlier tonight, she had felt an instant connection with the man in that bed. Now under the unforgiving blaze of medical lighting, he looked exactly like what he was, a stranger, someone she knew nothing about.

"I didn't see him." The momentary silence was interrupted only by the sound of his heart monitor, the sounds of life. "If you hadn't been here I'd be dead."

Michaela pushed the realization away before she could accept it. It was much too awful, too scary, too real. "I'm not certain I didn't just make a fool of myself."

"No." His voice was huskier than before, a mere murmur of words. She edged closer to hear him. "You were here when I needed you. Amazing. I thought I was dreaming." The smile that lifted the corners of his well-shaped mouth was more provoking than it had any right to be under the circumstances. "I should have known. You always bring me luck."

Michaela didn't know that to say to that. She reminded herself that he must be heavily sedated. Sitting up and reaching to punch the alarm button on one of his monitors had probably cost him whatever ground he had gained since entering the hospital. She hadn't caught much of what the doctors had said as they came rushing in in the aftermath of the alarm and her cries. They had been shouting about cardiac arrest and Code Blue. Then she had launched into her hysterical tale about a gunman and a murder attempt. That stopped the life-saving attempts but not before Guy had been manhandled in an effort to restart his still-beating heart. She could tell from the white line about his mouth that he was still in a great deal of pain. The only feeling in her at the moment was a great desire to escape.

She resettled the shoulder strap of her purse as she side-stepped back toward the door. "Now that all the shouting's over, I really must go."

"Wait. There's something I need you to do." He groaned softly as he reached out for the pad and paper on the table nearby.

"I'll get that." Michaela crossed over and picked up the articles. She started to hand them to him then realized that she was behaving badly. He looked as helpless as a day-old fawn and all she could think about was her own needs. "Would you like me to take notes for you?"

"Better than that. You can help me get out of here."

Michaela's gaze lifted from the pad she held with pen poised. "You've got to be kidding?" His lips thinned in annoyance but he didn't say anything. "You're serious." She let the hand holding the pad fall to her side. "You need to be in the hospital. Dr. Ramey says you're lucky to be alive."

His vivid blue gaze met hers and there was nothing helpless about the look in them. "I won't stay that way unless I get out of here, now."

She carefully placed the pad and pen back on the table. "I can't help you."

He reached for them and she pushed them into his grasp but made certain their fingers did not touch. She saw him wince and heard his groan as he propped the pad on his stomach and then tried to write while holding the pad still with the same hand.

She reached out to steady the pad for him. "I know you're upset, Mr. Matherson, but be reasonable." She kept her tone matter-of-fact. "The police have assured me that you'll be protected with an around-the-clock guard."

But he wasn't listening, he was busy writing. After a moment he tore the page off and handed it to her. "Call this

man and tell him where I am and why. Then tell him I'll be
in touch as soon as I've gotten out of here."

Michaela stared at the paper as if it were going to bite her.
"I won't do it. Somebody's trying to kill you. If I get any
further involved, he might decide to take a few shots at me
for good measure."

She saw by his expression that this possibility hadn't before occurred to him. "You're right," he said after what she
read in his face as a quick recalculation. "You need to get
out of here. Leave the hospital. Use a public phone. Just tell
Sam where I am. Tell him I'm about to get out. I'll call him
when I do."

"You mean you're going to try to leave on your own?"

His smile wasn't up to full wattage but it still had the
power to charm. "You're a smart girl."

"And you're an idiot."

"Oh, and take the money, Kiki. You earned it."

Michaela hesitated, rocking one boot heel as she sup-
ported her weight on the other. This was her cue to leave but
she couldn't just walk out. "You never said how or why I
earned it."

"I don't have time to explain." He looked away, sounding more weary with every second. "Let's just say I'm set-
tling an outstanding debt."

"Right!" Stubborn bullheaded idiotic male! Why was she
worried? There were doctors and nurses and even a police-
man between Matherson and the rest of the world. If no
unauthorized person could get in this room then he certainly couldn't get out. "Goodbye, Mr. Matherson."

He turned his head toward her. "Thanks, Kiki. Looks like
I still owe you one."

Michaela made it all the way to her car in the under-
ground garage before the shakes started. Once the car door
was closed and locked, her hands shook so badly she had to
grip the steering wheel to steady herself. Even then her teeth
chattered and her knees knocked. Cold sweat beaded up on
her brow and then trickled down her neck and back. Dizzi-

ness spiraled through her. Weak and sobbing, she leaned her head against the steering wheel and took several deep breaths.

After a few minutes passed she knew she wasn't going to be sick. Yet she was in no condition to drive out of the parking lot, not to mention all the way back to Baton Rouge. Several more minutes passed before she felt able to hold up her head.

Finally she sat up and groped around on the dark front seat until she found her purse. She opened it and pulled several tissues from the pack she carried. After dabbing her face dry, she released a few buttons of her shirt and whisked her neck and bosom. She had drenched her shirt, something a lady was never supposed to do. But a case of nerves didn't take into account gentility, Michaela decided with a returning flicker of her humor.

She flicked on the overhead light and then reached for her compact and lipstick. As she did so, she forced herself to think logically. She was perfectly fine. Perfectly safe. She had cried out before she saw the gunman's face. Which meant he may have bolted before he saw hers. He must have thought she was a nurse checking on her patient. He had taken a great risk in coming to the hospital yet he hadn't been so reckless or single-minded that he was tempted to kill an innocent bystander in order to get to his target.

"Which means you are safe," she said to her image in her compact mirror. Only Guy Matherson's life was on the line.

She closed the compact after replacing her lipstick then spritzed on her favorite perfume, White Gardenia. It was a protective gesture. The scent always made her feel more attractive and that meant she felt more like herself. She needed a little normalcy very badly at the moment. As she was tucking her things back into her purse, her bracelets snagged on a piece of paper. It was the note Guy had given her.

She held it up to the light. The letters were scrawled and barely legible but she made out the name Sam and a phone number. She had not promised to make the call but it

seemed little enough for her to do for him. It would be a
simple matter to go back into the hospital lobby and make
the phone call. Perhaps this Sam would be able to persuade
Matherson to stay in the hospital where he belonged. Then
too, by the time she was done making the call, her nerves
might have settled enough so that she would no longer be a
driving hazard.

She recrossed the parking garage floor at a rapid clip, glad
to see a security guard stationed within hailing distance. She
stepped into the elevator and punched Lobby.

The lobby lights were dimmed for after-hours but luckily
the public phones were located in an alcove just off the bank
of elevators.

Michaela put in her coin and dialed. The phone rang six
times before an answering machine picked up.

"This is Matherson. State your business." The statement
was dry to the point of rudeness. Much like the man himself, Michaela mused. She debated the merits of leaving a
message on Guy's own answering machine then the beep
sounded. "I'm calling Sam," she said, sounding foolish in
her own ears. "Guy says to tell you he's okay and that he'll
be in touch very soon."

She hung up before she remembered that she hadn't told
Sam where Guy was or why. But then, she wasn't even certain Guy had given her the right number. Perhaps he'd been
so spaced out on painkillers he had given her the wrong
number. Oh well, she had tried. She might even try again
once she was safely out of town.

She turned back from the phones to the hallway just as an
elevator arrived with a chime and the doors parted. She
didn't have to wonder what was wrong with the man inside.
The man staring back at her from its interior was Guy
Matherson.

He was braced against the back elevator wall, hands
splayed out along either side, his head hanging slightly forward. He had on trousers and dress shoes but no socks. His
belt was unfastened and his zipper was half open. His shirt

hung loose and was buttoned incorrectly so that one tail hung lower than the other. He looked like a man who'd been on a three-day drunk. And then he made a terrible guttural sound as he stepped forward to stop the doors from closing on him.

Michaela dashed across the distance and shoved her arm into the shrinking opening. The doors sprang instantly apart and she stepped inside.

"Are you mad?" she exclaimed as Guy Matherson staggered back against the wall with a groan of pain.

His face contorted grotesquely and then his eyes opened, watering with tears of agony. "Stay out of this!" he warned in a horrible voice.

"Oh, right!" Michaela stared at him, more angry than she could remember being in years. He had no right to drag her into his mess. She wanted no part of it. She didn't want anything to do with him. She punched the Garage button.

As the elevator began to descend, she moved toward him. She worked quickly and methodically for there was no time to think about what she was doing or why. She shoved his shirttail into his open fly, being careful not to touch his bandage, and then hiked up his zipper. She didn't let herself think about where she was touching him or even what she was touching. Then she ran his belt through the buckle and cinched it. She was on her knees tying his shoelaces when the doors opened on the garage level.

She rose to her feet and tilted her head back to look him in the eye. "Can you do this?"

"Sure, angel." The look of gratitude in his aquamarine eyes melted her heart—or perhaps it was her brain. It seemed that nothing inside her was solid anymore.

She slipped her shoulder under his right armpit. He hadn't seemed a heavy man until she tried to bear his weight. His lean physique hid a frame of iron, she decided as she staggered forward out of the elevator. He was a full head taller than she. Though he tried valiantly to support himself with one arm wrapped around her shoulders and the other locked protectively to his injured side it was tough going.

She thought they must look like a pair of sailors on the town as they swayed and staggered toward the Buick. She wondered fleetingly if security would stop them. They looked very suspicious. But when she waved at the man in the booth, he merely waved back. Nonsensically, she wondered why he didn't come out to offer his aid. She definitely needed it.

They got no more than ten feet from the elevator when Guy suddenly slumped against her. It was all she could do not to buckle under his weight.

Desperate to keep him from falling she swung them toward a nearby cement support post and shoved his back up against it.

She heard him bite off his cry of pain as the impact jarred him from head to toe.

"Oh, I'm sorry," Michaela whispered miserably as he groaned with the effort to stay upright.

He grasped her tightly about the shoulders and leaned closer until his lips were warm against her brow. "You smell good," he said thickly. "Feel even better."

"Don't," Michaela responded in an angry whisper edged with embarrassment. "Maybe we should just go back. We'll send down a stretcher for you."

The look in his eye belied the pain and weakness she knew he felt. It was implacable, unemotional, immutable. "I'm not going back. But you shouldn't get any more involved," he said softly then released her shoulders so that she would swing fully around and face him. "Just call me a cab."

"You're a cab!" Michaela actually giggled though he looked as if he would have liked to strangle her. Nerves were making her giddy. "OK, we haven't got time to debate the various degrees of my acts of idiocy tonight. Someone's going discover your absence any second now. Do you want my help or not?"

He shook his head as if to clear it then looked at her. His need was so stark he didn't have to say anything. "I can't ask anything of you. I don't have the right."

Michaela experienced a moment of misgiving as those black-engulfed blue eyes met hers inches away. Once in a moment of dire need she had asked him to help her. He had refused. Nothing he'd said or done so far implied he had changed in any way. But she could not walk away from anyone in distress. She supposed that was the difference between them.

"Stay right here. I'll bring the car around."

She turned and ran toward the Buick before she could change her mind, be sensible, or act responsibly. She was certain she would have turned him down if he'd asked for her help. But—damn him!—he hadn't. Whatever happened now would be all on her head.

It took under two minutes to bring the car around to where he stood supporting himself. Yet she could see, as she approached him, what every second had cost him. The Guy Matherson she had known had been very careful of his appearance yet now his shirt was sweat-sodden. As she reached out to help him, his perspiration-soaked shirt dampened her blouse where he embraced her. Beneath it, his skin was hot, scalding her shoulder and breast where his torso pressed along hers. In the bright lights of the garage she saw his profile stiffen with pain as she urged him the few steps to the car. Her eyes lingered a telling moment on his sensual mouth. She hadn't been this close to him in seven years but her reaction was the same. She felt in emotional jeopardy.

She murmured angrily to herself as she led him past the open door on the passenger's side. Nothing had occurred between them that she couldn't have told a stranger about without blushing. So why was she unable to think of anything but the pressure of his hard sweating body draped against hers and the clutch of his fingers under her rib cage just beneath her left breast? Why was she miserably happy that she was here to help him? The several shocks of the past few hours must be affecting her mind.

She angled her body so that she could lower him onto the car seat. Guy sank down heavily onto the vintage leather, the weight of his body pulling her down beside him. For a moment he held her close even as she tried to squirm away. "You're making a big mistake," he whispered against her ear.

"Let me go!" Michaela snapped because she was certain he was right.

He released her and tried to lift a leg into the car but paused in midmotion, issuing a sharp grunt in response to pain.

"Let me help you." Michaela reached for his leg but he shifted sharply away from her.

Guy grimaced as he leaned back against the seat. "I just need to rest," he said in a tight voice.

She reached up to smooth the black curls from his brow. "You're sweating something awful," she said and grabbed up the tissues she had used herself. As she daubed his face she gazed down into his light eyes darkened by pain. Whatever the doctor had given him was strong. His pupils were wide open. "You need medical attention."

That statement seemed to focus him. His expression became almost tender. "Are you certain you want to stay mixed up in this?"

"Of course I don't," she responded in a spurt of honesty. "I don't know you and I don't like your playmates."

"Right." She saw him make some mental adjustment and then he reached for the top of doorframe and tried to lift himself off the seat. A sudden stricken look of surprise came into his face, not so much pain this time as absolute stunned amazement. His lips moved and a whisper escaped. "Oh, sh—!" His hand fell from the doorframe as he slumped against her.

"You need help there, ma'am?"

Michaela swung her head around to find the security guard standing behind her. "Oh, yes." She knew she had to sound convincing. "I don't know what they gave my husband for pain in the Emergency Room but they said it would make him drowsy. I guess it worked faster than we expected."

"You want me to call the ER?" The gray-haired man squinted as he bent closer to get a better look at Guy.

"Oh, I don't think that's necessary. I could use your help in getting him in the car."

"Sure thing."

The guard helped her shift Guy back onto the seat and she propped his head against the seat back. Working quickly, she lifted first one and then the other of his legs into the car and then reached across him to secure his seat belt, the only new addition to the car in nearly fifty years. Despite Guy's one murmur of protest, he didn't say anything that would betray his real condition.

"This is really nice of you. Thanks," Michaela said by way of acknowledgment as she hurried around to the other side of the Buick and slid in under the wheel. She gunned the engine and took off at a pace that made the tires squeal. She knew it wouldn't be long before the search for the missing patient began. While she wasn't certain she was exactly breaking any laws by helping a patient leave a hospital without discharge, she didn't want to wait around to find out.

Minutes later, as she sat under a street lamp waiting for a red light to change, she realized she didn't know where to take her passenger. She looked across at him. The lines of strain in his face had eased. His color was better. His lids smoothly closed on a fringe of sooty lashes. He was sleeping. A daunting presence when his eyes were open, she had never before seen Guy Matherson look helpless or vulnerable. He seemed more human, more approachable.

An inconsequential thought crossed her mind. How many women had watched him as he slept beside them in the aftermath of lovemaking, and felt that for a few hours their worlds were complete? She suspected they had all learned the moment was a mirage. One had only to encounter his sneer and depreciating gaze when he was awake to know that Guy Matherson was a loner, his only interests his own. So why was she voluntarily tying her immediate future to his? Was it possible she was jeopardizing her life for the helpless look in a pair of aquamarine eyes?

Her troubled gaze encountered inky chest hair feathering out through the opening of his shirt. Beneath that shirt was a white bandage. Not everyone liked Guy Matherson.

That thought sent a sudden chill through her that had nothing to do with the breeze streaming through the open windows. She had felt an ominous sense of pending trouble ever since she had left her Uncle Leon's offices. She had thought perhaps Grand-mère was ailing. Now, she suspected the warning had been for herself. Was it a rare flash, like Grand-mère's legendary gift for fortune-telling, or good old common sense?

Guy's eyes opened. He blinked several times. Finally he turned his head slowly toward her as if it were a very heavy weight. "You stayed." His voice was low and harsh, a dry whisper.

Because she knew he didn't have a good grip on consciousness, she leaned close to whisper in his ear. "I need some help. Where do you want me to take you?"

His hand grasped her arm tightly just above her row of silver bracelets . "Don't...leave...me."

Michaela experienced a moment of misgiving as those black-engulfed blue eyes met hers three inches away.

She bent forward and brushed her lips against his hot cheek without thinking of the implication. "I won't desert you. I promise. I'll see that you're safe."

"Safe." He mouthed the word as if the sound had a taste as well as texture. His head nodded toward hers, the stubble on his chin grazed her cheek, and then his lids fell shut.

"No. Wait!" She touched his face but he didn't respond.

The car behind her blew its horn to signal that the light had changed. Rattled, she scooted back under the wheel and put the Buick in gear.

She heard Guy grunt as the car jerked forward under her unusually clumsy shifting. The uniquely male sound reminded her that even wounded he was first and foremost a man. She knew that, had known it from the very first moment she faced Guy Matherson seven long years ago.

Chapter 3

Las Vegas—seven years earlier

Michaela groaned in frustration as her thermal cup cracked and leaked the dregs of cold coffee onto her sequined heels. Maybe it was a sign that she should give up. She glanced at her watch. It was a little after seven a.m. She had been waiting two hours. Her eyes felt gritty. Her feet ached from the punishment of working an eight-hour shift in four-inch heels. Within the artificial world of Las Vegas casinos, one lost all sense of time. She had been faintly surprised to walk out and discover the pale light of another desert dawn pinkening the sky.

She tossed her leaking cup into a nearby trash receptacle then stood up and stretched. She ignored the bellhops who'd been surreptitiously watching her. Hanging around in the lobby of a hotel in a tight-fitting sequined gown encouraged the wrong kind of speculation. She should definitely go home. No, that was exactly what she would have to do if she couldn't replace the money she'd been saving for her college tuition.

"Stupid, stupid," she whispered as she subsided onto the hard uncomfortable sofa. If only she hadn't boasted to her roommates, all relative strangers who lived together out of expediency, about how she had saved nearly ten thousand dollars during the summer. A call from her bank the day before had shattered her belief in human nature. She went in to learn that someone had forged her name and wiped out her savings account. Her money was gone and, when she got back to her apartment, so was her roommate, Sherryl.

Michaela couldn't believe her own gullibility. What was worse, she couldn't tell anyone. She'd lied to her parents, saying she was working in Vegas as a secretary while in fact she'd been hired as a dealer. They had no reason to doubt her for they were living in Germany, far enough away not to even visit. Now, all she had to show for her efforts were ten one-hundred-dollar chips that a major jackpot winner had impulsively lavished on her as he left the casino the night before. It was a beginning, but it was going to take a miracle to recoup her future.

Though she'd spoken to him only once before when he'd approached her table her first night on the job, she'd been conscious of Guy Matherson for three solid months. He was flat-out gorgeous. No woman he passed was immune from taking a second look. If she'd been more sophisticated, or less shy, she might have tried her luck with him. As it was, she had stood back in mute admiration. Of all the rumors about Guy Matherson, one was the most persistent and therefore probably true: he had nerves of steel. While most professional gamblers developed pleasing personalities, Matherson remained a loner who gambled with the dispassionate yet single-minded intensity of a physician performing brain surgery. He was said to be extraordinarily, intimidatingly intelligent. Those who followed such things believed Guy would be one of the few to make it big. He had the brains, and the hunger, and phenomenal luck.

Michaela glanced around the seedy hotel lobby and repressed a shudder. Matherson must be down on his luck at the moment. Maybe it would make him more sympathetic to her situation—maybe.

The bellboys, lounging by the door, suddenly came alert, telegraphing their interest in an approaching guest. Even before she saw him, she knew who it must be.

Guy Matherson waved away the young men who inserted themselves into his path with anxious-to-please smiles. The admiration on their faces didn't surprise her. There was no denying Guy Matherson's unique physical attraction.

His curly black hair was not softened by shades of brown but was truly blue-black. The highly arched brows, prominent nose, jutting chin, and tender-tough mouth all belonged in a package marked Too Hot to Handle. Even if she hadn't heard the rumors, she would have guessed that beneath that handsome exterior beat the heart of a predator. He looked about as cuddly as a Bengal tiger.

When he paused halfway across the lobby to retrieve a cigarette from his jacket pocket, his slow deliberate movements betrayed a trace of weariness. This sense of his mood surprised her. Unlike her great-grandmother, her ability to read strangers was limited. Yet she knew without a doubt that he had lost tonight, and lost big. There'd be no penthouse suites for a while. Looking at him she thought he just might be the loneliest man in the world. Or, maybe he was just broke. Then she realized that he was moving toward her. This was her moment.

She moved to intercept him. "Mr. Matherson, may I speak with you?"

She thought for a moment he hadn't heard her, or was ignoring her as he continued past her toward the bank of elevators. Finally he paused and punched the Up button. His gaze ranged casually back across the lobby to where she stood. "You coming?"

As she hesitated, the door slid open behind him and he stepped inside. She saw him reach to push a floor button.

The action sent her hurrying toward the elevator but she was hampered by her ridiculously high heels. The doors started to close. At the last second his hand shot out, halting them. She stepped in beside him, brushing his shoulder.

She moved to the opposite side of the car, and his gaze followed. Those eyes said *Keep your distance.* "I don't usually pick up women in the lobby. Why should you be an exception?"

She kept her voice level. "I'm not a pickup."

His aquamarine blue gaze skimmed her revealing evening gown. When it again reached her face the jaded edge could have etched glass. "How much?"

She tapped down the impulse of anger. After three months in Vegas, she'd almost grown accustomed to men thinking her sexual favors were for sale—almost. "I'm not selling anything either, Mr. Matherson."

"Good. Because I never buy."

It was a boast but she believed it.

The elevator jerked to a halt on the third floor, metal groaning in protest. He didn't wait for the doors to finish opening before pushing through them. Michaela followed, a renewed reluctance dogging her every step. Perhaps she was making a mistake to think—no, the worst he could do was refuse.

He had turned the key in the lock by the time she reached him. He pushed the door open and reached in to flip on the light. "Go ahead," he said impatiently when she again hesitated.

As she passed him her gaze skimmed his lower jaw, pausing a fraction on the kissable curve of his mouth that invited a woman to ignore every other warning—at her own risk.

The room was neat but dingy. The designer label black leather baggage piled in one corner looked pointedly out of place, as did the silver-backed comb and brush she glimpsed on the sink as she passed the bathroom. A crystal whiskey decanter and glasses were the only other personal items on display.

He must have read something in her expression for he said, "What'd you expect?" His tone was curt, combative.

Michaela turned back to him and saw that he was standing with feet slightly apart, as though he expected her to come out swinging. "What do you want, Kiki?"

She was surprised that he knew the false name she went by, but then remembered being told that successful gamblers often possessed phenomenal memories. He probably made a habit of paying more attention to details than other people. "I want to hire you."

He didn't even blink. "That's a switch. What, exactly, do you want me to do for you?"

"Gamble."

"What?"

"I have one thousand dollars. I need ten thousand."

"Don't we all." He looked away, as if he were no longer interested.

She took a step toward him, and held out the ten one-hundred-dollar chips. "I want you gamble this for me. Anything you win I'll split with you fifty-fifty."

He looked at the chips in her outstretched hand but didn't touch them. "Why do you need ten thousand dollars? No, let me guess. Aunt Jessie needs an operation. No, better yet, you're trying to save the ranch."

The sarcasm in his voice would have sent her out the door if she hadn't been so desperate. "It's the second."

He burst out laughing. "Just that the hell are you going to do with a ranch?"

Humor was good, she thought. At least he was listening. She smiled tentatively. "First I've got to save it. Then I can worry about that."

"What if I lose your precious thousand?"

She shrugged. "Then, at least, I will have tried."

He folded his arms across his chest, his full attention on her now. "You're serious, aren't you?"

She simply looked at him, holding her breath.

He continued to stare at her for a moment then turned and yanked open the door. "Sorry. I never work for anybody but myself."

"Two-thirds." She stumbled over her words in an effort to hold her ground. "You can keep two-thirds of what you win."

He turned back slowly, watching her as though she were dull-witted. "What if I just took your thousand and kept it?"

"You wouldn't do that."

His gaze as now glacial. "Why not?"

"Because you wouldn't like word to get around that you steal from women."

"I don't give a damn what people say," he said scathingly.

"You'd care if people thought you were a cheat. A gambler's reputation is everything." She saw his eyes narrow and realized she sounded dangerously close to making a threat. She shrugged disarmingly. "Besides, I don't think you'd like yourself very much if you cheated me."

"Don't fool yourself," he said coolly. "I'd like myself just fine. My motto is never give a sucker an even break."

"But never cheat a friend?" she added with a small smile.

"You're no friend of mine," he thrust back and pulled out another cigarette. When he looked at her again his expression had changed. The look could have melted glaciers. "Or are you willing to do whatever it takes to get me to help you?"

"How about if I save your life?" Before she could lose her nerve, she whipped the cigarette from between his lips and stubbed it out in a nearby ashtray. "You'll live longer and better without that."

He snapped the lighter shut. "When I decide to reform, it won't because some woman nagged me into it."

"Someone should care enough to make you look after yourself."

Some new emotion skimmed across his features and disappeared. "Come here." He took her by the wrist and pulled her toward him. The dozen silver bracelets on her arm tinkled, distracting him from whatever he had intended to do. Instead, he reached out with his other hand and ran the back of a finger across the silver rings, eliciting another series of wind chime sounds. Faster than she could have imagined, he slipped the first silver bracelet off her wrist.

"What are you doing?" Michaela asked in alarm.

"I want a souvenir. Something to remember you by."

As he held it up for inspection, she reached out for it. "Give that back. Please."

He pocketed the bracelet and met her startled expression with a smug one. "You want it back? Offer me something else."

She lifted her chin a notch. "Like what?"

He glanced pointedly at the chips still clutched in her hand.

"You can't be serious!" The shock in her voice was genuine.

Irritation entered his expression. "Do you realize the position you're in? You came to my room, had evidently been waiting for me. I might do most anything to you now and there'd be plenty of witnesses to say you came with me of your own free will. Are you that naive, or just that desperate?"

"I—I don't know," she answered a little helplessly.

He leaned toward her, his chin thrust out. "I don't care how young you are or what kind of trouble you're in. I never take on causes. Never offer protection. Never show mercy. In my line of business I can't afford it."

She ducked her head, a blush warming her cheeks. "Grand-mère Delphine gave me the bracelets. I must have it back."

He ran a finger down her cheek. "What's it worth to you?"

She smiled though her heart was slamming uncomfortably against her chest. She'd learned a few things in Vegas. One of them was that when a pretty woman was dealing with an obnoxious man, she was better off smiling as she did so. "Are you that hard up?"

He smirked. "I'm hard. Is that enough for you?"

Her chin lifted a notch. "I suspect any woman who went to bed with you would find things a bit crowded. There'd be you and her, and your ego."

"Let's find out."

As he dragged her in against him, she braced both hands against his shirtfront in alarm. "No!"

He frowned. "You're not old enough, or tough enough to trade insults with me, are you, kid?"

When she didn't answer, he cursed and backed a little away. "I must be more tired than I thought," he mumbled before looking up at her. "Tell you what I'm going to do. I'll make you a friendly wager."

Her whole body tensed with expectation.

"If you win, I'll give you back the bracelet. If I win, I get a kiss. And keep the bracelet," he added as he saw the question forming in her eyes.

"I don't gamble."

"That's a pity. You might find you like losing."

"Right." She swallowed back her disappointment. "I can see now I made a mistake. I'm sorry I wasted your time."

"It's not a waste yet." He began shedding his tuxedo jacket. "Stick around. You might yet find a way to con me into helping you." He tossed the jacket on a chair before slowly turning back to her. "Why me?"

Suddenly she was acutely aware of how foolish she'd been. She couldn't very well tell him that the idea—that he—had come to her in a kind of flash of second sight. "I thought of the idea when I overheard a woman ask a man in the casino to place a bet for her."

"You overheard a woman buying a man's favors, kid. That's right," he continued as her eyes widened. "That's how it's done. The gigolo pockets half the bet and keeps any winnings.''

"Have you ever done that?" The question was out before she could stop it but he didn't react as she expected.

He plopped down on the bed and crossed his arms behind his head. "I've been hungry enough, and desperate enough a time or two. Haven't you?"

She shook her head. "Never."

"Lucky you." He patted the empty place beside him on the bed. "Come here. Don't look like that. I'm too tired to wrestle with an unwilling woman."

She didn't believe him. Stretched out like that, he looked like a jungle cat at ease. He lacked only provocation to strike. The only reason she was still in the room was that he had her bracelet and she wanted, had to have it back. She moved forward and perched uneasily on the edge of the bed. "Now what?"

"Now we're going to pretend that we've been out on a date and we've come back here because we wanted to be alone. Only I'm too bushed to jump your bones so you're going to tuck me in." She'd never known blue eyes could hold such warmth. "You can begin with the tie." He was playing with her, teasing her. Why? Had he read in her expression her secret attraction to him? Or was this the price she had to pay to get her bracelet back?

She glanced sidelong at his mouth as she began loosening his tie. He wasn't smiling but his lips were slightly parted, as if he couldn't get enough air through his nostrils. Suddenly she shared that feeling. She could smell his cologne, a subtle but heavy fragrance that only a man as overtly masculine as he could successfully carry off. She'd had daydreams about being this close to him, but had never thought it would become reality. The woven silk texture of his tie seemed the height of erotic stimulation as she slipped the knot free.

"Now the shirt," he said quietly as he pulled the tie from about his neck.

She didn't look into his eyes again, afraid of what she might see, and what her own gaze might reveal. The daydream was gaining reality. The heat of his body pervaded the fine cotton fabric as she reached for the first stud. She soon found it impossible to work it free without sticking her hand inside the placket. The warmth of his skin heated the back of her fingers. The fine dense hair tickled. She nearly withdrew her hand. Touching him was a mistake. Reality was crowding out speculation. She was having trouble breathing. If he said anything, one single syllable, she would bolt.

But he didn't say anything. He lay perfectly still until she held a handful of studs and his shirt gaped open on a tangle of crisp dark hair. Now what? she thought a little wildly, and raised eyes to his.

"You've never made love." It wasn't a question, which was just as well, she decided, because she wasn't capable of lying at the moment about anything. But she knew he knew the truth. It was there in the tender, half-amused expression on his face.

He reached up and cupped the back of her head, the pressure of his fingers an indication of his intent. As he levered forward he pulled her head down to meet his.

His kiss stunned her with its gentleness and sensual persuasion. His lips cushioned hers, altering their outline with the pressure of his. His tongue skimmed their surface, following the shape with warm, damp licks. She heard herself sigh breathlessly and felt his chuckle against her mouth. "Virgin kisses," he whispered into her mouth.

She wanted to protest, to say she'd been kissed many times by many men. But his tongue was slipping in and out between her lips with slow seductive strokes that made her aching toes curl inside her too-tight shoes. She realized with a shock that he was right. She had never, ever been kissed like this. Not even in her fantasies about him.

She reached up and touched his cheek, needing to steady herself with reality. He caught her other hand and tucked it between them into the opening of his shirt. "Touch me," he said huskily.

His skin was like heavy satin roughened by silk hair and then she felt the heat and hardness of his muscle and bones beneath. He was breathing hard, as moved by their kisses as she. As his mouth left a wet trail from her mouth down her cheek to her neck, her fingernails curled into the tangled furring on his chest. His fingers skimmed the opening at the back of her deep-plunging gown and then brushed soft as a kiss up her spine. Low down, she felt a flow of desire. The nature of her daydreaming would never be the same again.

His kisses changed, his mouth becoming an engulfing force. He pulled her down on the bed beside him and rolled them over so that his body covered hers. His lips slanted over hers and his tongue thrust deep into her mouth seeking, not demanding, her response. Her tongue tangled with his in a sexual tango as he tugged his shirt free of his trousers. His body was tense and hard. The blatant expression of his desire was pressed tightly against her. And then she felt his hand seeking her breast. He took his time, not hurrying any movement or action but giving her time to adjust to his touches and kisses, and respond in kind to his desire. She felt both ravaged and protected by the fierce wonder of his lovemaking. It was as if he knew what she wanted even before . . .

Suddenly she recalled his words. *Stick around. You might yet find a way to con me into helping you.*

But she had not come here for this.

She couldn't trade sex for help.

"No! Stop!"

She was amazed by the speed with which he released her and sat up. It was as if he had expected her protest. He raked the hair from his brow and smirked. "Changed your mind, huh?"

She sat up, shocked by his words. "I didn't—you don't think I—?"

The knowing look in his eyes killed her protest. He *did* think that. His bare chest was heaving slightly, otherwise he seemed unaffected by the desire that had erupted so suddenly between them.

She scooted off the end of the bed and stood up, sliding her dress down over her legs, acutely aware that his seductive hands had worked it up about her hips. "I didn't come here to seduce you. I came to offer you a business—"

"I won't help you," he injected bluntly into her speech. "I've never taken money from a woman for any reason. Ever."

She looked up sharply and saw the truth in his eyes. His admission was a double-edged sword. He was refusing to help her, but he was also admitting he'd never been a gigolo.

She nodded and backed away, realizing that while she'd gotten away, it was only because he'd let her go. Ashamed to admit that, even to herself, she looked around for her shoe. When had she kicked it off? Dear Lord! She'd almost made love to a stranger.

Without bothering to excuse herself she grabbed up her shoe and then the chips that lay scattered across the floor.

"I wouldn't advise you ask anyone else in Vegas to help you," he said brutally, as she hurried toward the door. "Another man might not be so nice."

She was on the elevator before she remembered her bracelet. She went back and knocked on his door several times. There was no answer. Finally, she gave up, too humiliated to complain to the hotel management. She thought the worst had happened until she was on the street and realized that she was clutching only nine chips. By then she hadn't the heart to go back.

Chapter 4

Michaela hunched her shoulders then arched her back. It was nearly daylight now. The Buick was sliding along the tarmac laid across the delta swampland as the silver-blue of predawn misted the sky. Not once in the past two hours had Guy regained consciousness. Because she didn't know what else to do, she had decided to seek help from the one person who might understand what she had done, Grand-mère.

She was taking the long way back toward Baton Rouge and Belle Isle, traveling the old river roads where her car would less likely be spotted. Using a '48 Buick as a getaway car was hardly a smart choice. Not that she'd been given much choice. Having given the matter some thought, she was fairly certain she hadn't committed a crime in helping Guy Matherson—unless the authorities knew something they hadn't bothered to tell her.

She didn't let herself think about what Guy Matherson had gone through to get himself out of that hospital room. He'd had to disconnect himself from things that didn't bear thinking about too closely. But she did wonder about his condition. He hadn't awakened even once during the drive, not even when she'd stopped to buy coffee and candy bars in order to keep herself going.

She had left Baton Rouge without lunch and then Belle Isle without dinner. All-night diners and service stations were not part of the back-road experience in Louisiana. Instead she'd had to stop at a honky-tonk and submit to being perused by the local gents while she waited for coffee. One thing Las Vegas had taught her and that was how to handle overly friendly boozed-up men. She had found she could handle about every situation and every man—except Guy Matherson.

She'd left Vegas that same day as her disastrous meeting with him, afraid of him and of the emotions he'd so easily aroused. Call it self-protection or cowardice but she'd run away to keep him from breaking her heart.

As she shifted on the car seat to relieve tired muscles, Michaela smiled in rueful memory. She'd never before or since felt what she'd felt in Guy Matherson's sophisticated embrace. She had eventually learned about sex and romance from a kinder lover. Guy had been right. She'd been too young and too naive to deal with him. Now, she told herself, she was too smart.

"At least I hope so," she said herself as she threw a glance in his direction. Grand-mère often said that all things work for good. If she thought about it, it might be said that Guy Matherson had done her a favor in turning down her offer. With her money gone, she'd had to remain at her old state college. Determined to make the best of it, she'd finished in three years. In the two years between college and law school she had learned a lot about the value of earning her own way in the world. She had put herself through LSU law school. She knew that nothing good ever came easy.

Yet, did that explain completely why she had turned down Guy Matherson's offer of $100 thousand? Only an idiot turned down cold hard cash. Hadn't she just the afternoon before been musing on the possibilities of shoring up Belle

Isle with the winning from a lottery or a sweepstakes? Beau Wilson was no Ed McMahon but that hadn't made the cash he carried less spendable. If only she had taken the money and stayed on Belle Isle she wouldn't now be trying to decide what to tell her great-grandmother about the injured man dozing beside her. But no-oo, she'd had to press her luck, look the gift horse in the mouth and slay the cash cow. Where had the cliché "Take the money and run" been lurking when she'd needed it?

Half an hour later, the sharp black silhouette of Yancy's shack took shape against the backdrop of the oaks and cottonwoods that lined the bank of the river. Dripping with moss and moisture in the eerie stillness, the drooped branches gleamed greenish black in the pale mists illuminated by the dawn. Instead of driving up to the house, she pulled the Buick up close to the pier and parked. She didn't want to have to explain any more than absolutely necessary to Yancy. With luck he wouldn't even notice her companion.

She approached the shack without trepidation. When two fleet-footed shadows emerged from the side of the house, their backs sloped like wolves', she didn't hesitate. The dogs came quickly toward her barking raucously.

Michaela checked her step. She had known the pair of mongrel pups since they were born last fall. She knew they were harmless as long as they were not challenged. Yet coming upon them in the dark had probably not been the best idea.

"Cayenne! Pipitoe!" she said forcefully. "Down boys. Good dogs."

They paused and fell silent with a suddenness that always unnerved strangers. For a few seconds the only sounds now in the misty air were the final night croaks of bullfrogs and sluggish lapping sounds of the river against the muddy shore.

Then she called loudly, "Yancy! Yancy? It's Michaela Bellegarde! Come out here this minute and curb your dogs!"

The sound of her voice seemed to revive the dogs. They fell into a frenzy of barking, each trying to outdo the other with yips and yowls that echoed horribly in the mist. Yet neither approached her.

Michaela stood her ground.

After what seemed an unconscionable time during which the animals made enough noise to rouse the zombies said to inhabit the swamp at the rear of the house, Michaela saw a light come on inside the shack. Moments later Yancy staggered out onto the porch with a high-beam flashlight in one hand and a shotgun in the other.

"Who the hell is there?"

"It's Michaela, Yancy," she replied with more relief than she had realized she felt.

She heard him swear vividly as he none too steadily propped his gun against the wooden pillar of his porch. "Guess I won't be needing the artillery," he finished in a mutter and stepped off the porch.

"Shut the hell up!" he roared as his dogs leaped happily upon him. He cuffed one with the butt of his flashlight but they both followed eagerly on his heels as he made his way toward Michaela. "What the hell's a woman doin' out here this time of night?" he demanded.

Michaela didn't bother to answer directly. He smelled like a brewery. A struck match would probably set his breath afire. "Good morning, Yancy. I need to cross to Belle Isle. Now."

He shined his light into her face all but blinding her. "Bless it all if it ain't you, sure enough."

Michaela threw an arm across her eyes. "Would you mind lowering that light? As I said, I need to cross to Belle Isle."

He lowered the beam to the ground and flicked it off. "Can't do it, leastways not till the mist clears." He turned and headed back for the house grumbling about city folks who woke up decent people in the dead of the night.

"I'll make it worth your while," Michaela called after him. "Twenty-five dollars. Cash."

As he turned back to her Michaela mentally checked her wallet and hoped she had that much.

She heard the mush-mouth smile in his voice. "I'll take it now."

"You'll get it on the other side," she said in a non-compromising voice.

She couldn't see his face clearly but she thought he gave her an ugly look. He only said, "I'll get dressed."

She turned back toward her car, satisfied that he would return. Only one thing motivated Yancy and that was whiskey. Only one thing got him whiskey and that was cash.

She didn't like Yancy. He was rude and a drunk and proud of both facts. If not for his pilot's license she suspected he would long ago have become a derelict and a street person. But he ran the only ferry to Belle Isle and a few of the other more remote spots along both shores of the Mississippi. In the summer he took fishing parties out on the river. In the fall he led hunters into the swamp for duck and goose hunts. The rest of the year he sat on his rickety porch and drank himself into a quiet stupor. As far as she was concerned his was a waste of a human life.

Five minutes later, he appeared out of the mist wearing overalls and carrying a thermos. She would liked to have believed it was full of strong black coffee but she suspected it was fifty percent booze. She slipped behind the wheel and waited patiently until he had opened the gate so that she could drive the Buick onto the flat surface of the ferry. The bargelike vessel rocked gently under the weight of the automobile. Minutes later the motor came to life, making the barge and its contents vibrate violently.

The shuddering roused Guy. He moaned and opened his eyes. "Where—? What—?" he muttered.

Michaela reached out to gingerly place her fingers over his lips. "It's okay," she whispered as she scooted across the seat toward him. If he drew Yancy's interest she'd have a lot of explaining to do. "It's only me," she said as she leaned in close so that his blinking eyes could focus on her. "See?" she whispered even more softly as she smiled into his eyes. "It's Michaela. You've got to be quiet. Understand?"

He stopped blinking and she felt his lips moved softly against the sensitive skin of her fingertips. The tingling sensation made her lift her hand. "What did you say?"

"What have we here?"

The gloating question barked at her back made Michaela jump even though she recognized the voice. She took her time in turning around, trying her best to shield with her body the man beside her. "Yes, Yancy?" she asked impatiently.

Unabashed by her tone, he stuck his head in the window on the driver's side. "I said, who's your fella?"

Michaela held her breath until the worst of the fumes subsided. She knew by the look on his unkept sun-baked face that he thought he'd caught her red-handed in a compromising position. Yancy didn't care for much besides his bottle. But he did enjoy gossip, the more scandalous and dirty-minded the better. He took delight in repeating what he'd heard to any and all comers. The tale of how he'd ferried Michaela Bellegarde and a man across the Mississippi at five o'clock in the morning would spread faster than the dawn.

"He's a friend," she said in annoyance.

"He don't look so good." Yancy bobbed his head right and left, trying to see past Michaela but she moved to block his every attempt. His grin turned lewd. "Looks like you done wore him out."

"Hardly," she answered curtly. "He did a little too much celebrating. At the convention," she added for color.

"Celebratin', you say?" Yancy's grin widened as he licked his lips. "Don't suppose you got any more of what he's been celebratin' with?"

Michaela met his greedy look calmly. "Sorry, no."

"Too bad. Looks to be it does the job nice and proper."

"If that's all?" It was an unmistakable suggestion he withdraw.

Yancy nodded. "'Bout time you got yourself another fella. Saw Larroquette on TV the other night. He done made a mistake trading you in on big boobs and a bleach job. You got class."

It was the closest thing to a compliment he'd ever given her but Michaela was hard-pressed to be polite. "Thank you." She reached for her purse and pulled out her wallet. She placed the two tens and a five she fished out of it into Yancy's calloused palm. "I appreciate you doing this so early."

He tipped his cap, grinning. "Anytime. By the way, you tell your fella there I said to drink a beer with a raw egg and three shakes of cayenne in it when he comes to. That'll fix him right up. Then he'll be ready to celebrate properly come evening." He winked. "Know what I mean?"

He relieved Michaela from having to respond by pulling his head out of the window. She slid across and rolled it up.

Only then did she turn back to Guy. His eyes were open but he sagged forward against the shoulder harness. She reached out to prop him up in a more comfortable position and felt something wet and sticky on her fingers. She withdrew her hand and held it up.

Even in the hazy light of daybreak she could not mistake what it was. When she turned to him she saw the source was the dark stain on his left shirtfront. It was blood, fresh blood. He was bleeding.

She looked up and saw the shore of Belle Isle emerge from the mist. She hesitated. Maybe they should go back to Baton Rouge. But who could she call for help who would be discreet? Doctors reported all gunshot wounds to the authorities. Maybe it would be better to get him in bed on Belle Isle then send for a doctor. That way, she'd have time to think of a reason to explain who Guy was and why he was with her.

She reached out to smooth the hair from his brow. Hours earlier his skin had been damp and cool. Now his face was hot and dry. In the gloom his eyes gleamed strangely but he didn't say a word.

"Hold on," she whispered as she continued to stroke his hair. "I'll get you help. I promise."

Her nerves stretched to the snapping point, Michaela ground her teeth as the minutes ticked away while Yancy lined the ferry up to the shore. He might be a drunk but he was a good pilot, did his job properly.

"You tell your boyfriend I said he can come by and hoist a few with me anytime!" Yancy called after them as she gunned the Buick past him onto the shore.

Chapter 5

All Michaela could think about on the drive to the house was that a man might be dying because she had acted foolishly when she knew better. She castigated herself because she couldn't afford to give in to the feeling of terror that was crowding in on her. She floored the pedal and sent the old car sashaying through the reeds and mud at breakneck speed.

She drove the car practically up the steps of the grand old house before stepping on the brake. She was out of her side of the car in record time and hurried to open Guy's door.

His face was hidden in the shadowed interior but was there was no mistaking the pain in his voice. "Just... help me... up."

He tried to force himself into a sitting position, keeping one arm wrapped protectively about his ribs. Michaela leaned in beside him and touched his shoulder and felt him shudder. When he turned toward her she saw his beautifully chiseled lips were pinched with pain.

A moment later the front screen of the house creaked

open and Michaela heard her great-grandmother's voice. "What's this? Who's there?"

Michaela straightened. "It's Michaela, Grand-mère." She kept her voice level in order not to frighten the older woman. "I have someone with me. He's hurt."

The elderly woman wasted no time with questions or exclamations of surprise. With amazing agility she hurried across the gallery and out onto the grass. A moment later she was standing beside Michaela, peering into the face of a stranger.

She felt his cheek. "*Mon Dieu!* He's burning up with the fever. Take an arm, 'Tite. We must get him inside where I can see to him."

"I—I'm okay," Guy said thickly, trying to brace his legs under himself as the two women struggled to get him to his feet. He failed, knees buckling even as he bit out an angry, "Damn it!"

As his body weight sagged between the them, Michaela looked across helplessly at her great-grandmother. "We must be careful, Grand-mère. He's hurt."

Tante Delphine studied her great-granddaughter a moment with alert black eyes then she nodded. "Quickly. This way." She pointed toward the side of the house. "We will put him in my bed. It's closest."

Michaela didn't reply. Too many sensations were throwing her system into overload. She was aware of Guy in every intimate shift of his body along the length of hers. The connection she had felt so briefly in the hospital came back. He couldn't die. She wouldn't allow anything else to happen to him. She had made a bargain with herself to prove to him that she was different from him. She would not turn her back on a plea for help.

When they reached the side entrance she angled her body through the shutters that opened into her great-grandmother's bedroom. A single oil lamp burned by the bedside.

"Gently!" Tante Delphine admonished softly as she pulled the bed's mosquito netting aside so that Michaela could lower him onto the mattress.

As Guy sank down heavily onto the feather tick covered by linen sheets, he pulled Michaela to him. For a moment he held her close. He brushed his lips over her cheek, his beard rasping her skin. "Get rid of the old woman!" he muttered. "I want only you."

On the other side of him, Tante Delphine chuckled. "The man's what's still got enough life in him to make love to a pretty girl—he's gon' be just fine."

Michaela wriggled free of his grasp, embarrassed by the fact that her great-grandmother had overheard his rude remark.

"'Tite, you take his shoulders and I get the feet," Tante Delphine said briskly. "Now you lay him back. Slowly, *ma chère*. Never mind the coverlet," she added as Guy tried to push it out of the way. She handed Michaela a pillow. "Put this under his head. When you done that, get my medicine bag from the front closet."

Guy grimaced as he lay back against the pillow. "You won't need that. I just need rest," he said in a tight voice.

Tante Delphine patted his leg affectionately as she pulled off one of his shoes. "We gon' see to it everything is fine. Don't you worry yourself."

His gaze shifted from the older woman to Michaela, narrowing in defiance. "Tell her I don't want her help."

Michaela gazed down into those angry light eyes and wondered how she had ever dared think he might respond differently to further attempts at aid. There was no gratitude in his expression, no grateful appreciation in his gaze, just a rude core-deep stubbornness. "He doesn't want our help, Grand-mère," she said tersely.

"What he don' want and what he's gon' get ain't the same," Tante Delphine answered implacably. She folded her arms and cocked her head with its silver coronet of braids to one side. "He don't seem no *bébé*. What's he afraid of?"

Behind the black stubble of a day's growth Guy bared his teeth in a very unfriendly smile. "Don't push me."

Michaela reached out to lift the coverlet over him, noticing as she did so that dark hair smoked the contours of his chest inside his open shirt. She had scarcely registered this before his hand released its protective caress of his lower left side and she saw that the bright red stain had soaked through the lower left side of his shirt onto his waistband.

"My Lord," she whispered in alarm as she heard her great-grandmother's echo in French: *"Mon Dieu!"*

"He's worse than I thought," Michaela said. "He needs a doctor."

Tante Delphine met Michaela's gaze across the prone body. "How we gon' get him one, 'Tite?"

"There's no phone," Michaela whispered miserably. How could she have forgotten? There had never been one on Belle Isle because her great-grandmother disapproved of them. In case of an emergency, they had always relied on a short-wave radio. Her eyes widened. "The radio?"

"Still in the repair shop," Tante Delphine replied calmly.

"I don't need a doctor," Guy said testily into the silence between the women. "I just need rest."

Tante Delphine patted his shoulder. "Don't you worry, *mon beau garçon.* Tante Delphine gon' take good care of you." She looked again at Michaela, a militant gleam in her black eyes. "Now you gon' get my bag, 'Tite, or must I?"

"I'll get it," Michaela said and hurried out.

She was gone less than five minutes but when she returned Guy Matherson lay under the coverlet, his upper body bare. Surprisingly, his shirt and trousers lay in a heap at the foot of the bed. Then Michaela spied the long scissors in her great-grandmother's hand. Appalled and amused, she realized Grand-mère had cut off Guy's clothing.

Her gaze strayed speculatively toward Guy's face, a question in her eyes as she approached. He looked thoroughly outdone but he merely rolled his eyes in response.

Michaela smiled. Guy Matherson might be a tiger in his own world but on Belle Isle, Tante Delphine was the power to be reckoned with.

Tante Delphine lifted back the sheet with which she had covered him and pointed to the bloody bandage partially taped to his torso just below the left ribs. "He's a sick boy, 'Tite. Someone done shot him."

Michaela's heart sank into her shoes. So much for her hopes that her relative wouldn't recognize what had caused his wounding. "Are you certain?"

Tante Delphine's unblinking gaze said that she didn't buy for a second Michaela's feeble attempt at deception. "Didn't I nurse half the hunting accidents in the parish most these last eighty-five years and more?"

Michaela's startled gaze flew to Guy's face but he had closed his eyes as if he wanted no part in what transpired next. She didn't know what to say or how much of the truth to tell. Embarrassment mantled her cheeks as she met her great-grandmother's sharp gaze. "Since he's been shot—" she began in a subdued voice.

"We got to close the wound before it gets infected."

"But, Grand-mère, we should—"

"Stop the bleeding," she answered firmly. "He's been seen by a schooled doctor." She held out two prescription bottles. "They were in his pocket. He just broke open his stitches."

Michaela's stricken expression lowered back to the silent man. Though she was certain he was listening to their conversation, he still chose not to take part in it. "It's my fault. I must have pushed him too hard when I was trying to get him in the car."

"You done no wrong, 'Tite. On a healthy man your shoving would have had no affect. *Mais, oui.* It would have encouraged him to kiss you."

Michaela frowned. Grand-mère no doubt had match-making on her own mind. This time she was way off base.

"Now, 'Tite. I need boiling water for to sterilize my needles. *Tout de suite!*"

They worked together for a quarter of an hour, Michaela holding the lantern aloft and dabbing at the flow of blood with antiseptic-dampened gauze pads when her great-grandmother directed. She had never before helped tend anything more serious than the removal of a fishhook from a hand but she felt strangely calm as she watched a few neat stitches close the wound.

It was only when she glanced up into the face of the man quietly regarding her with eyes so dark that they seemed black that she was forced to remember who he was and how he had come to be in this situation. For reasons she did not want to probe, she was strangely thrilled by his reappearance in her life. The only thing she wasn't happy about was the dramatic manner in which it had occurred. Everything she knew about Guy Matherson was steeped in mystery and edged with danger. Finding him in the hospital with a bullet wound in his side hadn't improved that image.

Finally, Tante Delphine finished a new dressing and gave him one of her secret potions. "For the fever. It's a brave man who takes the stitches with no anesthesia." After Guy had choked it down she reached out and tenderly pushed back the black curls that were plastered by sweat to his brow. She then took his face between her hands and bent down to look him closely in the eyes.

"Now you look at Tante Delphine. Can't no man lie to these old eyes. You been shot. What I want to know is if it's on account you done some wrong."

Michaela watched as Guy met the old woman's black gaze, a tender smile that she had never before seen curving his mouth. "I swear I didn't do anything wrong, Tante Delphine." His voice was husky from his ordeal but the foreign inflection of her name was perfect. "I was just in the wrong place at the wrong time."

Tante Delphine stared down into his face a moment longer then nodded slowly and patted his cheek as if he were a small child. "You gon' sleep now," she promised him.

She straightened and looked at Michaela in satisfaction. "You done good work, 'Tite. You can throw out them bloody things now and then put the kettle on for coffee."

Michaela did as she was asked, partly because it gave her something to do besides worry, and she had plenty to worry about. Even if Guy had told her great-grandmother the complete truth, and she doubted it, the question remained: what wrong place had he been in and why?

When she returned to the bedroom with two cups of coffee, her gaze went directly to the man in the bed. He lay so still her heart lurched. "Is he all right, Grand-mère?"

Tante Delphine nodded calmly. "What I give him makes him sleep deep." She stroked his bare chest above the tucked sheet. "So much fine black hair. Much virility as well as beauty, like my dear dead Julian."

She smiled as Michaela approached the bed. "I have wondered, child, what you were waiting for. It's no good, a life without a mate. Now I understand." She lightly caressed the young man's cheek. "This one, he has a touch of the old blood. *Oui.* He has what makes a woman happy."

Michaela's embarrassed gaze darted to Guy's closed eyes. "Hush, Grand-mère. He will hear you."

The older woman pursed her lips. "What will he hear? That he is handsome, and so strongly made? That just looking at him makes women want to share their bodies with his? You think he does not already know this?"

Michaela blushed despite the fact Guy's eyes remained closed. "It's not considered correct these days, Grand-mère, to talk about a man—or a woman—as if he were a mere sex object."

Tante Delphine tossed her head like a young girl. "You modern women. How careful you are around the young men. This—how do they call it?—this political correctness, it is speaking with no feelings."

Michaela set down the cups of coffee she had brought in on the nightstand before saying, "You never approve of modern ways, Grand-mère. That's why you have no phone."

Tante Delphine snapped her fingers dismissively. "There is no warmth in a voice without a face to go with it. Modern conveniences make for no more romance in the world." Her black eyes suddenly danced in the lamplight. "For romance there must be intimacy, honesty of feelings, and just a *soupçon* of mystery. In the old days, I had a dozen lovers at once. Once I marry, many a former suitor came to me for advice and a love philter to help him capture his second choice. But this one, this Guy will not need my help." She rolled her eyes appreciatively. "Your man has all you need."

"He's *not* my man," Michaela maintained evenly, aware that everything they said might be overheard.

Tante Delphine's silver brows became crescents of surprise. "You think not? I can make it so, if you wish."

"Please, don't." Michaela paused before she vented her frustration on the one person who was totally innocent in the matter. "We aren't even friends. You don't understand."

The older woman bristled in offense anyway. "Maybe I do, and maybe I don't. We will see who is right."

Before Michaela realized her purpose, her great-grandmother reached for the sheet that covered Guy's hips and lifted it for an appraising glance.

"Grand-mère!" Michaela whispered in a scandalized voice.

When she had patted it back in place Tante Delphine said smoothly, "If I am to heal him, I must know all things about him." She slanted another, pointed glance at the covers and smiled. "*Oui*, this one, he's gon' make lots of great-great-grandbabies!"

Michaela's jaw dropped as her great-grandmother chuckled wickedly. "You're incorrigible!"

"And you are too prim for such a pretty girl. But enough of that. You don't tell me who he is."

Michaela glanced again at the sleeping man. "This is Guy Matherson, Grand-mère. He's the man who offered me $100 thousand. But I still don't know why."

The older woman wagged her head. "Isn't it plain?"

"Not to me," she answered. "And if you think it has anything to do with romance, you're quite wrong."

"You think so?" Tante Delphine reached for Guy's arm as if to take his pulse. Once she lifted it, Michaela saw that a thin band of silver metal encircled his left wrist. It took a second amazed glance for Michaela to recognize it. She felt her cheeks again catch fire as the older woman said, "I thought you said you lost this bracelet."

Michaela couldn't think of a thing to say. She could no more explain why it spanned Guy Matherson's wrist than she could fly. Nor could she imagine why she hadn't noticed it before.

Shaking her head, Tante Delphine tucked his arm back under the sheet. "When I am rested, we gon' talk more about this man. But now I am most weary. He was too heavy a burden for this old back. You sit with him first. I will spell you after I've dozed awhile on your bed. *Bons rêves*, 'Tite."

Michaela stood a full minute in indecision after her great-grandmother left the room. Finally, she moved to the other side of the bed where she whipped Guy's left arm free of the sheet. She bent closer to inspect it. Her ponytail slid forward to whisk the sheet covering his chest but he didn't stir. There was no mistaking that bracelet. Eleven others just like it clinked together melodiously on her right wrist as she traced with a finger the fine floral etching on the one he wore. The etching was of a violet, the symbol for faithfulness.

For her thirteenth birthday her great-grandmother had given her a dozen bracelets, each etched with a different flower. Together they represented through the language of flowers all the things Grand-mère Delphine said she wished for her great-granddaughter. During the twelve years since, she'd never taken them off. Nor had she given away this one. It had been taken from her.

She reached out and fingered the silver circling his wrist. While her arm was slender enough to allow the bracelets to slide on and off she saw that this one had been cut open and fitted around his wrist, making it much too tight to ever slip off. In fact, there was a groove in his skin where the metal sometimes rubbed.

Why had he done that? Was it a private joke, a trinket to remind himself of the silly little virgin who'd gotten away?

"What else?" she whispered and hurriedly tucked his arm back under the cover. Whatever the explanation, she doubted it would make sense to her.

Guy drifted in and out of darkness, riding the swift, curling edge of the pain. Its power was all that kept his consciousness afloat. He knew he was badly hurt but he couldn't remember what had happened or where he was. Maybe he'd been mugged.

Then he took a deep breath.

A wave no longer, steel-edged pain jackknifed through his left side. He held his breath, waiting for the agony to ease. Instead his grip on reality blurred. His stomach pitched and heaved. He reached out for an anchor and grasped a slender arm.

"Shh! Gently." A woman's voice! A familiar voice but not really. A soft cool hand stroked his burning skin. Tinkling sounds like tiny bells reached his ear. The scent of gardenia teased his nostrils. "Breathe slowly," she cooed.

He blinked rapidly but his vision wouldn't clear. He tried to sit up but amazingly her hand on his shoulder was enough to pin him to the bed. He gave up the effort. "Where am I?"

"Don't worry. You're safe."

He grunted. *Safe.* When had he ever been safe?

He tightened his grip on the wrist in his grasp. That much seemed to be real. Yet, it roused his suspicion. Who was the woman? "Why is it so dark?"

"Why do you think?" came the humorous reply.

He relaxed a little, determined that no one should see him like this, hurting and vulnerable. He let her go. Why and where had he picked up the woman? Perhaps as a defense. Whatever the answer, he realized he was in no shape to be left alone. "I need . . . to rest. I'll make it worth . . . your while . . . if you stay."

"You're in no shape to strike bargains, Mr. Matherson."

He knew that voice! Kiki's voice. No, that wasn't possible. He was just dreaming again. Kiki wasn't real. She had never been real, not in the sense he had come to think of her.

His head ached like a sore tooth. His vision seemed clouded by a mist so thick it wouldn't yield even to concentration. And then Kiki's exquisite face was there, hovering just inches above him.

"You need to sleep," she said in the sexy whisper whose pitch he had never before been able to get just right in his dreams.

Of course! This was part of a dream.

He wanted to reach out and take her in his arms the way he'd done a hundred times before. But he found he couldn't even raise his hand this time. He was baked by fever, too drained of energy to move a muscle. So he simply lay there and stared at the vision in his best dream yet.

Kiki was his talisman, his very own Lady Luck. His recurring dreams had embellished his slender memories of her with thirty-one years of accumulated wishes and unrequited desires. She represented what he'd never had, someone he could depend upon, no matter what. Kiki was his good luck charm and in his dreams she never failed him. This dream of her was just more vivid than usual because he had nearly died. Might still die.

"I'm not ready to die."

"You're not going to die," she answered. "I won't let you." She touched his cheek, the cool palm of her hand a gift of comfort. She lifted his head and pressed a glass of cool water to his lips, coaxing him to drink all of it. God, he was thirsty. He dropped his head back on the pillow with a sigh.

"Do you need anything else?"

He felt his face ease into a smile. "You. Just you."

Her elegantly shaped brows drew into a slight frown and then she was gone.

Mistake. The word flashed in his thoughts like a gaudy neon sign.

Other thoughts drifted through his fever-riddled mind. Memory eddied backward. Snatches of his past seemed to confirm his suspicion that his life so far had been a great pitying waste of time. He had made many mistakes in his life. The biggest one was letting Kiki get away.

He remembered the first time he'd seen her, seven years ago. Guy had never seen a pretty woman look more bored. She was dealing blackjack at a table placed outside the entrance of the biggest casino in Vegas. The spot was usually staffed by an experienced dealer who knew how to entice patrons through the door. He knew all the regulars by name. She was a recent addition.

He'd awakened with an indefinable restlessness. He knew how to handle the anticipation that accompanied the eve of a big game. This was something altogether different. Despite a sharp mind and killer instincts, he never discounted the importance of luck. No gambler worth his luck discounted a premonition. His nerves were all but tingling. So, he'd come out into the night looking for a reason for the hunger gnawing at his psyche.

Then he spotted her. She was dead center, ground zero of the crazed hard-edged excitement that made up Las Vegas nightlife. She wore a shimmering gown of silver beadwork that set off rainbow-hued sparks with the slightest movement. Yet she might as easily have been playing solitaire for all the interest she showed in those around her. She was alone, isolated, in but not of the world swirling around her.

He knew plenty about isolation, had learned how to survive by sheer self-determination and despite the fondest wishes of others. He knew about loneliness. He had endured a bitterness so deep and dark that by comparison a moonless night seemed full of warmth and color. Was she the sign he sought? Was she a muse for his loneliness or an oracle of his future?

He never played blackjack. He never bet against the house. It was a sucker's bet. He crossed the lobby to the blackjack table.

She barely glanced at him but he felt the effect of her enormous black eyes in the pit of his stomach. Her gaze hooked into his libido as surely as if she had leaned across the table and offered him a long, wet, openmouthed kiss. To cover his surprise, he took a long drag on his cigarette.

"Would you mind not smoking?" Her voice was pitched so low he had to lean forward slightly to catch the final husky words. "It's bad for you."

The other players looked at him expectantly. He smirked. Didn't she know the rules? No one discouraged anything pleasurable in Las Vegas.

"Anything to please a lady."

As he stubbed his out in the nearest ashtray he noticed that it was full of half-smoked cigarettes. His gaze returned speculatively to her as he placed a modest bet. The pretty woman knew she had power...and how to use it. "You have a name?"

Her gaze never rose above the knot in his tie. "Kiki."

"What kind of name is that?"

"Mine." The single syllable was uttered with the finality of a door swinging shut. A rare smile of amusement lifted the corners of his mouth. An enigma. Perfect.

As she dealt the first hand he studied her. The silver gown she wore was high-necked and long-sleeved and fit her body as if it had been poured on. Yet with her thick black wavy hair pulled tightly back from her lightly made-up face she looked almost prim. That impression vanished when she turned away to speak to one of the casino's floormen.

His gaze followed the incredible plunge of the back of her dress, down the satin surface of her spine past the indentation of her waist to within a fraction of indecency. He looked away, stricken by a deep-down tug of desire. Okay. He was getting the message. She was like Lady Luck herself, unpredictable and full of contradictions, and practically impossible to resist.

As she placed two cards before him he heard something tinkling. Surprised, he glanced down. A dozen thin silver bracelets cuffed her right wrist. The sounds they created made him think of sultry nights, island rhythms, the dark undulations of a restless sea in the moonlight. Desire pushed him hard. But he pushed it back. He never let lust—or anything else—get in the way when he was gambling. In Vegas desires were easily satisfied. Only life was hard.

With a slim finger she lightly stroked the surface of his top card: an ace of hearts. It was as if she were taunting him or offering him a gift. "What's your pleasure?"

He lifted his eyes to hers but she wasn't looking at him. He wondered what she'd do if he answered honestly, "You." One thing was certain. She wouldn't understand the more subtle implications of his remark. He was half seduced and she had yet to even meet his gaze directly.

He lifted the edge of the facedown card. An ace of spades. The odds against drawing two aces were high. He flipped it over, separating the two cards. "Split."

She placed an additional card facedown on top of each of his aces then dealt the house a second hand.

Guy turned up the edges of his new cards. Shock raced up his fingers to his brain like an electric current. She'd fed him two face cards! Was it coincidence? In a town where everything was for sale, where life was bigger and better and magnified out of all proportion to reality, she was an in-

triguing mixture of reluctance and mystery. Or was this her
idea of foreplay? He was tantalized.

He dropped the shield of his poker face as he looked up.
"I'm feeling lucky, sweetheart. Are you?"

This time her gaze met his. He knew what she saw: a man
with *I want you* written all over his face. The startled recognition that flared in her dark eyes was as unexpected as it
was spicy hot. The next moment it was gone, replaced by the
stricken look of a doe caught in a car's headlights. More
contradictions.

"What are you doing here?"

Guy glanced over his shoulder. Ted Barlow, the casino's
manager, was standing behind him. Barlow's disapproving
gaze shifted from Kiki to the bruiser behind her. "Tom, you
know new girls don't work out front."

The floorman hunched his shoulders. "Wasn't my call,
Boss. I was just told to keep an eye on her."

"You're holding up the game, Barlow," Guy said in annoyance.

Barlow jerked in pleased surprise as he recognized Guy.
"Mr. Matherson. What brings you to one of my tables?"

Guy let his gaze slide toward Kiki. "I liked the view."

"Then please, continue." Barlow smiled at Kiki. "We'll
talk later."

But the mood was spoiled. Kiki had retreated into herself. Her self-imposed isolation lowered the atmosphere
surrounding her by several degrees. Suddenly she looked like
what she was, a frightened young woman—too young and
too frightened to suit him.

After he won his bet, Guy stood up and tucked a tip in her
tip glass. He saw her eyes rest for a moment on the edge of
the hundred-dollar bill sticking out and then watched the
deep blush that flowed up from her neck into her cheeks.
She didn't look at him again.

He turned away, unable to decide whether she was angry
or mortified. He suspected she was both. Well, like Lady
Luck, there was no accounting for the moods of a woman.

Yet, as he walked out of the hotel, he felt unexpectedly lighthearted. Women came and went so fast through his life he often didn't even bother to learn their last names. But he knew he wouldn't forget Kiki. It had little to do with the fact she'd aroused him. She'd done something infinitely more rare. She had altered for a moment his abiding sense of isolation. And, more rare, she had made him smile.

Guy's first impression upon opening his eyes was that he must be dead. The world was swathed in white as far as he could see. Golden light suffused the mist while the pungent floral scent of gardenia filled his senses. His next thought was that he must have pulled off an inside straight to beat the odds of a man like himself reaching heaven. Too bad he wasn't ready for it.

Then the haze parted and the lovely face of Kiki again hovered above his. A funny choking feeling knotted in his throat as she smiled.

"Grand-mère! He's awake."

"About time," he heard another woman say.

Against his will his eyes closed and he drifted off.

A minute or perhaps an hour later another face, that of an older woman in silver braids, replaced Kiki's in his line of vision. "You gon' be fine, aren't you, *mon beau garçon?*"

Guy decided that perhaps he hadn't reached heaven after all, not unless angels wore saffron yellow bathrobes.

"Where am I?"

"You on Belle Isle," the woman replied.

Something about her features struck him as strangely familiar but his usually sharp discernment had deserted him. His head seemed filled with helium and he wasn't certain how well it was tied to his neck. Though obviously well on in years, her face was as smooth and unlined as a sixteen-year-old's. Then she smiled and the parchment-thin skin pleated in a hundred fine wrinkles around her eyes, cheeks and mouth.

A dozen questions swam through the fog of his understanding. When he opened his mouth one leaped out. "What happened to me?"

"Someone done tried to separate you from this world. Only I don' allow it. Sleep now." Her black eyes seemed to see clear down to the bottom of his soul. "You gon' be as good as new."

Then she vanished into the pale mist surrounding him.

"Wait!"

Chapter 6

"I think I made a mistake," Michaela said as she entered the kitchen and dumped several bags of groceries on the table.

Grand-mère Delphine looked up calmly from the sweet potato she was peeling. "What the papers say?"

"They said a lot."

Michaela perched on a stool and plucked an apple from one of her grocery bags. After giving the apple a brisk rub on her sleeve she bit into it. It had been three days since she'd arrived on the island. But Guy's fever had remained normal overnight and so she had dragged herself from bed just after dawn and gone to the mainland for supplies and news. Luckily the local grocery store, a mom-and-pop affair that offered bait and ammunition as well as groceries, kept stacks of unsold papers to use as wrapping paper. She'd been able to get several back issues. What she'd learned wasn't heartening. So, she hadn't brought the papers home.

"Where are the papers?" Tante Delphine asked. "I want to read for myself what they say about our guest."

"Oh, I didn't think to bring them," Michaela answered and took an even bigger bite of her apple.

"You gon' finish the whole apple before you tell me what the man done makes you think it was a mistake to save his life?"

Michaela swallowed the half-chewed chunk, feeling every inch a villain. "I didn't mean that, exactly. It's just that I wish I hadn't gotten us involved."

"Why's that?" The rest of the Bellegardes might use subtle influence. Grand-mère used blunt speech.

Michaela adopted her judicial voice. "For one thing, we know nothing about him."

"You must know something," Tante Delphine pressed calmly. "What do you know?"

Michaela pointed to her full mouth as she debated for the hundredth time whether or not she should tell Grand-mère about Guy's past as a gambler. She had confessed about her summer working in Las Vegas but let her great-grandmother believe Guy was a customer she'd met at the blackjack table. She couldn't bring herself to admit that, in a moment of weakness, she had succumbed to superstition and had tried to hire his professional services as a gambler. Nor had she mentioned the fact that someone had attempted to take a second shot at Guy in her presence. That was why she hadn't brought the papers home. Though they didn't mention her by name, they mentioned the second attempt and a visitor who had saved Guy's life. If she was deceiving her great-grandmother, it was for the best of reasons. She didn't want to needlessly distress her. Guy would soon leave, never to return. Still, she had to say something.

She swallowed. "The papers describe Matherson as a prominent businessman in the computer industry." The sarcasm in her voice peaked her great-grandmother's dark brows. "He was shot while hosting a political fundraiser at his New Orleans residence in the Garden District. You're not going to believe who the guest of honor was." Her dark eyes danced mischievously as she took another bite of her apple. "Daniel Larroquette!"

Tante Delphine nodded as if she had expected that answer and picked up another sweet potato. "Go on, 'Tite."

Michaela knew she was playing a losing game. At any moment her great-grandmother was going to call her bluff. "I'll know more by this evening. After I've helped you with the housework, I'm going into Baton Rouge to make a few inquiries of my own."

"These papers, they say nothing more about who done the shooting or why?"

Michaela shook her head. This at least, she could answer truthfully. "The police can't or aren't saying if they have any leads. Still, the reporter who wrote the piece in today's paper wasn't shy about suggesting that Matherson will most likely turn up dead in a ditch."

The older woman stiffened in disapproval of her great-granddaughter's flippant tone. "You think this is cause for amusement?"

Michaela shook her head. "Sorry, no." She had sat by Guy's bedside day and night for two days and watched him battle for his life. The thought of him losing that battle had kept her from getting much sleep. "I'm going to call a friend in New Orleans and have him verify Matherson's business connections."

"Why you gon' do that?"

"Because we could be harboring a criminal," Michaela said in exasperation, the only hint of her darkest suspicions.

"If the thought so disturbs you, 'Tite, you should go back to Baton Rouge and leave this man to me." Tante Delphine dropped a long ribbon of potato peeling into the paper bag and began slicing the pared potato into chunks. "I don' believe he's a criminal. What you know that says different?"

"From what I've read? Nothing," she answered reluctantly. Lying by omission was a tricky business.

"That one." Tante Delphine jerked her head toward the bedroom at the front of the house. "He's got eyes like the tiger. I look into them and see his powerful hunger. But, down deep, he's got an honest soul."

Not wanting to argue but certain her great-grandmother's affection for Guy had nothing to do with facts and everything to do with her belief that he might harbor romantic designs on her great-granddaughter, Michaela changed the subject.

"Yancy was so drunk today he couldn't dock the ferry without my help. I told him if he takes me or anyone else out on the river when he's been drinking heavily again, I'll inform the authorities."

Tante Delphine clicked her tongue in disapproval. "You are hard on the man. The burden of his drinking a cruel one."

"That's why they invented A.A."

"Ah 'Tite! Where is your modern tolerance? No! Don' say it. When you have more experience of the world you'll find compassion is a better healer of wounds than self-righteousness." She smiled fondly at her great-granddaughter. "Yancy is a broken soul yet even he must earn his bread."

"He doesn't have the right to jeopardize the lives of others."

"*Tiens!*" Grand-mère's black eyes lit up. "Yancy forced you to take the ferry?"

"No but—" Michaela took a deep breath. "The relevant fact here is that the ferry is the only reliable source of transportation. The outboard limits what I can bring across."

"*Tout à fait.*"

Michaela shook her head. When Grand-mère wished to be her most provoking, she resorted to French.

Guy reached out and snatched open the mosquito netting. The room beyond it looked like something out of a stage set for a historical romance. He scanned it, looking for hints to his whereabouts, but nothing was familiar.

The walls were whitewashed. A palm-leaf-shaped punkah hung from one of the high ceiling beams. The floor-to-ceiling windows were shuttered and the floor was covered with what seemed to be reed matting. The few pieces of wood furniture were massive and dark and would not have fit within the modest contours of most modern homes. Kerosene lamps with hurricane shades provided the only source of light. Directly across the room from the bed a framed Audubon print offered the only color in the room.

The sound of footsteps echoed through what he calculated to be a large plantation-style house. He recognized the tread as female. So far, so good.

He rolled his head to look up. The bed in which he lay was an ornate rosewood half-tester carved with a floral motif. It was superior in every way to a similar one he had been negotiating to purchase for his own bedroom from a New Orleans antique dealer in Magazine Street. Simplicity and contrast. Light and dark. Contradictions that blended into harmony.

The sheets beneath him rustled with starch as he readjusted himself. Pain nudged him low down on his left side. He tucked a hand beneath the sheet and touched the bandage that strapped his left side. Beneath it his body ached but the mind-numbing pain was gone. His hand moved lower in a quest. It seemed the bandage was all he wore. Someone had taken his clothes.

Someone don' tried to separate you from this world.

The old woman had said those words to him. Her phrasing had given them the lyricism of an incantation. The truth came back in brutal simplicity.

Someone with a gun had tried to murder him. Jackson Pike, to be exact.

His mind locked onto the details in quick ugly flashes of remembrance. He had been shot on the balcony of his New Orleans home, in the midst of a dinner party he was hosting. He had been warned about Pike's parole and the man's threat to get even. Yet he thought he would beat the odds. He'd left the world of high-stakes gambling behind four long years ago. Still, he'd bet on Pike losing interest. The roll had come up craps. But he was hard to kill. Or maybe fate was toying with him.

Pike had tried again. In the hospital. And...

"Kiki saved my life!"

No, that wasn't right. Her name was Michaela Bellegarde. He had learned that much about her by chance less than a week ago. Strange how fate had decided all at once to toss his past life back in his face.

He smiled smugly. She had come all the way to New Orleans to learn why he was offering her $100 thousand. He couldn't think of one other person of his acquaintance who wouldn't simply have taken the cash and run. Or, maybe she'd been just as curious about him as he was about her.

Her name was different, she was older, more womanly, yet still full of unexpected contradictions. And still having an unexpected impact on his life. She'd saved his life...and nearly been killed because of him.

Hissing a curse, Guy rolled onto his side and swung his bare legs over the side of the bed. "Got to get away from here," he gasped. "Protect her!"

He struggled into a sitting position. In retaliation, the dull ache in his side became a scream. He gritted his teeth and looked around for his clothes. The single planter's chair in the room was empty. Where could they be? His gaze zeroed in on the mahogany armoire across the room.

He stood up, groaning loudly as the muscles that tightened to hold him upright clamped down on his wounded side. When his head stopped spinning he let the sheet slide from him and concentrated on the armoire. But the cabinet might as well have been a mile away. He took three steps before the floor tilted wickedly. He caught the chair back in both hands to keep the floor from rushing up to kiss him.

"And just what do you think you're doing?"

He hadn't heard her footsteps but there was no denying the reality of Michaela standing before the open shutters with brows arched in disapproval.

He glanced down to assure himself that the chair offered strategic modesty. "I need my clothes."

He saw her expression change into outright anger. Then, to his dismay, she stepped into the room, her arms full of folded sheets. "Are you crazy? Do you want to undo all of Grand-mère's hard work?"

She crossed the room in an ankle-length sleeveless dress of pale green gauze that drifted over her body like a caress. Her hair was loose and billowed in long, loose, dark waves over her shoulders and bare arms. Angel tresses, he thought.

She dumped the sheets onto the chair that stood between them and then her fists settled on the fullest part of the curves of her hips. "Well? What are you waiting for? Get back in that bed."

His jaws remained locked together as he said, "Go away."

She tilted her head to one side and gave him the fish-eye. "Think again."

He met her gaze squarely. "I . . . can't . . . move."

"You—?" Michaela's gaze shifted to where his hands gripped the chair's back. His knuckles were white from the pressure he exerted on them. Despite having seen him without even the modest covering of a sheet these last days, she remained impressed by how much bigger he looked upright. The neat white bandage taped to his lower left side accentuated the fan of black hair that tapered from his broad chest to a feathering that flanked his navel before disappearing behind the barrier of the chair. Her gaze flew back up to his face.

"You should have known better," she said as she skirted the chair to reach him. She reached for his hand, pried his fingers loose, and transferred it to her shoulder. "Here. Use me as a crutch."

"Towel."

Michaela frowned at the strangled sound. "What?"

"Hand me a towel," he said between locked jaws.

"Oh." She reached for the top one in her pile and handed it to him. Why hadn't *she* thought of that?

He wrapped the bath towel low on his hips and tucked the ends together beneath his navel. The towel gaped open over one long, hairy, masculine thigh. She wondered if the ends would stay tucked against the strain and had her doubts.

Guy shifted his balance to face her more directly and grunted. If she hadn't cared that he was as naked as the day he as born, why the hell had he? Maybe it had something to do with his sense of helplessness. He was certain she wouldn't have been so nonchalant about her own nakedness before him. Or had she changed that much?

He looked down at her. The top of her head only reached his chin. She didn't seem strong enough to bear his weight even though he knew she had the night he escaped the hospital. Then as now, she gave him little choice.

"Come on," she encouraged. "You shouldn't be standing yet. It will only take three steps at most to reach the bed."

Because his knees were buckling under the strain of his weight, he moved his other hand to her shoulder and stepped out from behind the chair back.

"That's right." She smiled up at him. "One step. Now another. Easy!"

Guy leaned heavily on her as he forced his feet to move one slow step at a time. To distract himself from the pain he concentrated on the woman before him. Her hair smelled of sunshine and her skin of gardenias. He had assumed the floral scent had come into his room on the breeze. Now he realized it must have been her presence that accounted for the fragrance that wrapped seductively around his consciousness each time he awoke. If that was true, then she must have remained by his side the entire night. That thought triggered others—of how often he had dreamed about her when he was too tired to protect himself against useless yearnings, or when he'd won big. Her presence had hovered at the edge of his awareness during every big game, every time he took a calculated but necessary risk. He had counted on "Kiki" being there, just out of reach but as real emotionally to him as the young woman now before him.

He lowered his gaze. She was frowning in concentration as she backed slowly toward the bed. As he watched she tucked the ripe fullness of her lower lip under the edge of her very white teeth. She had braced her hands flat against his shoulders for counterbalance. He could feel his heart beating hard and fast under her right palm. Eleven silver bangle bracelets tinkled as they moved, the only music to their awkward dance. Suddenly he was aware of how flimsy her dress felt beneath his hands. It was the kind of garment a man could easily slip off or lift aside. The thought did nothing to improve his delicate situation.

Michaela realized the most difficult part was going to be lowering him back onto the mattress. She moved in close to him and slipped her palms under his elbows to offer additional support.

"Take your time," she said calmly. "Just unlock your knees and let yourself drop onto the bed."

He shifted his hands from her shoulders to her upper arms for better leverage and flexed his knees. Pain knifed into him, forcing a sharp grunt from him.

"Wait a minute." Michaela moved in against him to take more of his weight onto herself. Her action brought their bodies together. She embraced him, careful to make certain her arms were above his bandage. At eye level she saw nestled in the mat of his black body hair one small male nipple. It was nugget hard. His skin was hot, but no warmer than warranted by the fact that he was a vitally alive man. And one that was blatantly sexually aroused. The bulge prodding her middle couldn't be mistaken for the tuck in the towel.

She felt her cheeks warm but immediately told herself not to take it personally. Men's bodies were different than women's. They behaved in the most unlikely fashion under the most unusual circumstances. He was in pain. He couldn't control his body's actions. But it was flattering all the same.

"Okay, now try," she directed a little breathlessly and hoped he mistook it as the result of her exertions.

As he slipped inch by inch down her front, his lips grazed her brow and then cheek. She stepped in between his spread knees to keep his weight shifted toward her and heard his sharp intake of surprise as her hip brushed his arousal. Somehow his towel had come undone and slipped to the floor.

Concentrate she told herself. Just a few precious inches to the bed. "You're doing fine," she whispered. "Just a few inches more." *Oh dear!* That sounded like a clumsy double entendre.

Guy had his own concerns. Sweat broke out on his forehead and his teeth suffered under the strain before his hips met the bed. By then his face was buried in her bodice. His lips felt the texture of gauze, and beneath that the slight scrape of a lacy bra cup. He shut his eyes for an instant, intently absorbing the delicious warmth and scent of her skin where his nose poked through the space between two buttons. All he had to do was pull down and she'd be in his lap. He knew he had no right to be thinking such things but nothing—not even the pain prodding under his ribs—could stop the drag of desire deep down.

He didn't look up at her. Did she feel it, too? Every instinct told him she did but that didn't mean she welcomed that awareness or that she would even acknowledge it.

The contact lasted only an instant and then she was backing away from him. She tossed the bedsheet with economical accuracy over his lap before moving to the head of the bed to fluff his pillows. Then she took the weight of his shoulders as he maneuvered himself back against the fresh linen.

It occurred to him as she resettled the sheet up over his nakedness that someone had changed the bedding. He remembered vaguely his regret that he had bloodied the linen the night before. When she backed away, he finally looked up. There was a polite but impersonal smile on her face yet the tension level in the room hovered at the awkward moments level.

To break the impasse he said, "How long did I sleep?"

"Two days."

"Two—!" He did some rapid recalculation. "Then it's Thursday?"

She frowned at him. Her eyes were enormous in her delicate face. "It's Friday."

That sent an electric shock through him. He had lost four days from his life thanks to a bullet. "And you've been here, the entire time?"

"Yes."

His brooding gaze remained on her. For days he had been lying helpless in her care. That thought unnerved him more than the loss of the days. "Why?"

She smiled. "I would think the past five minutes would be self-explanatory."

He allowed her that moment. How polite she sounded, as if she had not spent the last few days taking care of the most intimate details of his needs. He felt suddenly more vulnerable than he had earlier standing naked before her. He never let anyone this close, not ever.

He felt stripped of his privacy and dignity. He wanted it back. If he had to take it out of her hide he would. "What's in this for you?"

She arched a dark brow. "I beg your pardon?"

"I asked what's in it for you, looking after me?" He let his gaze wander with insulting deliberation from her face to her breasts. "Was it the opportunity to exact revenge?" His gaze shifted to the tented lump in his lap before rising back to her face. "Or just female curiosity?"

Michaela folded her arms as annoyance tugged at the corners of her mouth. The last minutes had been awkward and embarrassing for both of them. Another man would have let it go. Guy Matherson was running true to form with cold, calculating and crude honesty. "Does it matter?"

He leaned back deeper into the pillows. "Call it self-protection. I want to know what your Florence Nightingale act is going to cost me."

Michaela saw his gaze shift away, dismissing her, but she didn't rattle nearly as easily as the nineteen-year-old he remembered. And there was something more. She had been waiting three long worried days to have this conversation with him. "What if I said I wanted nothing?"

Beneath heavy dark brows, his vivid blue gaze tracked her down. "Nobody does anything for anyone unless they figure there's something in it for themselves."

To his surprise she didn't react emotionally. "Is that grammatically horrendous statement another of your mottos?"

Inwardly he smiled. She had changed. The new maturity suited the refinement of her features. The girl was a woman now, a very intriguing woman. He changed tactics. "Where am I?"

"At my great-grandmother's home, Belle Isle."

He grinned. "What the hell is Belle Isle?"

"An island, Mr. Matherson, a delta river island in the Mississippi."

"No sh—no kidding?" He sat up a little higher. "You own a whole island?" She nodded. "Well, well, ain't life grand?"

This time she did react. Her face lost its wary neutrality. "I don't know you but I do know a man like you doesn't catch a bullet by mistake. Somebody is looking for you to finish the job. You can't hide here."

Because her words matched his newly forming hopes too closely for comfort he reacted in anger. "Did I ask? Did I ask you to come to New Orleans? Did I ask you to get involved? I told you to mind your own damn business. The way I see it *you* hijacked *me!*"

She recoiled from the remark. There was an underlying bitterness in his voice to which he had no right. "And how far do you think you would have gotten without my help?"

"Far enough to suit my needs." He smirked. "What's wrong, did you think I'd take back the money?"

"You really are a lowlife, aren't you?"

The insult told him that he'd gone too far. His initial curiosity about her that had first made him notice her in Vegas returned and edged out his hostile wariness. A moment ago she had been touching him, vibrantly warm and real. Now she seemed a cold and remote if lovely woman. He wanted her warm generosity back. That admission surfaced in his conscience reluctantly.

"How about a truce?" he murmured sulkily. "I can make it worth your while to shelter me."

He saw anger flatten the luscious curves of her mouth. "I can't be bought."

He doubted that was true but decided not to further antagonize her. He looked away after a moment of silence. "Look, I don't expect anything more from you, if that's what's worrying you." Suddenly he was annoyed again, almost angry that he let her maneuver him into the admission. He wanted lots from her, more with every moment. "I'll be out of here as soon as I can move."

"I think there's something you should know."

"Yes?" He deadpanned the word. Here it came, the punch to the gut. He *knew* there'd be something, some payoff owed.

"I'm an attorney, Mr. Matherson."

"Congratulations."

"You may want to restrain your approval when I tell you what that means. As an officer of the court, I should to report your whereabouts to the authorities."

"Have you?" He didn't know he still knew how to hold his breath.

"No."

Suddenly he wanted to kiss her. It was the only clear thought in his head. "Why?"

"Call it self-protection. I don't want my great-grand-mother dragged into your problems. I suspect there was some illegality involved in your wounding."

Yeah, like assault with a deadly weapon. "You mean you think I must have deserved to get shot?" His mouth was a flat line of irritation. "If I were to tell you I was shot for doing my duty as a citizen, what would you say?"

"Were you?"

He glared at her. "You don't believe it's possible I could do a good deed?"

Michaela shrugged. "I once appealed to your better nature and discovered you don't have one."

His confusion fused into anger. Why did she insist on pushing when she obviously wasn't about to believe anything he had to say? He shifted on the bed, the throbbing of raw-edged pain further souring his mood.

"Where are you going?" he demanded when he saw her turn away.

She turned her head but the smile on her face had no humor in it. "This is my home, Mr. Matherson. I come and go according to my own whims."

"You're going to call the cops," he accused.

She stared at him. "Do you really think I'm that petty?"

Yes! No! Maybe. The last thought shamed him. It wasn't true and he was glad it wasn't true. But her brand of open honesty frightened him. Some deep secret place inside him recoiled from it.

"I haven't thanked you for what you did for me in New Orleans." The statement sounded phoney and flat, too formal after all they'd been through. But he didn't know how to apologize. "Why didn't you just call Sam?"

"The number you gave me got an answering machine with your voice."

He grunted. "Must have given you the wrong number."

"That's what I decided. You were pretty doped up and in no condition to tell me anything more. So I did what I always do when I don't know what else to do. I came home."

"Lucky you." She cocked her head in question. "You have a home to go to," he added for clarification.

Michaela regarded him quizzically. "Don't you?"

"No, and don't get maudlin on me. The reality of life is that we're all alone. When the chips are down, it's always every man for himself. The name of the game of life is solitaire."

"What about love?"

His handsome face turned stony and the impact of that was like a shove into a wall. "What about it?"

"Never mind." Michaela turned to pick up her laundry. "You must be hungry. I'll bring you something to eat. In the meantime, if you need anything, just ring the bell on your bedside table."

"Michaela?"

She turned toward him, braced for another insult. "Yes?"

But his face was void of all emotion. "You saved my life. I promise, I'll find a way to repay you."

Michaela debated accepting his thanks. If only he knew the truth! Nothing he could have offered her would have made her willingly step into that hospital room had she known what was about to happen. And yet, she had not hesitated to help him escape the trap of a hospital bed—not because he had asked—but because he needed her. She'd responded to his need because it was her nature.

Yet as she looked at his tense face and wary eyes, she doubted he would accept her explanation. What sort of life had he led to believe that every act of human kindness had a price tag attached?

She came back to the bed and reached out to him. She didn't know why but she couldn't touch that hauntingly handsome face with its bristle of beard and pained blue eyes. Instead she plowed her fingers into the black hair above his right temple and then bent to place a kiss in the hair she'd mussed. "You're welcome."

Guy watched her leave, too touched to trust his voice. And really, there was nothing to say in answer to her tender gesture. Just looking at her made something squeeze hard on his heart. She had gone out of her way to protect him, brought him home like a stray kitten with a broken leg, and nursed him back to health. And all he could do was snipe at her generosity and make light of her personal code of ethics.

That painful realization was as close as he'd ever come to admitting that he didn't much like himself. Another man might call the complex set of emotions she had set in motion inside him love. But he didn't think it was that. He didn't expect or even want that.

He had known the first time he saw Kiki that she was going to impact his life. What he hadn't known was that later, in denying her the favor she asked of him, he would lose more than the chance to woo a pretty woman. Some of his self-respect had walked out the door with her.

He'd made a big mistake when he'd hit pay dirt at a big game the night after they met at the blackjack table. He believed she had been the source of his good luck yet he had forgotten her in a single-minded pursuit of ever bigger games and ever bigger stakes and ever bigger winnings. In his experience women were easily come by. Some waited patiently for him to notice. Others thrust themselves upon him for that recognition. Over the course of that summer he had grown arrogant and reckless. He even got careless at the table, relying too much on luck. By the end of the summer his winning streak had abandoned him along with his notorious powers of concentration.

Guy murmured a self-deprecating curse. By the time Kiki sought him out he'd lost his bankroll, and his nerve. When she asked him to gamble her last dime, he had choked. He was afraid of her belief in him. Convinced his luck had run dry, he had turned her down. Then he'd committed the most selfish act of his life. He had tried to steal luck from her by taking her silver bracelet. Strangely enough, it had worked. His luck returned, better and stronger than ever.

He rubbed the smooth cool strip of silver circling his left wrist. Call it superstition or just a gut level hunch but he didn't think it was coincidence that Michaela had come to the hospital the night Pike had made a second attempt on his life. What he did not know was why she had come at all. Any other person he knew would have taken the money and run. She had come seeking answers. Now he wanted answers of his own.

For the first time in his life he was not thinking about running away from something but toward something. The pounding of fear deep inside him redoubled his heart rate. What if it was too late? What if men like him didn't get second chances?

Chapter 7

"Why haven't you returned my calls?"

Michaela glanced down at the phone in her hand. She hadn't heard Daniel Larroquette's voice since the day she broke off their engagement nine months earlier. He sounded almost as hurt and offended now as he had then. But that was Daniel. Everything that affected him personally was by definition important. "I've been busy. Didn't get your messages until today."

"Your uncle didn't contact you? My messages said it was urgent," he replied testily.

"Your messages always say urgent. You operate in italics." Michaela heard his snort of amusement and hoped she had defused the moment. "So tell me, what's so urgent this time?"

To her surprise there was a moment of hesitation on the line. Then she heard him say, as if he had turned away from the phone, "Right. Ask him to hold a moment." His voice came back to the receiver as he said, "I've got to take this call, Michaela. It's—"

"Urgent," Michaela supplied. "Fine. But I may not be here when you call back. I'm staying out on Belle Isle these days."

"You can't leave until we talk." There was no possibility of a request in that dictatorial tone. "I'm flying into Baton Rouge this evening from a political rally up in Shreveport. Meet me at the airport and I'll take you to dinner. No, better, a drink."

"You're getting cheap, Daniel."

"All right, dinner. Pick me up outside luggage pickup about seven."

Michaela didn't get to reply because he hung up too quickly. It took her only a moment to realize what she'd done—made a date with her ex-fiancé. "Not a bright move, Michaela!"

She slumped back in the leather wing chair behind the desk in her uncle's law office and stared out into the middle distance. Something had been gnawing at her for days now, something she had tried hard not to put into words.

She was in Baton Rouge because she had to get off Belle Isle, away from Guy Matherson for a while.

He had awakened from a midmorning nap in the sullen mood she had found him in earlier in the day. He had blocked her and Grand-mère's every attempt to make things more pleasant for him. Having confined him to the bed as much for health reasons as his lack of attire, they had tried to bathe and shave him. He had behaved as badly as any child, ordering Michaela out of the room. The bath water had ended up equally soaking the mattress and the floor before Grand-mère finished. Only the straight razor Grand-mère then produced had had a calming effect on him. Perhaps he thought he'd end up sliced to ribbons if he fought her attempts to shave him. Sneaking back in, Michaela had watched in fascination as Grand-mère deftly scraped four days' growth of black bristles from his cheeks while cooing soothingly to him in her lilting French tongue. When his clean-shaven face emerged from the hot towel Grand-mère had wrapped it in, she had felt a sudden unexpected of hot flash of desire.

Michaela slumped farther down into the chair as if she could hide from her thoughts within its butter-soft contours. She had been so surprised that she hadn't guarded her expression. She'd seen his blue eyes flare in recognition of her reaction.

Suddenly she was remembering how he'd looked in the nude, his jaw set against the pain while his body arrogantly ignored all proprieties. Her experience with men was strictly limited but to her eyes he *was* impressive.

"So that's all it was," Michaela said aloud to herself. "It was lust for an Alpha male."

Grand-mère was right. A woman only had to look at Guy Matherson to want to crawl into his bed. Passion without regard for reality. Primitive urges that leaked through years of civilized training. She wanted him. That astonished and embarrassed her. So she'd borrowed the Buick and come into town for the afternoon. She needed breathing room.

"Problems with Larroquette?" inquired Leon Belle-garde as he entered his office and noticed Michaela's scowl.

Michaela rose from behind his desk and scooped up the half dozen yellow phone message slips she had been handed when she dropped into the law firm on a whim. "Daniel's just being his usual the-world-revolves-around-me self."

Her uncle's eyes narrowed. "He's not pressuring you in any way?"

"Of course not. He just needs a lift from the airport tonight." Michaela didn't want to admit that she'd been maneuvered against her better judgment. "Thanks again for the use of the phone." She offered him a quick kiss as she passed him and headed for the door.

"Did he tell you his lead is slipping in the polls?"

Michaela turned back. "No. But, personal feelings aside, Daniel is the best candidate. I will reassure him tonight."

Her uncle frowned at her as if she had said something of which he very much disapproved. "Some men get a little nervous when they realize they're closing the door on their bachelor days. Larroquette may be suddenly regretting what he lost in letting you go. Don't offer him too much comfort.''

Michaela laughed. ''What makes you think I'd even consider it?''

Uncle Leon pursed his lips as he did whenever he was considering a decision. ''Something's happened since I saw you here a few days ago. You look like a young woman whose emotions have been deeply stirred.'' He held up a hand as she opened her mouth. ''I don't need to know what it is. Prefer not to know. But you've got what Grand-mère Delphine calls a 'womanly look' about the eyes. You're searching for something. Don't let Larroquette confuse you or get in your way.''

Michaela glanced away from him in disconcert. ''You sound every bit as mysterious as Grand-mère when she's had one of her visions. And all this time I've thought that you were the most sensible head in the family.''

He chuckled. ''I am. Grand-mère's the one with the power.''

She hesitated only a moment before asking him the question that had often come to mind but that she'd been too embarrassed to ask. ''Do you think Grand-mère has special powers?''

His eyes twinkled. ''I know it. She helped me win Corrine. She was engaged when we met at a Mardi Gras party to a fellow by the name of Samson.''

Michaela feigned indignation. ''Uncle Leon, you don't mean you actually stole another man's fiancée?''

He nodded with a sly smile. ''Corrine hadn't married him so to my mind she was free to change her mind. Only she didn't want to sell herself cheap. It was 1942. I was a sailor on a three-day pass in the port of New Orleans. I didn't have much time to spend convincing her that she should spend at least one of those nights with me.''

''So you seduced her, you old rascal!''

"I did not! I married her!" He chuckled again, the youthful swagger of the man peeking through. "We got a special dispensation from the parish. We had one night before I shipped out."

"So how did Grand-mère help you?"

"She gave me the love philter which turned the trick."

This time genuine surprise colored Michaela's tone. "You drugged Aunt Corrine?"

"No such thing!" Her uncle looked offended. "The potion merely filters out distractions so that the user can see clearly his or her heart's desire."

"How romantic."

"Exactly." He winked at her again. "Every woman deserves a little romance and adventure. Find a man who can give it to you."

"Advice to the lovelorn, Uncle Leon?"

"Advice to a pretty young woman who's a little afraid of her own attractiveness. Don't be too nice to Larroquette. He won't be grateful. He'll think you've changed your mind."

"I'll remember that," Michaela said as she reached for he doorknob. "See you at Belle Isle next Saturday."

Later that evening, Michaela remembered her uncle's words of caution. She was threading her way from the powder room through the tightly packed tables in the dimly lit jazz club toward the booth where Daniel Larroquette sat.

The evening had started off well enough. When they met at the airport Daniel had kissed her lightly enough to be called friendly and yet long enough to be called more than perfunctory.

Despite the latest polls, Daniel looked remarkably well for a man on the last leg of a dead heat campaign. His face was tan and his sandy blond hair had been expertly styled to withstand wind and humidity. He had doffed his jacket and rolled his shirtsleeves back as if he had been hard at work up to the moment he stepped off the plane.

She had worn her long hair in a loose dark cloud and changed into a very feminine softly shaped dress so that he wouldn't be able to think to himself that his memories of her were better than the reality. She'd seen his gray eyes move approvingly over her yet he had wisely refrained from anything more than "Wow."

Dinner had been easy and fun. He'd taken her downriver to a place where she had been dozens of times before, a catfish house where the menu was written on a blackboard and the smoking hot fried fish was served on butcher paper with a bottle of Tabasco sauce. While they ate with their fingers he'd entertained her with stories of life on the campaign trail. He had even managed to make her a little envious of the fact she could have been working with him—if they'd stayed together.

She couldn't remember now which of them had mentioned music but somehow they'd found themselves here in this little bar tucked into a corner of a quiet street in Baton Rouge that featured a live band.

Daniel came to his feet as she reached him. "Dance?"

Michaela hesitated as he held out his hand. Once that look in his eyes had made her eager to be alone with him. Now it just made her cautious. Only now did she realize that by coming here with him she might have implied an intimacy she didn't want. He had yet to say why he needed to see her tonight. "Doesn't Morgan mind when you dance with other women?"

The mention of his fiancée made him smile. "She's going to be a politician's wife. She'd better get used to it."

"Then I suppose one dance won't wreck your career," she said baitingly.

She saw him glance around before he could stop himself. She moved with him out into the dark, postage-stamp-size floor with a few other couples. There wasn't much room to do more than sway to the music.

After a few seconds, she leaned back against his arm and looked up into his face. "We've been together three hours and you still haven't said why you wanted to see me to-night."

He nodded. "Truth is, I don't get much of a chance to unwind these days. I've been having such a good time, I didn't want it to end." When she didn't respond in agreement he went on a little more stiffly, "I'm not quite certain how to begin."

"Why don't you name the topic and we'll go from there."

She could see his light eyes gleaming in the dimness and wondered if he was really as uncomfortable as the shadows made him look. "Fair enough." He bent close to whisper in her ear. "The topic is Guy Matherson."

Michaela's mouth dropped open but she snapped it shut as he leaned away from her. The parental voice inside her head began issuing orders like a drill sergeant. *Think! Keep a clear head! Don't rush! Don't give anything away!* "Who?" she said blankly.

She saw by the slight frown that appeared between his sandy brows that she hadn't reacted as he expected. Perhaps, because she didn't trust herself to react at all.

"I've never known you to be coy, Michaela. I know you went down to New Orleans to see Matherson two days after he was shot. I want to know why and how you know him."

She smiled and shook her head, reminding herself to stick with the surface problems until she knew where this was going and why. "You spent three hours working up the nerve to ask me if I'm seeing another man?"

Daniel's expression soured. "You're *not* seeing him, are you?"

Michaela forced herself to keep her voice light. "Perhaps you'd like to take this conversation back to the booth?"

Daniel nodded once and followed her back to the table.

As she slid into the booth she turned to face him. In law school she had learned that a good offense was the best defense. "What makes you think I even know Guy Matherson?"

His lips thinned into twin lines of displeasure as he slid in behind her. "I'm the one who gave him your address."

Michaela digested this startling news. "How did he know we knew one another?"

"He saw that damned footage of us celebrating our engagement last Christmas that played all over the state last weekend," Daniel groused. "Seems my opponent has friends in the media and they didn't want the electorate to forget Morgan wasn't my first choice as a wife."

"I'm sorry about that," Michaela said sincerely.

"It's politics as usual. The thing is, Matherson has been a heavy contributor to my campaign. Don't tell me you didn't know that he was hosting a fund-raiser for me the night he was shot. My God! I thought, at first, the shot was meant for me."

"How awful," Michaela murmured. *Trust Daniel to think first of himself. How strange was this going to get?* "Do you know why Matherson was shot?"

His gaze narrowed. "That's what I thought you might be able to tell me."

"What do the police say?" she countered.

"They're pretty closemouthed." His expression said he didn't like that one bit. "Ken, my campaign manager, says that could be good news. The less attention brought to the case the better, until after the election. But now Matherson's disappeared. It could get ugly if he doesn't turn up soon."

"Or not at all?" she suggested.

He nodded glumly. "The rag sheets will have a field day. A major contributor to *my* campaign was gunned down practically in my sight. After a second attempt on his life—in a hospital for God's sake—he disappears."

"Maybe Matherson is just taking himself out of the line of fire until he can recover," she suggested.

Daniel put both hands on her shoulders, lightly squeezing the sheer fabric of her dress. "Do you know something, Michaela? You've got to tell me."

Michaela shook her head. Daniel's interest in Guy was strictly self-serving. He didn't want any surprises to surface in the final days of his campaign. If his self-interest reminded her uncomfortably of Guy's, it didn't matter. She wasn't about to consider divulging Guy's whereabouts without much better cause. "Sorry. I can't help you."

Anger flared up and died in his eyes as he leaned closer to her, all persuasion and smiles. "Don't be stubborn, Michaela. You may soon need my help. The police are questioning everyone connected with the case. You were the last one to see him before he disappeared. It could get messy."

Michaela allowed her growing annoyance with Daniel's manipulations show in her face. "How did you learn about that? It wasn't in the papers."

Daniel smirked. "I have my sources."

"What else did your sources tell you?"

"That you lied about being a relative to get in to see him after-hours. Which means you must have more than a passing interest in the man." He seemed to sense he was stepping over the line and backed off. "Look, Michaela, I'm sorry about that crack about you and Matherson. I don't care what he is to you. But my possible future could be on the line here."

"And you thought I would help you find Matherson?"

Daniel's attractive face eased into a grin. "Exactly."

"No."

"What?"

"No. You know the word."

His frown deepened. "The police could decide at any moment that you are a suspect."

"Right," Michaela said sourly. "I confess. I kidnapped Matherson from the hospital. I made my escape in Grandmère's old Buick. He's being held prisoner on Belle Isle. Oh, but I need a motive. Let's see, he's there to be my love slave because a certain candidate for public office is marrying someone else. Is that how you figured it?"

Daniel's expression turned smug. "Why didn't I expect this? You're still harboring resentment over our breakup."

Michaela turned to reach for her purse on the seat beside her. "The stress of campaigning is getting to you." She looked back at him and said in a perfectly composed voice, "I left you, remember?"

Daniel reached for her as she slid away. "Now just a—"

Michaela jerked away so quickly his hand had caught in the neckline of her dress. She heard the fabric give and one of the pearl buttons that closed the front popped off, hit the tabletop and bounced off into the darkness.

"Gee, Michaela, I'm sorry."

She looked back at his stunned expression and said, "Yes, Daniel, you are. Don't call me again."

"Hey! Aren't you going to take me back to the airport?"

She looked down at her missing button before replying. "Call a cab, Daniel. It's cheaper than buying me a new dress."

Michaela sent turf and gravel flying as she stepped hard on the Buick's brakes before Belle Isle.

As she exited the car she noticed the silhouettes of two people standing in the veranda, Grand-mère and Guy Matherson.

The question neither the media nor Daniel could answer was what was the motive for the shooting. Well, standing on her great-grandmother's veranda was the one person who could answer that question.

As she stalked across the yard, laughter floated out toward her across the grass. For reasons she didn't pause to sort out, the sounds of amusement made her angrier. She had been hoodwinked twice this week by two different men from her past. If Matherson had answered even one of the questions she had put to him, she wouldn't have walked blindly into Daniel's trap. She resented, too, that Daniel had thought he could manipulate her for his own selfish reasons, as if she were still gaga over him. As if she had ever really been gaga over him! Only once in her life had she been that impressed with a man and Guy Matherson had turned out to be the biggest letdown of all.

"It's nice to see someone's having a pleasant evening," she said ungraciously, "but I wouldn't believe anything this man has to say, Grand-mère."

Tante Delphine's disapproval of her great-grand-daughter's tone registered in her black eyes. "This gentleman has a name, 'Tite. It's Guy. I tell him it's a good name, a strong name." She turned to Guy with amusement in her voice. "Michaela is my most favorite if provoking great-grandchild. But then, you know this about her."

Michaela turned a suspicious gaze on Guy. What had he been saying about her? And, why was he looking at her as if she'd just jumped out of a cake?

"I was about to win a generous wager from Guy," Tante Delphine continued smoothly. "After a most pleasant meal, I bet him that the number of bats to pass the porch would number twelve before the hour was out. I would have won, too, if your noisy arrival hadn't frightened them away."

"She's a con artist," Guy said with a chuckle. "I didn't suspect I'd been set up until after the wager was made."

"The bats are hers," Michaela said and found, to her annoyance, that her voice sounded choked with emotion. Anger, she assured herself, not a flustered response to the fact his blue gaze remained fixed on her.

"The bats are messengers for my psychic powers," Tante Delphine replied without embarrassment.

"Really?" Guy's considering glance took in the tiny silver-haired woman dressed in a flowing emerald caftan who was smiling serenely at him. "I believe in luck and omens."

Tante Delphine nodded slowly. "I know you do. And they favor you. The signs are strong. You must allow me to read your palm before you leave. I sense a change in your life, a—"

"I'm sorry, Grand-mère." Michaela interjected herself between them. "But I don't think Mr. Matherson should be up yet."

A challenge entered his shadowed gaze. "As you know, I would have been up yesterday, if I'd had clothes."

Michaela noticed belatedly that he was wearing one of her brother's faded denim shirts and a pair of the jeans he kept there for bumming around the island. The clothes reminded her that the last time she'd seen Matherson, he'd been stark naked. She forced herself to look away. "Did you give Mr. Matherson these clothes, Grand-mère, or did he just take them?"

"Such a question, 'Tite. Of course I give them to him." Tante Delphine rolled her eyes. "You aren't yourself tonight. It must be the heat. You sit with Guy while I fetch a frosty glass of lemonade for you."

When the screen banged shut behind the elderly woman, Michaela faced Guy in challenge but he beat her into speech.

"Where the hell have you been?" The abrupt anger in his tone stunned her. "Don't you realize how worried Tante Delphine has been? You left at noon and promised to be back before dinnertime. It's now," he checked his watch, "after eleven." His gaze slid up and down her. "She made gumbo especially for you and you didn't even bother to let her know you wouldn't be here to eat it."

"I forgot that," Michaela said in a subdued voice. "Anyway, there was no way to call."

That didn't appease his temper. "Now you come back looking like you've been in a brawl and smelling like you've been in a bar."

Michaela put a hand simultaneously to her hair and her bodice. With the top button missing, it gaped open to reveal the lacy upper edge of her bra. She had forgotten about the incident with Daniel. Yet, she didn't feel the need to explain herself to this man who was staring at her like a betrayed husband. "I stood on the ferry deck on the ride over. The wind must have tossed me around a bit."

His eyes narrowed. "Since when does the wind wear aftershave?"

Michaela groaned in frustration, sorry she'd tried to duck the truth. Daniel wore enough cologne to be recognizable fifty feet downwind. Some of it must have rubbed off on her clothes during their dancing. No wonder Yancy had leered at her and asked about her new boyfriend. Still, the fact she had been out with a man didn't give Guy Matherson the right to chastise her.

She dropped her hand from her bodice, letting the edge of lace once more peek through. She wasn't a teenager or an adulteress. "I had a date," she announced smugly.

"You deserve a better class of ape," he shot back without missing a beat.

He reached up and fumbled with his right hand until he had withdrawn a battered cigarette from his shirt pocket. The action was surprisingly clumsy for a man whose physical grace she had once admired. Perhaps he was still in pain. The thought disturbed her. Yet, she was too provoked to ease her stance.

"My great-grandmother doesn't approve of smoking," she said in her most censorious tone.

"Liar." He placed the cigarette between his lips before continuing. "She had her nightly pipe before you arrived. Some awful concoction that smelled like a combination of vanilla extract and shoe leather."

"She cures her own tobacco," Michaela replied, admitting momentary defeat.

He produced from his trouser pocket a silver lighter. He flicked it open and in the glow from the flame that emerged she saw his profile. Her stomach did somersaults. She felt stifled by the night. When he looked up, he was smiling— had she ever seen him really smile? His smile—damn it!— was quite effective. The realization made her angrier than before.

"Why didn't you tell me you knew Daniel Larroquette?"

"Why should I?" A second later his head snapped toward her, his eyes widening in understanding. "Was *he* your date? I'd have thought you had more pride."

"For the record, I'm the one who broke off our engagement."

"That's not the way he tells it."

Something about the way he said that made her resist the temptation to ignore the jibe. Out of curiosity she said, "What is Daniel telling people?"

He glanced at her from beneath arched black brows, his lower lip illuminated in seductive curvature as he dragged on his cigarette. "Larroquette maintains you were both in love but you were afraid that you couldn't measure up as a politician's wife."

"What?"

Guy nodded. "You believed he was going straight to the top and you didn't think you had what it took to go there with him."

"He wouldn't have dared say that," she replied confidently.

Guy shrugged. "He said more. He said he tried to bolster your confidence by giving you every opportunity to be with him. But ultimately, as much as you loved him, he had to accept that what he needed and what you were able to offer weren't enough."

"But that's not true!" she exclaimed. "Why would he tell you such lies?"

"Maybe because I'd asked your name and he was feeling territorial."

"There's nothing to feel territorial about," she murmured. But it made a certain sense, considering how Daniel had behaved when questioning her about Matherson. "Daniel and I were over months ago."

Guy's gaze flicked over her. "But not so long ago that you didn't allow a friendly kiss."

"There was no kiss!"

"Really?" He leaned back against one of the columns that held up the second floor gallery and blew a puff of smoke her in her direction. "You look like something went too far, or not far enough. If I'd kissed you, you wouldn't look like you got left standing at the starting block, sweetheart."

Michaela stepped back from the blue-white haze wafting her way. "God, I hate your habits."

He looked at her from beneath dark brows. His aquamarine gaze sought her out across the width of the porch. "Once you thought very highly of some of them, especially my way of kissing you. You were purring from the first one. Or was it only because you wanted something?" he finished sarcastically.

Stunned by his sudden change of mood, Michaela rounded on him. "Why do you always do that?"

"Do what?"

"Introduce selfishness as a motive for every human action."

"It's self-explanatory. Everyone is out for himself, what he can get. You figure the odds and take your chances, same as everybody else."

"I'm not like that."

His gaze flickered over her. "Aren't you?"

It was a direct challenge and one she wasn't about to back down from. "You're so good at assigning motives to others, let me offer my observations of you. You think everyone else has an angle and everything has a price because that's how you operate. You might be surprised to know," she continued primly, "that some people do things for the sheer pleasure of the experience."

His expression changed, suddenly alert, as if he were a predator who had spotted something of great interest to him. "Maybe you're right. Maybe some things should be done for the sheer pleasure of it."

He tossed his cigarette away.

Michaela watched the glowing ember make a slow somersault in the air and then wink out in the grass like a dying firefly. She watched it because it seemed safer than acknowledging his approach. From the periphery of her vision she noted that her brother's shirt was tucked into jeans whose waistband rode low on Guy's leaner hips. She saw his bare feet in his dress shoes. He had left the hospital without socks. Belatedly she remembered that he hadn't bothered to struggle into underwear, either. The erotic image that thought summoned disconcerted her.

When he reached her side he lifted a hand and lightly encircled her throat with his fingers.

Because she didn't expect so gentle a touch she recoiled before she could stop herself.

His hand lifted from her skin. "What are you afraid of?" To her surprise he sounded hurt.

"I just—you surprised me."

He didn't reply but after a moment his hand returned. For several seconds his thumb simply moved slowly up and down the side of her slim neck. Beneath the pad of his roving thumb Michaela felt her pulse beat faster than before. Still, she didn't look up at him. She stared out at the night and saw a bat swoop across the moon.

"You've got a face that drives me crazy, you know that?" His thumb curled inward to delve into the shallow spot at the base of her neck. "All those nights you sat by my bedside. All those times you leaned over me in comfort. I felt you haunting me in every muscle and bone of my body. And each time I wanted to touch you." He raked his thumbnail lightly along one of her collarbones. "Want to know what else I wanted to do?"

"No." She said the word reflectively, automatically, a lifetime of proper training coming to play before the woman in her was consulted.

"No?" His tone was light but skeptical.

"Yes."

She heard the smile in his voice. "That's better." He moved in close until their bodies were almost, but not quite, touching. "I wanted to get so close to you that I couldn't tell where you left off and I began."

Michaela knew she should resent his aggressiveness. Yet, strangely she didn't. She sensed that he didn't know much about real intimacy. Passion was something he understood. He was attracted to her and she to him. That, for the moment, seemed enough.

She could no longer see the night. She could only see the white buttons of the shirt he wore. She could smell the clean scent of his skin, feel the heat rising off him. She could sense in his hands the potent masculinity of a man who took what he wanted and made no apologies afterward. She wondered if she could match his blasé attitude. "Go on."

His hand lifted to cup her chin as his thumb splayed across her lower lip. His rough whispering continued. "I like watching your lips when you talk. I like the way they form words. You have an incredible mouth. Soft and ripe and sexy. It makes me want to taste the woman in you."

The words sent shivery feelings through Michaela. "Is this how you talk to all women?"

His thumb paused in the fullest curve of her lip. "I don't usually talk much to women."

"They just offer themselves for the sheer pleasure of the experience?" she asked lightly though her heart was a set of bongo drums beating out a wild tropical rhythm.

His finger dragged provocatively at her lip. "Is that what you want to do?"

She jerked away from his touch but his other hand came out to grasp her waist. He smiled down into the hot angry expression she turned up at him. "Don't quit now, sweetheart. Things were just getting interesting."

He sidestepped to bring them closer together again. His hand moved caressingly over her cloud of hair and then scooped in underneath to cup her head securely. Strangely his eyes, nearly black in the dark shadows of the veranda, held the only light. "Which is the real you, Michaela? The straitlaced lawyer or the adventurous Kiki?"

Michaela shrugged under his hands. "We're both cowards."

"I wonder." His voice was a rough whisper. He lifted her chin as his blue eyes reached for and trapped her own gaze. "Your dark eyes hold about a thousand secrets. They make me want to dive in and find the answers to every one."

"I have no secrets." Michaela didn't know why she was whispering, too. It just seemed right.

"Oh, yes you do."

Guy reached out and tenderly traced the shape of her lips with a forefinger. In her gaze he saw the illusive fragility and vulnerability always lurking there, and something more, a desire and eagerness to match his own. "Let me show you."

He pulled her closer, tilted her face up to his and caught her lips in the hot embrace of his.

Chapter 8

Michaela didn't resist or push him away. She told herself she didn't resist because he was injured and she might hurt him. Yet once his lips settled with deliberate possession on hers, she knew the reason she hadn't resisted was because this was the moment they had been building up to ever since she had voluntarily linked her life with his four days earlier.

The kiss was devastating. She felt his hands sliding over her, one moving up to tangle in her hair while the other moved low down on her hips. Bone and muscle pressed into her womanly body, molding her perfectly to his harder frame. The combination of masculine assertiveness and raw hunger awakened in her an answering need.

Somehow her hands found his back and then clutched his shoulders. He was tough and sinewy beneath the soft cotton shirt. He smelled of aftershave—she wondered where it had come from—and the faint bitter taste of the tobacco he had barely inhaled, and the subtle indefinable scent of his skin that she inhaled every time she was near him.

She was clutched so tightly against him that his softest sigh warmed her lips. And all she wanted was to kiss him and go on kissing him. She welcomed the intrusion of his tongue, wanted his lips to remain on hers and persuade her that devastation was exactly what she needed.

Then suddenly he let her go and they were again staring at one another. The kiss left them both breathless and more than a little leery of one another.

Guy recovered first. He had set out to make a point but standing in the deepest shadows cast by the house, he couldn't remember exactly what it was. His voice sounded far from detached. "I've been wanting to do that since the moment I saw you in the doorway of the hospital."

"Well that makes one of us," Michaela lied. One kiss and she was having trouble standing on her feet. The thought appalled her. She wasn't about to simply dive into his arms and kiss sweet reason goodbye. Instead, she retreated behind frosty politeness. "Well, if your curiosity is satisfied."

It was a mistake.

"Like hell!" Guy dipped his dark head like a bull that had sighted a red flag as he hauled her forward against him for another kiss. This time there was no pretense at moderation or control. He engulfed her mouth and body in his physical embrace.

Panicking, Michaela back-stepped, desperate to elude his kiss but he simply walked her backward until she met the barrier of one of the porch columns. Trapped between it and him, she gave up the fight. But he was not finished. He leaned his heavier weight against her, angling his lower body to fit the softer contours of hers until she was pinned against the post by his hips. It was impossible to deny the level or strength of his arousal as raw need poured from his mouth into hers.

A sudden sound from deep within the house, a reminder that they were not alone, broke them apart.

Michaela took a self-protective step away from Guy, her expression anguished. He was staring at her as if she had snatched away something that belonged to him. She put a hand to her throbbing lips. The romance of moments before had disappeared.

His need! It had nearly overwhelmed her in the simple possession of her mouth by his. He kissed with his whole body, every muscle strained with aching need. His desperation frightened her.

She remembered once thinking that he looked like a man who had never had a taste of life that satisfied him. She very much feared at this moment that he had decided she was tiger's meat. She was too smart, too savvy, too frightened by her reaction to him to accept that.

"If you have any decency, you'll go inside before Grand-mère comes back." She shifted away from the column and him. "Or I will."

As she turned Guy caught her by the elbow. "Look, I didn't mean to—"

"Don't touch me!" She shoved backward with her elbow and caught him just below the ribs. She heard his grunt of pain and instantly swirled around, her own expression pained with regret. "Oh, I'm so sorry, I forgot. Are you all right?"

His face was hidden in shadow but was there was no mistaking the pain in his voice. "Just...give me...a minute...okay?"

He forced himself to stand upright but he kept one arm wrapped protectively about his ribs.

Concerned, Michaela moved in closer, a frown ridging her brow. "Are you all right?"

He stepped out of the shadow and into the lantern light streaming through one of the floor-to-ceiling shutters. When he met her gaze his eyes were dark with pain. "Maybe you better check and see."

Michaela cautiously reached out and unbuttoned his shirt. When she was done, she spread his shirt wide. The dressing was pale pink with seepage but he wasn't bleeding. She touched him gently, her fingertips testing for the telltale signs of infection: swelling and fever. There were none.

"You seem okay," she said and began rebuttoning his shirt. When she looked up at him after fastening the last button there was no longer repressed desire but wariness in her dark gaze. "Who shot you?"

The muscles about his mouth formed bitter lines. "You want to know? You really want to know?" His tone said she didn't.

Suddenly she was again a little afraid. "No, never mind."

His eyes warned her that it was too late. "Oh no. You asked and I'm going to tell you."

He took a few stalking steps toward her and took her by the upper arms to steer her toward one of the peacock-back wicker chairs. "Sit right down and let me tell you a modern bedtime story, Ms. Bellegarde."

With a forceful push, he sent her backward into the chair. "It all began five years ago. I made a mistake. A big mistake. I'd broken a few laws before. But this one was a beaut."

Michaela bounded up out of the chair. "As an officer of the court I don't think I want to hear this."

He swooped down on her, thrusting his face to within inches of her own as his hands settled with leveling force on her shoulders. "Well that's too damn bad, counselor. I've just decided this confession is going to be good for my soul." He shoved downward and she had no choice but to sit.

"Very well," she said primly, "but keep it short. Grand-mère could return at any moment."

He glared at her but lifted his hands from her shoulders as if he feared he might do her some harm if they remained. "Now where was I? Oh yeah, I went into partnership with a man named Pike. He was a Vegas hustler who knew certain people I needed an entrée with in order to set up the very lucrative but illegal private game I wanted to run. Pike got me inside to get that permission."

He paused to gauge her reaction but she seemed too entranced by his story to balk at his oblique mention of organized crime.

"Right, so for nearly a year everything went well. I ran a small gambling parlor for a very exclusive clientele, some of whose names you'd recognize if I was stupid enough to mention them. These people wanted to gamble big in discreet circumstances. For a cut of the winnings, I provided what you might call an elegant safe house. We didn't keep records and we didn't pay taxes." He saw her squirm but she didn't say anything.

"Pike and I made so much money I thought we must have been vacuuming pockets as clients left. But I was greedy." His expression darkened as the sudden memories released a little of the cold controlled fury he still harbored for his own gullibility.

Michaela gripped the armrests and sat perfectly still, her back ramrod straight in the chair as she watched dark emotions play over his face. She had always known Guy Matherson was a proud and smart man. He would not like to have found himself duped. And that, she suspected, was where his story was headed.

"It took me exactly nine months to realize that not even I was that lucky," he said in a low tight voice. "We'd cleared well over a million by that time with no end in sight. Then one day I tallied the receipts and compared them to the evening's betting. I came out with fifty grand more than was bet. I let it go but every night for nearly two weeks I watched the tables and the receipts."

"I thought you didn't keep records?" Michaela replied, her legally trained mind pouncing on the inconsistency in his story.

Guy shook his head. "We didn't. Once I started watching the games I just kept a running tally in my head."

"That's some head."

A small smile. "I've always been good at figures. It got me an offer from MIT but I couldn't swing the tuition." Before she could respond to his throwaway line he went on. "Anyway, it happened again, twice, a sizable amount of cash came into our coffers that hadn't been bet at the tables. Yet when I checked the bank records later, it was gone. That's when I realized something was going on. Somebody, probably with Pike's help, had developed a little side business of laundering money through my tables."

He raked both hands through his hair. "I may not be what you'd consider an upstanding citizen but I don't steal and I don't do business for the mob."

"So what did you do?" Michaela asked skeptically.

"I went to the bosses I had cut a deal with and told them that I was nobody's errand boy. I hadn't agreed to do that kind of business and that I wanted out."

Michaela leaned forward in her chair. The man knew how to tell a story. "And?"

"Turns out they didn't know about any deal but they were very interested in whose money Pike was laundering. I thought they'd take care of Pike but Pike had a few too many irons in the fire. The police caught up with him first, only he shot a bystander while trying to get away. I turned state's evidence to convict him."

"What about the mob?"

"They weren't very interested in anything but getting Pike off their turf. Jail was as good as dead. But it was clear I wasn't welcome back in Vegas. So I cut my losses and left."

"With a considerable bundle of illegal money."

His expression shuttered down. "I never claimed to be an angel. The money was mine by default. But I learned a few things from that experience. I had been so certain of myself when I went out to Vegas, a young man in great hurry, you might say. I thought I could stay clear of the worst the city had to offer, do things strictly on my own terms. If I got my hands a little dirty, I could wash them later.''

He stretched his hands out and flexed his long fingers. The action pulled back his cuffs to reveal the thin silver bracelet spanning his left wrist. "I didn't understand then that there's no such thing as being 'a little dirty.' Dirt attracts dirt. I nearly got swallowed up in a slime pit.''

Smiling, he touched the thin silver bracelet spanning his left wrist. "But then I got lucky again. I escaped.''

He glanced across at her. "I've been trying to make up for past mistakes these last four years. Become the model citizen, run my own business, do good deeds.''

"Get involved in local politics?" Michaela suggested.

He hunched his shoulders and slipped his hand back into his jeans pockets. "I'm sure this all sounds like a pack of lies to you. But I'm clean and I plan to stay that way.''

"You don't have to lie for my benefit, Mr. Matherson.''

He smiled. "Right. I should not insult your intelligence. You think I want something. You think I found out who you are, who your family is, what you're part of. I did. The Bellegardes are practically a dynasty.''

"A poor dynasty," Michaela observed pointedly.

"You think you're poor when you own a whole damn island?''

"It belongs to Grand-mère.''

"And one day it's going to be yours, if you continue to play your cards right.''

"What makes you say that?''

His smile wasn't pleasant. "You've got Tante Delphine practically eating out of your hand. She can't string three sentences together without mentioning your name. This birthday bash you're about to throw her should close the deal.''

Insulted to her shoe tips, Michaela rose to her feet. "I don't think I care for the tone of this conversation.''

"Right. So now you've convinced yourself I must be after your family's spotless name and reputation. What else do you want to know about me, sweetheart?"

Michaela hesitated, torn between the desire to leave him standing there and to get at the truth while she could. He didn't impress her as a man who could be induced to talk that often or that much about himself. "Is the $100 thousand you offered me part of the dirty money you left Vegas with?"

"No. That particular bundle went into a savings account the year after you left. It's your share of what I won beginning with the hundred-dollar chip you left behind in my hotel the day you disappeared."

"Oh really!" Michaela laughed in spite of herself. "You expect me to believe you turned $100 into $100 thousand?"

For the first time he looked less threatening as a genuine smile hovered as if waiting for permission to land on his lips. "Actually, it was more like $200 thousand. We were to split fifty-fifty, remember?"

Michaela's lips made a little O of surprise. "But you refused my offer."

He shrugged. "You left the money. The deal was done."

She studied his expression alternately in shadow and warmed by the golden glow of lantern light. What she saw quite surprised her. He was looking at her with singular intensity, as if it were very important that she believe him. "You're serious, aren't you? Why do I find your brand of chivalry so doubtful?"

He smiled. "Because you're scared of the strings that you think come attached to the money."

"What sorts of strings?"

"Oh, maybe like this."

This kiss was still different from the others. The long drugging persuasion of sensations kept altering even as she tried to record and understand each one. He was no longer angry or even trying to get the upper hand. He wanted to take her somewhere, to entice her to go with him and, boy oh boy, she was ready to go with him.

Yet when she came out of his embrace and found herself caught in the hot glare of ambivalence in his gaze, she grabbed at straws of sanity. "This is what you expect in thanks for the money? To sleep with me?"

He shook his head. "Women. You're always overestimating a man's perception of the value of money. I kissed you because I wanted to. Isn't that enough for you?"

"Yes," she admitted begrudgingly, "if I thought I could believe you."

His eyes lit up. "Is that an invitation for more?"

This time he pulled her in slowly, giving her every chance to protest or back off. But she didn't. Suddenly she wondered what it would be like if she equally participated in one of their kisses.

She reached up and touched his cheek as his mouth found hers. His mouth was hot. She felt as if she had opened the door on Grand-mère's cast-iron wood-burning stove. But the touch of those lips was tender, softening under the pressure of her own, offering an impressionable surface for her desire. She cupped his hard face between her hands, plying his hot mouth with little fleeting kisses that seemed the more powerful for their insubstantial brevity. She heard his hiss of indrawn breath and felt a shiver course through him. Guy Matherson wasn't made of stone after all.

When she moved back a little so that she could look up into his face she saw surprise limned the desire pulsing in his gaze.

Guy's fingers flexed on her upper arms, drawing her breasts against his chest. "Come on, sweetheart, let's tumble into the clean sheets on my bed. We'll make them sweaty with loving."

But Michaela leaned away from him. She, too, was trembling and the vibrations weren't all good. He had the power to move her, to take something very precious from her, and she was not at all certain he would handle her gift with the care and attention it deserved.

She put a hand on his chest and felt the heaving of his deepened breathing. "I can't do that. I can't handle any of this right now. I don't know what's going on. I can't explain it and I don't like it." She looked up at him with a wounded expression. "I don't even think I like you."

A look of exasperation replaced his scowl of passion. "There *is* no rational explanation for the attraction between two people," he countered in annoyance. "It just happens. Like being struck by lightning. It happened to us seven years ago. It's even stronger now. You feel it. I sure as hell feel it. It's like magic, alchemy. Destiny. Ask your Grand-mère to explain it to you."

Michaela refused his explanation with a toss of her heavy hair. "I don't believe in random strokes of madness."

She saw his eyes narrow. Like a semaphore they flashed alternate signals of warning, frustration, and desire. "Then let me put it in more scientific terms for you, counselor. Surely you had physics in high school. Call what's between us electromagnetic attraction. There's a force enveloping us, a kind of vibratory transmission field. It's elemental, unknowable, like the Heisenberg uncertainty principle. Yet, it follows the laws of nature. Why don't we just go with it, see where this natural attraction takes us?"

"You mean to bed?"

He smiled. "Maybe that will take care of it. Sure, why not?"

His hopeful tone that a roll in the sack might defuse the elemental passion between them wasn't the answer she wanted. "No, thank you, Mr. Matherson. I'd rather take my chances with a swamp gator."

He laughed. "Too bad. You chose the door with the tiger."

"I didn't choose you," she observed tartly.

"No, and I didn't choose you. But it looks like we're stuck, like it or not."

Michaela let his words sink in slowly, afraid of the ripples they caused in her composure. He was baiting her with her own desire for him.

For several long moments they stood staring at one another, neither wanting to make the next move.

"Then what?" Michaela asked a little desperately. "After tonight, if it doesn't end, then what?"

Guy shifted uncomfortably from one foot to the other, felt the throb of his need pushing him. She had been his lucky charm these last seven years, a powerful antidote to a life of loneliness and uncertainty and desperation. But he'd been a loner too long to simply lay his cards on the table with Michaela Bellegarde. He needed his own back. He needed to break the connection before he hurt her or broke his own heart.

"Take the money," he said finally. "If it bothers you that it comes from me, give it to charity or give it to your great-grandmother. Give it all away, but take it."

"I will, if it means that much to you," Michaela said slowly.

He looked at her sharply then nodded his head once. "I guess that settles that." He shoved his hands into his pockets and turned away.

"It settles nothing," she shouted at his retreating back.

Guy swung around, his head down as if he were a boxer sizing up an opponent. "I know." He sounded as miserable as she felt. But the bell had sounded for that round and they both knew it.

"Wait, you didn't tell me who shot you and why."

He was too far away and wrapped in shadow for her to see his expression. "Pike."

"But you said he was in jail for murder."

"He was." He resumed his stroll along the porch until the turn in the veranda gallery took him out of sight.

A little later the front screen creaked open and Tante Delphine said, "What's this? Where is everyone?"

Michaela's voice rose from the interior of a peacock chair. "Over here, Grand-mère." She kept her voice level in order not to startle the older woman. "Mr. Matherson has gone to bed."

Tante Delphine chuckled as she offered her great-grand-daughter a frosty glass of lemonade. "You mean you done run him off, 'Tite?"

"I'm sorry, Grand-mère, but I simply can't be nice to him."

"That man, he's got some powerful needs driving him."

"What he has is a rude, conceited, selfish ego."

"Sometimes a man is most rude when he aches to be most tender," she answered with a slow nodding of her head. "It is hard for the gentlemen sometimes. Their hearts are telling them one thing and their bodies are saying something else. Most confusing for the young ones."

"Guy Matherson strikes me as the kind of man who is more than capable of saying exactly what he means."

"That's what I say. It's most hard of all for a man like this, an honest soul who knows he is capable of so many other things besides what he allows himself. Then he meets you, the gentlest, most trusting, most open of souls. No wonder that he chose to keep your memory alive by solder-ing a piece of you to himself. There's a powerful need in that man—if it don't frighten him off."

"You're speaking in riddles."

"You're not listening, that's all. But I keep my thoughts here." She pointed to her head and then her heart. "You best see about him. Maybe he needs something."

"What he needs is a good lawyer. And, no, it won't be me."

"We see about that," Tante Delphine whispered as she watched her great-granddaughter enter the house.

Though her hearing wasn't as keen as it once was, she had heard more than enough of their conversation to know that Michaela wasn't indifferent to Guy Matherson. While the young man...

"My poor, *beau garçon*," she chuckled. "He ain't even know what's hit him is cupid's arrow."

Guy lay awake in the dark wanting, just wanting Michaela. Wanting just to hold her body next to his. He had gotten up once before and gone as far as her door. But he didn't open it and he didn't knock. He had seen the look of trepidation in her eyes after their last kiss. He understood her fears. He shared them. What he wanted from her frightened him, too.

She had not lost her fascination for him. Whether called Kiki or Michaela, she remained an enigma. He had thought that the most direct way to get to the core of a woman was to arouse her passion. But Michaela's passion had only confused and overwhelmed him with his own answering desire. He hadn't gotten to the core of her fascination but sunk a pipeline in a volcano of emotions. More than ever he wanted to crack the code, solve the mystery, answer the riddle. For that, he had to get close to her.

He heard the old clock in the parlor chime three times. He tossed back the sheet and rotated off the mattress and onto his feet in one smooth motion. Wrapping a towel about his nakedness he stepped into the hall. He didn't need light to find her room. There was only one hall. His room was the second door on the right. Hers was the third.

When he reached it, he lay his hand on the knob but again found he didn't have the guts to open it. He stood barefoot in the dark listening for any sound of the woman inside. Finally he heard her bracelets tinkle and imagined her turning in her sleep. Encouraged by the tiny sound, he shut his eyes and conjured up an image of her lying on her bed in a

SILHOUETTE®

AN IMPORTANT MESSAGE FROM THE EDITORS OF SILHOUETTE®

Dear Reader,

Because you've chosen to read one of our fine romance novels, we'd like to say "thank you"! And, as a **special** way to thank you, we've selected <u>four more</u> of the <u>books</u> you love so well, **and** a Porcelain Trinket Box to send you absolutely *FREE!*

Please enjoy them with our compliments...

Senior Editor,
Silhouette Intimate Moments

P.S. And because we value our customers, we've attached something extra inside ...

EDITOR'S FREE GIFT SEAL · THANK YOU

PEEL OFF SEAL AND PLACE INSIDE

HOW TO VALIDATE
YOUR
EDITOR'S FREE GIFT
"THANK YOU"

1. Peel off gift seal from front cover. Place it in space provided at right. This automatically entitles you to receive four free books and a beautiful Porcelain Trinket Box.

2. Send back this card and you'll get brand-new Silhouette Intimate Moments® novels. These books have a cover price of $3.75 each, but they are yours to keep absolutely free.

3. There's no catch. You're under no obligation to buy anything. We charge nothing—ZERO—for your first shipment. And you don't have to make any minimum number of purchases—not even one!

4. The fact is thousands of readers enjoy receiving books by mail from the Silhouette Reader Service™ months before they're available in stores. They like the convenience of home delivery and they love our discount prices!

5. We hope that after receiving your free books you'll want to remain a subscriber. But the choice is yours—to continue or cancel, anytime at all! So why not take us up on our invitation, with no risk of any kind. You'll be glad you did!

6. Don't forget to detach your FREE BOOKMARK. And remember...just for validating your Editor's Free Gift Offer, we'll send you FIVE MORE gifts, *ABSOLUTELY FREE!*

YOURS FREE!

*This beautiful porcelain box is topped with a lovely bouquet of porcelain flowers, perfect for holding rings, pins or other precious trinkets — and is yours **absolutely free** when you accept our no risk offer!*

SILHOUETTE®

WITH OUR
COMPLIMENTS

THE EDITORS

YES! I have place
seal in the space provide
books and a Porcelain T
I am under no obligatio
explained on the back a

NAME

ADDRESS

CITY

Thank

DETACH AND MAIL CARD TODAY

THE SILHOUETTE READER SERVICE™: HERE'S HOW IT WORKS

Accepting free books places you under no obligation to buy anything. You may keep the books and gift and return the shipping statement marked "cancel". If you do not cancel, about a month later we will send you 6 additional novels, and bill you just $3.12 each plus 25¢ delivery and applicable sales tax, if any.* That's the complete price, and—compared to cover prices of $3.75 each—quite a bargain! You may cancel at any time, but if you choose to continue, every month we'll send you 6 more books, which you may either purchase at the discount price...or return at our expense and cancel your subscription.

*Terms and prices subject to change without notice. Sales tax applicable in N.Y.

white cotton gown so sheer he could easily discern the woman beneath.

After a few moments more, he laid his head against the smooth dark wood of her door, as close to as he dared to be. The ache in his groin was almost a comfort for it kept him focussed and alert. He didn't want to have to explain to Tante Delphine why he was standing in the hallway lusting after her great-granddaughter. He suspected she already knew how he felt. The only question was, did Michaela? And would she welcome him if he opened this damned door?

Finally the cool damp air sent him back to his lonely bed where he held on to a pillow instead of her.

Chapter 9

Michaela knelt in the attic amid the dust bunnies and spider webs so heavily powdered with fine grime that they appeared to be lacework doilies festooning corners and crannies. The room was dim, the air stale, the corners deeply shadowed. Morning sunlight slanted through the narrow attic window illuminating only a three-by-four-foot area on the floor. She had dragged an old leather steamer trunk into this spotlit space but she had yet to slip free the buckles that held it closed.

Instead, she rubbed idly with a forefinger at the gray layer covering its surface. First she made swirls in the dust. Then gradually cursive letters appeared behind her finger's trail, spelling out the name Guy.

She stared at the name for a moment then obliterated it with the heel of her palm before rising to her feet.

Her sojourns at Belle Isle usually refreshed and centered her. Belle Isle had always been her refuge, a world away from modern life, a place where she could gather her strength, shrug off her cares, and ease back into a serenity that suited her nature. But yesterday, she had run away from the island ... because of Guy Matherson.

Annoyed that her thoughts had circled back to him, she looked around for something with which to distract herself.

She spied several old hatboxes stacked in one shadowed corner. She smiled in recognition for she had played with their contents often as a child. She carried them back to the center of the room, placed them on the trunk, and opened the smallest first.

It was tied with a satin ribbon that was no longer bright pink but bleached by age to a rusty beige. She knew what was inside even before she lifted the layers of tissue paper. Lying in the box's depth was a twenties cloche hat made of sheer ribbon which had been stitched in one continuous spiral from crown to the deep brim that flared like a trumpet bell.

Michaela reached in and reverently lifted it out. The fragile-bit of champagne silk with its bronze velvet band had belonged to her Grandaunt Adelle, who was said to have been a real 'pistol' in her day. The cloche slipped sleekly over her head for she had pulled her hair tightly back and clipped it low at her nape before coming up here. Its sheer brim dipped low over her neck and cheeks before swooping up coquettishly at eye level. She smiled, not needing a mirror to envision herself in the hat she had donned so often in the past.

She bent forward and placed both hands on her flexed knees like a flapper, lifted one slim shoulder, made a moue with her lips, then tossed her head to offer an imaginary admirer a simply irresistible flirtatious glance through the veiling of the sheer ribbon brim.

"Very nice. Very nice, indeed!"

That voice of masculine appreciation evaporated Michaela's joy in the moment.

She straightened with a start. As her eyes adjusted to the dim recesses where the access door to the attic stood open she saw a head poking through from the floor below. Guy's head.

"I knew I should have pulled that ladder up after me," she mumbled.

She turned to open another hatbox, ignoring the man who climbed up without invitation.

"What are you looking for up here?" Guy demanded in amazement. "It's filthy and stuffy. Wow! Would you look at the size of that spider's web?"

Michaela glanced in his direction. "If you're afraid of spiders you shouldn't be here. There are black widows and brown recluses everywhere. It's the river," she went on conversationally as she lifted the box lid. She peeked inside then set it aside. "We occasionally even find a snake coiled under the eaves."

At the edge of her vision she saw him start. He didn't, however, retreat toward the ladder as she'd hoped. She paused before lifting up the lid of the largest box. He was wearing the same denim shirt and jeans as the night before. The lower half of his face was dark with new stubble. His beard was heavy and grew quickly.

"What are you doing up here?" he asked when he'd come near enough to see her clearly.

"Minding my own business," she answered. She lifted the lid and delved into the tissue paper which made dry whispering sounds as she pushed it aside. "Oh! *Oh!*"

Michaela jerked her hand out and stepped back. The hatbox tumbled from its perch and landed open side down on the wooden floor. As dust rose from the old boards two tiny shadows emerged from the overturned box and streaked for opposite dark corners.

"Rats!" Guy shouted and jerked her back toward him out of harm's way.

"Mice," Michaela replied and shrugged free of his protective efforts. "Just teeny tiny mice. They startled me, that's all."

As an afterthought she reached up and rubbed her hands up and down her arms. It wasn't goose bumps but nerves of another kind that made her do it. Her upper arms tingled where he had touched her.

She bent to pick up the box but he was there before her. "I'll get it."

She backed a little away from him, crossing her arms as she watched him. For days she had struggled with the sexual tension that ran like a riptide through their every encounter. She had formed excuses, given labels to, compartmentalized and rationalized each of her feelings concerning him. Some men, like rock stars and movie studs, could raise the temperature of a room by simply stepping into it. Guy had that kind of incendiary appeal. It was an indiscriminate appeal, available to all.

She had been so certain that it was the accumulated tension of the past week that had made her vulnerable to his brand of blatant sexual attraction.

There had certainly been enough recent turmoil in her life to weaken her defenses: Daniel's announcement of his engagement to another woman, her disappointment that her job had not yet come through, and then a near-death encounter with a stranger and a gun in a hospital room. She had decided she was drawn to Guy by nothing more than shared circumstance. When her life returned to normal and the tension wore off, so would her attraction to him.

Then he had kissed her. Now she had to face a different reality.

She was smitten with Guy Matherson. No, that was a silly teenage crush word. What she felt for the man illuminated by the shaft of light five feet away was much more powerful than a mere infatuation grounded in rampaging hormones. What had her uncle called the strange haunting awareness of herself that had begun the night Guy came back into her life? A "womanly look" about the eyes. Is that what Guy Matherson saw when he looked at her, a restless sensuality she had not felt until she saw him again?

Aware of her antagonism but unwilling to retreat, Guy delved into the box he had picked up and pulled out a matted collection of chewed straw, mangled velvet and satin. An artificial rose dropped to the floor by his left shoe as he held it out.

"Aunt Hélène's hat!" Michaela said in dismay. "The little beasts have ruined it."

Guy smirked. "It's a regular rat's nest."

Offended, she snatched it from him and then bent to retrieve the fallen rose. "It once had a broad straw brim with a black velvet crown that was ringed in pink roses and a huge turquoise ribbon. The most beautiful hat in the collection!"

Guy eyed her suspiciously. "You're kidding, right?"

She turned her back on him, batting her lashes in a vain attempt to best the stinging in her eyes. "I don't expect you to understand."

"What's to understand?" Guy dipped his head as he edged around to her to try to catch the expression hiding behind her cloche's deep brim. He reached out to touch her face and his fingers slid wetly along her cheek. "Are you crying? Over a collection of scraps?"

Embarrassed and resentful of his intrusion, Michaela hunched a shoulder to fend him off. "I know. It's a foolish bit of vanity that's lain forgotten for years." She tossed it back into the box. "It won't be missed."

"Except by you."

His oddly gentle tone when she had expected more sarcasm made her glance briefly at him.

He was smiling at her. "You're a funny thing."

She lifted a hand to wipe surreptitiously at her damp cheek. "I don't usually cry so easily. I think I must be a little under the weather."

Guy tried again to look past the edge of the downturned brim of her hat but in the dim room its sheer cover was as concealing as it was flirtatious. He saw only the full pout of her lips and delicate chin line. "I didn't come up here to

bother you. There's only so much time I can spend in one room without going stir crazy. I decided to browse the house.''

She turned a resentful stare on him. ''If you're feeling all that wonderful why don't you simply leave?''

''All right.'' He casually lifted and braced a foot on top of the leather trunk then leaned an arm on his bent knee. ''Where shall I go?''

''Why should I care?''

His smile relaxed in a grin. ''Thought you might be feeling a bit proprietary about my body.'' Seeing her stiffen he added, ''Since you're as responsible as any doctor for my recovery, I thought you might not want to see your efforts blown to bits.''

Though he said the words lightly, Michaela was aware that he had risked his life to keep from making things easy for the man who was gunning for him. ''I didn't mean to imply I'm not concerned for your health.''

''It's just my personality you dislike, right?''

Michaela smiled in spite of herself. ''Something like that.''

''Okay, then let's compromise. I won't force myself on you if you promise to keep me company for a while.''

She glanced down at the trunk. ''I was looking for something to wear to Grand-mère's birthday party. I thought I'd better locate it now, in case it needs mending and cleaning.''

Guy's arched brows rose half-up his forehead. ''You're looking for a party dress amid this filth?''

''It's not filthy. This is a cedar-lined attic. It's just dusty, and stale and—''

''—Old,'' Guy supplied in distaste. ''What sort of party dress do you think you'll find?''

Michaela pointed to the trunk. ''Unless someone's moved it, there should be a champagne silk mousseline dress in there.''

"Champagne silk?" He lifted his foot off the lid. "This I've got to see."

Michaela once more knelt in the dust, uncaring that it streaked her jeans. She was surprised when he followed her example but she didn't protest as he reached for one buckle after she began unfastening the other.

The lid hinges creaked like those on Dracula's coffin as they pushed it open. The first thing she saw was a dove gray fedora. She picked it up with a smile. "This belonged to Grand-mère's husband."

Guy reached for it and turned it over to look inside. "Satin-lined with a Saville Row trademark. Your great-grandfather must have been something of a blade."

"His name was Julian," she pronounced with a French inflection. "Grand-mère says he was the most handsome man she ever saw."

"You don't remember him?"

"No, he died before I was born. But there are pictures of him in the parlor."

"I'll check them out." He stroked the wool felt brim then started to lift it to his head. "Do you mind?"

Michaela shook her head.

He took the crown in the fingers of his right hand, using them to pinch and reinforce the impressions steamed into the crown. He raked a hand through his hair to lift a curl off his forehead then bent his head forward and set the hat on it. As he lifted his head back he gave the brim a little jerk with his thumb and forefinger that cocked it ever so slightly over one eye.

Michaela gasped softly in surprise. It was just the sort of gesture she had seen Bogart and Garfield make countless times in films of the thirties and forties. They most often played men with good hearts, hiding behind tough exteriors while trying desperately to reform bad lives. At this moment, she could almost believe Guy was of their ilk. "You've worn hats before."

He shook his head. "No. Why? Do I look stupid?"

"You look—" She smiled to hide her enthusiasm. He looked perfect, a natural. The hat added the final touch of old-fashioned glamour to his masculine good looks. "You look very nice," she said simply.

He smiled, a slow seductive curve of his lips that she felt in the pit of her stomach. "Maybe I'll wear it for the party."

"Yes, if Grand-mère says you may."

He reached out and touched her nose with a forefinger. "You look sweet in that hat, like a little girl playing dress up in her mother's clothes." The light shifted in his blue eyes. "But you aren't a little girl."

Michaela felt again the tidal pull between them. It had been there from their first encounter. That's why she had not been able to forget him, because he had not forgotten her.

Guy hadn't forgotten her. Maybe it was only lust based in ego but lust that lasted seven years couldn't be lightly discounted.

She suddenly understood why she had spent so much time with Daniel the night before when she knew it would end awkwardly, or worse. Meeting Daniel had been an excuse to keep from returning to face Guy.

"I'd better find that dress and get back downstairs before Grand-mère misses me."

She rose to her knees and bent into the trunk and began lifting back layer after layer of clothing wrapped in tissue paper. Tucked between the layers were satin cachet bags.

Guy patiently watched her progress through the clothing as the scent of lavender rose from the trunk's depths to tease his nostrils. He preferred her fragrance. The tinkle of her bracelets entertained him. As she arched gracefully over the edge of the trunk he lifted his hand with the intention of sliding his hand down the indentation of her spine and over the fullness of her hips. But common sense stopped him. She would think it a cheap trick, that he was copping a feel. She wouldn't understand how it would make him feel to move in behind her, to embrace and mold her body to his, to hold all her shining happiness and womanly softness in his arms. He wanted sex, yes. But he wanted it because of her.

He had never struggled harder for inner balance or been less certain he could maintain it. His hand began to tremble and his mouth went dry watching the temptation she presented.

When she finally straightened with "Aha! Pay dirt!" he had to wipe the sweat from his face with a forearm before he could see her clearly.

"So, show it to me," he said when she held on to the bundle tied up in what appeared to be pale pink linen.

"Oh, no," she said and hugged it to her breasts. "Nobody sees it until Saturday."

"I could use a few clothes myself." He tugged at the armpit of his shirt. "Things and people get ripe pretty fast in this heat."

"You're right." Michaela had momentarily forgotten that her brother's borrowed clothes were the only ones he had. "You need everything, shirts, trousers, socks, underwear."

He grinned. "Didn't think you noticed."

"I noticed." She ducked her head. "You make up a list and I'll go into town and get what you need."

"Why don't I just go with you?"

Her eyes widened. "Are you kidding? Your picture has run on the cover of every newspaper in the state since you disappeared. If you waltz into Baton Rouge someone will certainly recognize you."

He grin widened. "You think I'm that unforgettable?"

"You have a certain uniqueness of feature," she countered. "Are you ready to go to the police and save them the trouble of tracking you down? Once they've heard your story I'm certain they will protect you."

He scowled. "It's my private business."

"People with guns who shoot other people fall into the category of public nuisance at the very least."

"It's my problem."

Michaela had heard that end-of-story tone of voice often enough to know there was no sense continuing. "Suit yourself. I've got things to do in town, anyway, last-minute business for Grand-mère's party."

"What are you doing to go with me while people are here celebrating next Saturday?"

She feigned indifference. "I assumed you'd be gone by then."

"You mean you hoped I'd be gone."

She met his gaze through the barrier of her diaphanous brim. "Won't you?"

"Tell me to go and I'm out of here right now."

Her gaze lowered to the left side of his shirt beneath his breast pocket. "Are you still in much pain?"

"Yes." The husky expression brought her gaze back to his face. She never knew blue eyes could look so hot. "You just misjudged the source, by about twelve inches."

Her gaze dipped again before her brain told her that that was possibly not a good idea. He was kneeling beside her, legs spread apart. One knee was braced on the floor while the other was cocked at an angle that drew the denim tight against his crotch. She felt her face catch fire.

"Michaela?"

Her name sounded like a caress in his deep, hushed voice. She decided the only place she might look that would be more disastrous to her composure, was his face. She was right.

His expression as so tender, so understanding, so confident. "We'll take it slow. Not like last night." He brushed the cloche brim back from her cheek with a finger. The brim of his fedora nudged her forehead as he leaned forward to kiss the place he had exposed. "I'm willing to wait," he whispered by her ear. "You're worth it."

"You don't play fair," she murmured.

"No," he agreed. He plowed her silky brim back with his nose and touched his lips to her brow. "I'm a professional. I know how to stack the odds in my favor."

"You mean you cheat?"

"Not exactly." He leaned back a little so he could look at her. "But you don't win if you always play fairly. And I want to win you, Michaela." He moved in toward her again, angling his head in order to slant his mouth across hers.

She lifted her chin in anticipation but their lips did not meet.

She opened her eyes and found her view filled by smiling aquamarine eyes. His lips hovered an inch away. "Ante up, Michaela. You have to pay to play."

There was only one answer to his challenge.

She licked her lips, first the upper and then the lower. She scooped one hand in under his chin and used the other to pluck the fedora from his head. Then she very deliberately placed her lips on his. But she wasn't done. Her tongue darted out of her mouth and licked first his bottom and then his top lip, taking the time to trace the entire outline of each. Only then did she press the full contours of her damp, slightly open mouth on his.

He groaned or maybe she moaned, or maybe they both surrendered soft sounds of passion.

When she opened her eyes again she was smiling. "Good enough?"

His expression made her stomach clench. "Sweetheart, you just upped the ante."

She lay a hand on his left shirt pocket, curling her fingers into the opening. "Then do something for me to even the bet."

He strained toward her. "Name it."

"Throw these away." She plucked a crumpled pack of cigarettes from his pocket and held them up.

"Gladly." He reached up and closed his fingers over hers, crushing the pack within her grasp. "It was the first pack I'd bought in five years."

She frowned. "Why?"

"Some vices are harder to resist than others. Right?"

She knew he was no longer talking about his nicotine habit but her own attraction to him. "Right."

She saw a change in his face she didn't recognize. And then she had it. He had relaxed. There had always been a tightness about his mouth, even when he smiled. It was a watchful predatory look that said he lived in a world where his next meal might be his last for a very long time. Now that ever-present strain that pulled his skin too tightly over his bones had eased.

She heard the sounds of a car plowing across the island and rose to her feet. "Wonder who that could be?"

She had to stand on tiptoe to see over the sill of the high attic window. Even so, she could not see down into the yard. Guy came up beside her. "Can you see anything?" she asked.

He leaned in close and rubbed the foggy glass with a finger. "Yeah." When he turned to look down at her, the bones of his face were once more stretching his skin. You've got company. Official business, probably. It's the sheriff."

"Morning, Tante Delphine." Sheriff Proctor stood in the open kitchen door.

The elderly woman turned toward him with the pie she had just lifted from the oven clutched between two bright yellow oven mitts. "Ah, little Leopold. Come in, come in."

The fifty-year-old lawman hitched up his pants over the paunch that not even a three-times-a-week workout on gym equipment could defeat. "What's that I smell?"

"Don' you know? It's my sweet potato pie."

The expression on his face turned rapturous. "Sweet potato pie!"

"*Oui*. Made with molasses and lots of sugared pecans on top."

"What's the occasion?"

"My great-granddaughter, she's visiting me."

"That'd be Ms. Michaela." His smile sobered. "Good, I was hoping she was here. I've come to talk to her."

Tante Delphine bristled indignantly, tossing her head like a woman one quarter her age as she balanced a hand on one hip. "Time was, you came to see me. What I'm gon' tell your wife about you coming here to see a girl younger than your Jim?"

Sheriff Proctor produced a belly laugh. "You're about going to get me trouble, sure enough."

"Sheriff?"

Sheriff Proctor looked over his shoulder. "Come on in, Riley." He motioned into the kitchen a much younger man. "Riley, this here is Tante Delphine, matriarch of the Belle-garde family. Tante Delphine, this is my new deputy, Riley Talley."

She nodded slightly as she placed her pie on a rack to cool. "How you do, young sir?"

He doffed his cap, "Well enough, ma'am."

"You gon' have a slice of my sweet potato pie, like the sheriff?"

The younger man shook his head. "No, ma'am. We're here on business." His gaze shifted to his superior. "Urgent business."

"Business that don' wait on pie?" she teased and winked at Proctor.

"No, ma'am. We need to speak to Ms. Michaela Belle-garde. She is here?"

"She's no place else." She reached for a knife and placed it beside the pie plate. "This pie got to set fifteen minutes before I slice it. You want coffee while you wait?"

"Now, Tante Delphine, you heard Riley. We need to see Michaela. You want to call her or shall I?"

"No need to call. Most likely she heard your car." She glanced at the younger man. "We don' get much traffic through here, except during the migratory season."

"Hunting season," Sheriff Proctor translated for his deputy. "You haven't had any trouble with trespassers so far this year?"

She smiled and pointed to the corner near the stove. "I keep my shotgun loaded with saltshot. Ain't no poacher gon' come away from here with anything more than a backside full of fire."

"Now I told you, you don't want to go shooting at folks," the sheriff scolded. "You might injure someone."

Tante Delphine's dark eyes danced. "What I aim to injure I do. But, no, we don' get no poachers this year. The water is higher than usual 'cause of the summer flooding upriver. The gators come out the swamp to snap up them for me. Have a seat, Michaela come down soon enough."

But after nearly three minutes, Michaela had not appeared. "You got any predictions about the winter?" the sheriff asked to fill in the silence but glanced anxiously at the doorway that led to the front of the house. Riley had moved to stand there and was peering into the hall beyond.

"You, Riley!" Tante Delphine barked with surprising energy. "You want permission to roam my house? You ain't got it."

The younger man flushed and stepped away from the door. "Sorry, ma'am."

He sounded humble. He seemed clean-cut and serious. But in the split second their eyes met Tante Delphine saw deeper. His eyes, narrowed and constantly moving, were like searchlights. Emanations came off of him in ripples of hostility. The sound of his shifting muscles whispered menace. This one was trouble. If he didn't find it, he would make certain trouble found him.

The sheriff shifted uncomfortably. "What's taking Michaela so long?"

"Could be she just come out the bath." Tante Delphine cast a sidelong glance at Riley and smiled at his expression. *Oui,* she knew his kind. She turned away. "You still using my blister salve, Leopold?"

He guffawed again, turning bright red. "Now, you know I haven't required that in nearly half a century."

She nodded. "Time was your mama come and leave you with me. Said she couldn't bear to see your little fat bottom like one huge open blister." She glanced at Riley. "The worst case of diaper rash ever in ten parishes, on account of his fair skin."

The younger man sniggered until he realized Tante Delphine's black eyes remained riveted on him. "You got a rash, too. You stay away from Josey's girls and get to the doctor else it's sure enough gon' fall off!"

The outrageous exclamation provided the perfect pause for Michaela's entry. "Sheriff Proctor!" she greeted warmly as she stepped into the kitchen through the garden door. She shook his hand. "Tante Delphine, why didn't you tell me we had company?"

Her great-grandmother shook her head. "All the time you say you know things I try to tell you. Why I gon' waste good breath?"

"I need to ask you a few questions, Ms. Bellegarde."

"Certainly, Sheriff." She moved forward to claim one of the pair of kitchen stools, vaguely aware of the interested stare of the younger man in uniform. "How may I help you? Grand-mère did offer you gentlemen coffee?" she quickly added.

"Yes. Thank you, no." He reached into his pocket for his notepad. "Now Ms. Bellegarde, I understand you went to see a Mr. Matherson in New Orleans last Monday."

Michaela nodded. "Yes, it was Monday. I'd spent the afternoon at Uncle Leon's law firm."

The sheriff met her bright gaze over the top of his pad. "Duly noted, Ms. Bellegarde. Now would you like to tell me why you went to see the gentleman?"

She smiled. "Certainly. What would you like to know?"

"Why you drove at night all the way to New Orleans to see a man who'd been shot," Riley interjected from behind her.

Michaela turned an inquiring gaze on him. "I didn't know Mr. Matherson had been shot when I went to see him."

"Why did you think he was in the hospital?" Riley rejoined.

Michaela didn't bother to glance over her shoulder this time. "Because a mutual friend told me he was."

"Yet this mutual friend didn't say why?" The smirk in his voice needed no facial cues. "Isn't that a bit hard to believe?"

"You would think so," Michaela answered agreeably and smiled at the sheriff. "I won't ever accept anything at face value again, I assure you."

"Why are you all dirty, Ms. Bellegarde?" Riley again.

Michaela looked down at her dust-streaked jeans. "I've been cleaning out the attic. Why?"

"Is that where you were when we drove up?"

She tossed him a mystified look. "Should I have been somewhere else in particular?"

His gaze held hers. "Your great-grandmother thought you were in the shower."

Michaela turned to the sheriff. "I thought we were discussing Mr. Matherson. By the way, have the authorities located him?"

"No, ma'am, that's why we've come to talk to you."

"The New Orleans police seem to think you might know where he is," Riley added at her back.

Michaela turned her head toward him again. "Is this some interrogation technique you picked up on TV? As a practicing attorney, I must tell you it's quite ineffective. It only makes you seem like a hovering mosquito that needs to be swatted."

The level of hostility between them jumped several floors. "You might as well cooperate with us, or you may find yourself having to deal with the FBI."

"Actually, I think I'd prefer to talk to anybody else than you." She turned deliberately away. "Sheriff Proctor, is it against the law to visit a sick friend?"

"No, ma'am, but you were the last person to see Mr. Matherson before he disappeared."

"I see. Has he committed some crime?"

"Not that I'm aware of."

"Then whether or not I saw him first, last, or even helped him leave the hospital doesn't really signify, does it?"

Riley stepped around to face her in challenge. "Is that what you did? You were the only one who claims someone tried to shoot Matherson while you were in his room."

She gave him a debutante smile. "Thank you for that reminder but it's not the sort of thing I would forget."

"How well do you know Matherson?"

"Better than I know you," she shot back.

"Are you lovers?"

"Are you jealous?"

Riley bared his teeth. "Would you like to take this—?"

"Whoa!" Sheriff Proctor spread out his hands as if to stop traffic. "Let's not get ugly. This isn't a formal interrogation," he added with a meaningful glance at Riley.

"I'm so glad," Michaela answered in the first hint of anger. "Because I can tell you, you'd have the beginnings of a harassment case on your hands." She deliberately did not look at Riley. "I can also tell you that when I last saw Guy Matherson, he seemed to be all right. Now if that's all, I've got a thousand things to do to get ready for Grand-mère's birthday party next week."

She slid off her stool. "You are coming, Sheriff, and bringing your family?" She glanced in the general direction of Riley. "Your deputy is welcome, too, if he'd like to come."

She didn't hear what Riley mumbled but she hoped it was a negative.

Sheriff Proctor cocked his head at his deputy. "You go ahead and radio in from the car. Say that we found Ms.

Bellegarde and she couldn't shed any light on Matherson's disappearance.''

Riley smirked. "I'll tell them she had nothing to say." He sauntered out with his thumbs hooked in his belt.

Tante Delphine, who had stood apart, now came forward again with a bundle in her hand. "Sweet potato pie," she said as she pressed the covered dish into the sheriff's hand.

"Why, thank you!" He beamed.

She nodded but her smile dissolved. "This Riley, he's your deputy some long time?"

"Naw. He's a city boy from up in Memphis. Looking to get back there, too, soon as a position opens up."

"You best find him that position before the new year. 'Else you may have a death you don' want in your parish."

Sheriff Proctor recoiled. Like all residents of the area, he had grown up hearing stories about Tante Delphine's powers. The true stories were amazing enough to make the lies believable. "What have you seen? It is the rash?"

Tante Delphine shook her head, her gaze downcast. "I don' see nothing. I just tell you, the new year book don' got his name writ very large."

"I see." His face wore a doubtful scowl.

She looked up and caught him lightly by the sleeve. "Maybe it's writ bigger in the Memphis edition, *oui?*"

A smile broke through his scowl. "Now that's a thought." He dipped his head. "Good day, Tante Delphine. See you next weekend."

Michaela followed him to the rear door then waited until he had rounded the house and was out of sight. When she turned back from the door, Tante Delphine's black eyes were blazing.

"You never say nothing about no man with a gun in the hospital! What else you don' tell me?"

"I think I should answer that." Guy stood in the hallway door.

Chapter 10

Guy stood on the levee at the riverbank above Belle Isle's dock and looked west across the Mississippi River. The sun was a bloodshot egg yolk on the horizon. Four feet below him the muddy water churned and eddied. Gleaming like an oil slick in the encroaching darkness, it made sloppy wet noises as it sluiced past the timbers of the pier. Behind him the island vegetation had grown dark and still. From the umber shadows upriver, a hot wind dragged at his clothes. That brisk wind was all that kept the mosquitos and gnats droning in the darkness behind him from feasting on his exposed skin.

Though it was late October it could as easily have been June. That was the one thing he had never gotten accustomed to, living so deep in the South. Even in winter the weather never left semitropical levels for more than a day or two. It was just as well he hadn't adjusted. That would make moving on a little easier.

It was time to leave.

One look at Tante Delphine's face after the sheriff left had forced on him a reminder of what he had wanted to forget, that a man was looking for him—to kill him.

Pike was angry or desperate enough to walk into a public place, a hospital, in order to get the job done. That meant as long as Guy Matherson was around people, people were in danger. Innocent people. People like Michaela. That's the fear he had read in the older woman's face, that as long as he was on Belle Isle, Michaela was in danger. Strange. He understood intuitively that neither of them feared for themselves. But they shared the same protective feelings for the same person. Nothing must happen to Michaela.

He wasn't sentimental. Whether he lived or died didn't really matter, beyond the human instinct for survival. He could be unflinchingly honest. He had had a good run during his life. Had achieved, if only for a short time, the goals he had set out for himself. He was thirty-one, a success on his own terms. He hadn't planned beyond that. No children, house in the suburbs or pet collies in his future. It was time to fold his hand and saunter away into the night. No regrets, no losses, no debts.

Finally he saw what he was waiting for. Beyond the opposite bank, high-beam lights ricocheted wildly off the trunks of the dozens of trees that lined the bank. Growing steadily stronger, like police searchlights trailing a suspect, they ultimately sliced through the woods and became the twin headlights of Tante Delphine's Buick.

He stood watching as the ferry cast off on the opposite side a few minutes later and began its short journey to the island. That ferry was bringing Michaela back to him and he didn't know what he would say to her.

His stomach muscles clenched and unclenched and clenched again as he tried to think clearly. He wasn't going to take her down with him, not if he could help it. She needed to let him go. She had to, for both their sakes. But he knew she was going to fight him.

Chivalry wasn't his game, or his style. He was out of his depth. He didn't know how to say goodbye. He didn't know how to be gentle. He didn't know how to thank her. There was only one way he knew how to help her get over him. He knew how to be cruel, how to be a bastard, how to make it so she'd be glad he was gone.

Michaela stepped out of the car once the ferry cast off. The ride up from Baton Rouge had been hot and dusty. She felt sticky and tired and bone weary. She leaned her elbows against the ferry railing and faced into the wind. At least she had had a reason to get her out of the house and away from the confrontation over Guy Matherson.

She had known what was going to happen the moment she saw Grand-mère's face. The argument—no, it had not been an argument that had taken place in the kitchen. Grand-mère was too powerful, her speech too blunt. It had been a reckoning, a judgment. The verdict was guilty.

"That man knows better than to bring death trailing after him!" Grand-mère had said. "Does he track mud in my house? *Non!* Yet he brings in the scent of blood with a hell hound on his trail. Not right, Michaela. God don' like it when a man brings trouble to his flock."

Michaela had tried only once to defend Guy who stood like a pillar of stone as he accepted the older woman's disdain. "It's my fault, I brought him, Grand-mère. He didn't ask to come. Besides, you knew he had been shot."

The anger in her great-grandmother's black eyes had reached proportions of Biblical wrath. "You don' say a man tried a second time to kill him. That the gunman could have shot you instead. You don' say he's still out there waiting his chance again." She hadn't even spared Guy a glance as she pointed a crooked finger at him. It was as though he no longer existed except as an object of contention. "You don' say I invite a snake into my garden in protecting *him.*"

The last accusation had no defense and Michaela knew it. She had told her great-grandmother only as much as she thought absolutely necessary about Guy's wounding. She had lied about what had taken place in the hospital by omission and that was her crime, not Guy's. That's when she realized the argument was about family, about truth, about loyalty. In this, Guy was the outsider.

Then she had seen her great-grandmother's chin tremble ever so slightly and new guilt had whipped through her. Grand-mère had not only been angered but hurt and insulted by her lack of trust. "What you think I gon do, 'Tite, you tell me the truth? Huh?"

"Put him off the island," Michaela had admitted in shame.

"Oui." The tight jerk of her silver head had confirmed her great-grandmother's implacable position.

"I'm going."

Michaela had stared appalled at Guy after he spoke those two heartbreaking words. She had no right to ask him to stay. Belle Isle was not her home. Yet she didn't know how else to protect him. The realization of her helplessness had further demoralized her.

"We'll think of something," she remembered promising, but he had looked at her with a sad patience that she knew she would not be able to conquer. He had made his decision, just as Grand-mère had, and neither of them would be moved.

So she had done what she could, what Guy had asked her to do. She had driven into Baton Rouge to call a man in New Orleans named Sam, buy Guy several changes of clothing, and a plane ticket.

She didn't see him standing on the shore, a dark silhouette against a darker backdrop of twilighted trees, until the ferry was nearly across. He had walked a long way out to meet her. That thought should have made her a little happier but it didn't. She had only one problem left. How was she going to say goodbye?

He didn't give her chance to try.

The moment she had gunned the car up the embankment to the levee top, Guy yanked open the door, stepped inside, and slammed it so hard the chassis rocked.

"You took long enough." He rolled his head on his neck as if it were stiff, not looking at her. "You make my call?"

"Yes. Sam said he would meet you at the airport. I have your ticket and all the cash I could muster. The clothes are in the back seat." Michaela paused, waiting for him to look at her, to say something more, something personal. He didn't.

He turned and rolled down the window. "Give me thirty minutes, Yancy! There'll be an easy fifty for your time!"

After a few seconds he half turned, frowning as he looked at the steering wheel. "Something wrong with the car?"

"No." She felt like weeping.

"Then let's get this heap the hell outta here!" he said roughly and slapped the dashboard.

Michaela waited until she thought he'd had enough time to change and then she knocked at his bedroom door.

"Come in."

He was standing by the bed with his back to her, tying one of the two ties she had bought for him. She admired the tapered blue dress shirt that emphasized his shoulders and slim waist. The dark gray slacks she had had hemmed to his inseam specifications seemed a perfect fit. He had named articles and sizes, not colors or fabrics. She had liked buying clothes for him, had liked the idea of dressing him in her mind and now seeing him wear the things she thought he would look good in. He did look good. He looked normal, more like the Guy she had once known.

He turned around finally, his arms outspread. "Well?"

"I have good taste," she said simply.

He half smiled as he fingered the silk tie, a sumptuous design in rich jewel tones. "It's a little flashy but I suppose buying for me made a change from Larroquette's conservatism. Are you responsible for his blue suits and striped ties?"

Michaela didn't like the tone he was taking. At least she now recognized his jibes as a sign of stress. "I never dressed Daniel."

He smirked. "Just undressed him, huh?"

She hadn't really expected him to back off but she didn't expect a brickbat, either. "If you're trying to anger me you won't succeed, not this time." He was going back into the world to face a killer and she wanted something from him before he did. "I'm sorry about what Grand-mère said this morning."

"Why?" He reached for the suit jacket he had left lying on the bed. "She spoke the truth. I admire that."

"But she was too hard on you."

"She was defending you the only way she knew how."

"Yes, well, you know how relatives are."

He shrugged into the coat and settled it around his collar. "Not really."

She frowned. "Don't you have family?"

His expression flattened out. "None I'd want to claim."

Strangely, she thought he meant that. "I don't know what I'd do without Grand-mère," she said to keep the conversation going. She wouldn't let him close her out until she had to. "Especially with my parents living overseas these last years." She smiled. "Of course, I have about forty relatives in and around Baton Rouge. You will—would have met them on Saturday. Any excuse for a party brings us together—weddings, birthdays, anniversaries."

"Funerals?" Guy suggested rudely.

A little of her happiness dimmed. "Yes, even funerals. We're very close. Share everything, even the pain. Everybody keeps up with everybody else."

Guy rolled his eyes, not wanting to take responsibility for the sudden wistfulness in her voice. "Sounds claustrophobic."

"Really? I don't know any other way of life. I tried to go it on my own once. I didn't like it."

"You mean your gig in Vegas." He adjusted his jacket sleeves, more pleased with her choices than he dared admit. "You didn't give yourself enough time. You could have made it, once you'd toughened up."

"One summer was long enough for me."

"Standing on your own two feet is hard. You get knocked around a bit but you learn very fast how to handle yourself, how to take a punch and come back fighting."

"I try to avoid punches where possible," she admitted.

He shook his head impatiently. "No pain, no gain."

"I suppose that has some validity. No one can avoid all life's hard knocks. But there's always been my family to cushion the blow."

He looked up sharply. "You're lying to yourself. Nobody can take your blows for you." Across the distance of the room with only lantern light to illuminate it, his eyes looked opaque. They gave nothing away. "When people run interference for you, they're really denying you your independence. As long as you think you can't do without them, you can't. You're not an adult. You're an emotional cripple."

Michaela blinked back the criticism. "Everybody needs help sometimes."

"I don't."

She tried, oh, how she tried. She even smiled. "Then why did you let me help you the night you left the hospital?"

"I didn't ask for your help."

That particular thrust drew a little of her anger. "But you sure as heck needed it."

"Did I?"

She met his gaze. "I suppose we'll never know."

He smirked. "I'll tell you this much. I'd figured out my angle before I let you hijack me. So tell me. What was yours?"

He came toward her now, his shoes making soft sounds on the rattan matting. "Did it make you feel superior to see me so helpless, to show me my moral shortcomings by helping a man who wouldn't help you seven years ago?" He paused at arm's length. "You got a charge out of that. Admit it."

Michaela lowered her gaze to the middle button on his shirt. "I keep forgetting why sometimes I don't like you. But then you say something that reminds me."

She heard the satisfaction in his voice. "You just don't like to hear the raw facts of life. You'd rather label your motive a selfless sympathetic act of Christian charity."

"Something like that," she responded, wanting to slap him for being so good at being cruel.

Guy nearly laughed until he saw the flat-out misery in her gaze as her head came up. His self-loathing doubled but the predator in him told him he was too close to his goal to back off.

"I'm going to give you a piece of advice," he said shortly. "Don't try that Good Samaritan act with any other stranger. You'll just be dealing yourself in on a lot of trouble."

"That's the first sensible thing you've said," she answered as she reached out to pull his tie straight. "By the way, what was your angle?"

She saw the ice in his blue eyes melt. "Read my mind."

"No, thanks." She patted his tie with a slightly trembling hand. "I don't care for cheap fiction."

He smiled at her. "Right. I knew you'd be okay about this." He looked away. "I'd better go. Yancy won't wait long."

"No, wait!" She stepped forward and flung her arms about his neck, appalled by her actions but more afraid to lose him. "I don't want you to go, just yet."

He pushed her back to arm's length. His eyes were warning her. "Why, Michaela? Is this just sympathy? Or lust?"

She bit her lip then laid her head on the chopping block. "Does it matter?"

She thought for a moment that he would simply drop his hands from her shoulders and turn away. He saw rage, confusion and—was it possible?—panic flare in those remarkably blue eyes. "You're a fool!" he said roughly but pulled her back into him.

She ground her head against his shoulder as his arms closed in tightly around her. "I hate the way you make it so hard to be tender with you."

"You should remember that when I'm gone." His voice was harsh, as if he had been running a long way. "I'm not a nice man. I never make it easy... for suckers."

Her head snapped up. "Is that how you see me, an easy mark?"

He touched her face. "Never easy, but a sucker all the same. Why else are you standing here with tears in your eyes over a man you don't even like?"

"How do you know what I feel?" she said with a sniff.

"Look at me, Michaela. Right square in the eye."

He stared a long time into the dark depths of her gaze. What he saw was what he never thought to see in a woman's eyes: love for, and directed at, him. "You really are a fool." He bent his head quickly and kissed her.

All the breath went out of her as he crushed her to him but Michaela didn't struggle. She put all her heart into that kiss. When he finally let her go she was dizzy and clutched his shoulders to stay upright. "Promise me, you'll call me."

"You don't have a phone."

The word that escaped her sent his brows winging up in amazement. He had never even heard her whisper *damn*.

"Call my uncle's law firm in Baton Rouge." She curled her nails into the fabric of his new suit. "Please promise me you'll let me know, sometimes, that you're okay?"

He shook his head. He wouldn't lie to her. "It wouldn't make it any easier for you."

"How do you know?"

"Because I can't promise I'll ever come back."

Michaela studied his face. She knew what she was about to do was a stupid, hopeless, desperate act, but she knew she would never regret it. She grabbed his hand. "Come with me."

She led him quickly out of his room and to the back of the house where stairs led to the second story.

He had been up them before, but had never explored this particular part of the house. The second story hall was dark except for the reddish dying ember glare of the sunset that poured through the tall open shutters at the far end.

Michaela opened the first door they came to and led him in behind her. She didn't release his hand even after she shut the door. The room was in twilight. The only thing she could distinguish in it was the bed, for it was draped in fine mosquito netting that seemed to glow faintly in the gloom.

She drew him after her to it and then let go of his wrist as she turned to part the netting and attach it along either side, exposing the bed.

"What do you think you're going to do?"

She turned to him. He could see she was smiling, but just barely. Yet he certainly felt her hands sliding up his shirt-front. "I'm going to get so close to you that I can no longer tell where you leave off and I begin."

He had said those words to her just the night before. He had meant them but now, coming from her, they sounded like the most honest, most naked expression of longing he had ever heard. "I don't want to make you sorry." He wondered what had happened to his voice. It sounded strangled.

"Then do it right," Michaela answered in a whisper. She tentatively ran her fingertips down the left side of his face. "Do it without regret, without doubts, without promises."

He smiled tenderly at her. "You just aren't going to make this easy, are you?"

She reached up and began unbuttoning the front of her dress. "I'm going to make it impossible," she said, her eyes never leaving his face.

He stopped thinking, stopped calculating the odds, stopped wondering about the risks, the advantages, the stakes and the outcome. There was only one way he could lose: if he dropped dead of a heart attack right now.

Michaela was amazed by how brave she felt as she pushed
the tiny pearl buttons through their holes. The softly shaped
dress had dozens of buttons from its heart-shaped neckline
to its midcalf hem. Guy let her open every one, his hands
resting with absolute stillness upon her shoulders. His eyes
remained on hers as she gathered the fabric up in her hand
as she went. When she was done, she dropped the hem and
let the dress slide open on her bra and panties.

He looked down slowly from her eyes, pausing first at her
lips then at her breasts straining against the laciest bra she'd
ever owned. It was no more than wisps of champagne lace
held together by a hook hidden behind the rosebud in the
center. It was totally unpractical for daily wear. She would
have spilled out of it. But it wasn't meant for another day.
She had bought it today, for him. She couldn't see his eyes
but she saw the lines of his face reshape into a smile.

His hands moved from her shoulders down to her arms,
dragging the open edges of her dress with them. When he
reached her wrists he released her. She shook her hands and
the dress drifted to the floor.

He reached for her again, this time his warm hands set-
tling on her naked waist above her panties. Slowly he pulled
her in against him until they were touching from shoulder
to knee. And he held her, just held her as if it were enough
for both of them.

The gentle hands on her waist began to move, gently
stroking her—her spine, her flanks, her hips, her thighs. She
felt his quickened breath against her hair but he didn't say
anything, made no other sound at all.

After a moment one hand found her hair and tackled the
clip that she used to keep her hair back from her face. When
he could not find the catch she reached up and loosened it
for him. His fingers met and laced through hers. Together
they worked to pull her hair loose and free until its curly
masses were a full dark cloud around her face and shoulders.

''Better.'' It was the first word he had uttered since she began to disrobe. It sounded so good, so sharp, so urgent.

Michaela reached up and unknotted the tie she had spent forty-five full minutes choosing. She had bought everything he was standing in with the same care and attention. And now she wanted to take every piece of it off of him.

She began unfastening the buttons of his shirt. So many buttons. Why so many buttons? They became in her mind symbolic of the barriers, layers, reminders of the separateness they were defying. Time was short. He was leaving, but not yet. Not yet!

Guy's mind was so filled with the red mist of wanting her that he didn't even feel substantial any more. He felt like flame, a pure blue-white blowtorch of flame wavering under the faint eddies of heat rising off her delicious skin. He wanted to do it right for her, do it so that it would remain forever as the one right thing he had done in his life. But there wasn't enough time for that sort of perfection. He'd steal Paradise. Heaven would have to wait.

He shrugged out of jacket and shirt together and then he plucked the hook of her bra loose. The two shells of fabric snapped apart like a cut rubber band, freeing the dark-tipped globes of her breasts.

He drew her nakedness onto his own. Her breasts spread across the planes of his chest. She was hot everywhere they touched. He was hotter. He felt the edge of his bandage drag against her midriff and then her hand was there, her fingers questing over it.

''Can we?'' Her whisper came against his mouth.

''Just try and stop me!''

He caught her hand and brought it up to their lips. He tucked her forefinger into his mouth. He saw her eyes widen and her mouth fall softly open as he sucked the tip. Leaning forward, he caught that erotic sigh in his mouth. His tongue stroked in on hers, played with it, and then he sucked it into his mouth. She tasted of sunshine and long bayou shadows, of sultry evenings and tropically scented gardens, of hidden places where long slow wet kisses led to a passion that could not be denied.

Finally, he drew back a little, cupping her face between his palms. He wanted her, wanted nothing but to push her back on that waiting bed, push her thighs apart, and push himself into her. Instead, he tried one last time to save her.

"I don't want to hurt you." He was surprised that he sounded as desperate as he felt. Her kisses had left his detachment in shambles. "You can still walk out of here with your pride. Because, believe it, I'm walking out, now or in an hour."

Michaela trembled as his eyes dared her to up the ante. "Then leave. In an hour."

He blinked. "Are you protected?"

He saw her blush before she reached down to pick up her discarded dress and fish into one pocket. Then she tucked a small metallic packet into his palm. He saw her back up one step before she looked up at him.

"I thought, as long as I was shopping for you..." Despite the quiet surroundings her voice trailed away.

His fist closed over the offering. "I like the way you take care of me." He moved in against her and kissed her warmly, deeply. "Thank you."

His tongue slipped in and out of her mouth in a deep hard motion of love as his hands found the waistband of her panties. She gasped as one hand dove under the silk and down over the rounded cheeks of her bottom. The other delved into the front and found the mossy tangle of curls. Her hands gripped his shoulders and she shuddered as his fingers curved into the eager wetness below.

"Damn it, Michaela!" he muttered savagely against her mouth. "You win!"

Guy made love to her with his hands until she was clinging to him, sighing so that he thought he must be going deaf because he couldn't hear anything else. He didn't know which of them was a greater fool. He suspected he was.

Nothing less than the full blast of a fire hose would get him off her now.

They were moving, he slipping down her. His open mouth encountered the sweet flesh of her neck which he licked until it, too, was beyond him. He found the velvet nugget of her nipple under his tongue. His arms clamped around her to hold him there. But, ultimately, he was on his knees, his lips and tongue stroking the exotic scented garden of her femininity as she lay sprawled back upon the bed. He was so hard he ached.

He loved her with his mouth, couldn't get enough of her. This once, this first and last time. He wanted her to have everything, wanted to experience everything good with her. It was uncalculated, unplanned, no strategy but that this once-in-an-eternity would be enough for them both. Yet there was a meter ticking in his head. It was ticking off the remaining moments of his happiness even as he resisted seeking it.

Michaela rolled her head back and forth over the coverlet, her gasps coming in little sips of air as she reveled in the pleasure he gave her. Yet the pleasure was not enough. There was an emptiness even this intense pleasure could not fill. What she ached for most was to hold him, to feel him on her and in her, to rock him in the cradle of her thighs and obliterate the separateness that might forever after hold them apart.

"Please! Please, Guy!" she murmured. Her hands dove into the thick curls at the back of his head. Her fingers flexed and tugged. She heard him grunt in response but his arms remained wrapped over each thigh and he did not budge until she suddenly arched against him as sharp unsteady cries rose from her and then subsided.

Glazed in a sheen of perspiration, he slid slickly up over her, his skin massaging the dampness into her skin. Her hands found his waistband, unbuckling him and sliding down his zipper. Then her hands were inside, cupping and pressing and lifting him as he shoved his clothing down his hips. Within seconds all his splendid new clothes lay in wrinkled ruin by the bed.

She could not see him clearly in the dark depths of the veiled bed but she knew he wasted no time making use of the gift she had handed him. Then he was arching over her. She lifted her arms in welcome, the music of her bracelets accompanying the gesture.

For all he had tried to prepare her, there was that first shocking moment when she realized that he was much more massive than her touch had hinted at.

"Wait!" Her embrace turned into a barrier of arms as she pressed her hands into his heaving shoulders, her hips tilted and her heels dug into the mattress.

Guy nodded and arched his back, fighting for control. His body wasn't cooperating. He was so close to the goal he sought his stomach muscles bunched and cramped in protest. Just a shove, his body urged. Just one hard thrust!

For the first time in his life he understood why some men didn't take no for an answer after a certain point. But this was Michaela. He had tried to warn her, had tried to ward off the temptation. And this was his punishment. He shuddered and started to pull back.

She clutched his shoulders. "No!" He heard her whisper of extremity like a shout in the dark. He opened his eyes.

She was staring at him, the startled awareness of his impressive size making her eyes wide. Then her mouth twisted in a wry smile. "And I thought you were bragging."

He rolled his hips into hers. "I never brag."

She nodded, her lower lip catching in her teeth.

That action bothered him. He didn't want her braced against an onslaught, as if he were about to assault her. He leaned in against her straining arms and licked her upper lip. Once. Twice. The third time she sighed and he caught her released lower lip and dragged it into his mouth. He sucked at it, tugging until she relaxed her arms a little and he could rest his chest on hers. He kissed her everywhere, her eyelids, her cheeks, her ears, chin and mouth. He kissed her until her thighs were squeezing his hips and her hands were kneading the hard muscles of his back.

He lifted himself again and with the certain prerogative of the male not only to conquer but to unite, thrust hard and deep. She didn't stiffen against him this time but allowed him to slip into her warm welcoming tight wet warmth.

She was, as Guy had known she would be, a perfect fit. He was home, physically and emotionally, as he had never been in his entire life. He gathered her to him, cradling her derriere in his hands as she lifted her hips to bring him closer and deeper with each stroke. He whispered her name, and many other things he didn't let his mind in on. They were not only words of praise and thanksgiving but things he had kept locked away even from himself.

It seemed like a race now, their deep breathing like two thoroughbreds racing one another toward the finish line. But he was already there, hot and hard where she was warm and moist.

Michaela clutched him tightly, loving the feel and smell of him, letting his expert stroking direct them. She wanted the moment to last forever, to never end, to never reach the climax that would be both a victory and a defeat. This mustn't be all she'd ever have of him. Even now she knew it wasn't enough.

She began to cry, silent tears sliding across both her cheeks. She bit her lips to keep back her sobs, not wanting him to think he was in any way harming her. But he was. He was breaking her heart with his lovemaking, and she didn't know how to keep the pain from shattering her.

She heard him speaking to her, whispering his pleasure in words that might have offended her in any other place or time. But she knew by his tone that they were dragged out of him, forced by the urgency of his desire, a need she shared. When his mouth again found hers, she tasted that need and then even the world dropped away.

Guy lay in the dark wondering how much more he could take. He tried not to feel the hand lazily stroking his stomach. He resisted the feel of her lips on his chest on a quest for his nipple. He ignored the press of her breast against his arm, her nipple prodding his skin.

They were playing a game, pretending that they were lovers who had all the time in the world to learn what made the other happy. The truth was, Yancy had been waiting for him well over an hour now.

"Enough, Michaela."

Guy half turned to her. He touched her hair, her face, his fingers traveling down over her profile. He touched her breast, her waist, and then one full curve of her hip. "Stay here a while after I've gone. I want to think of you here, in this bed."

Michaela nodded, her dark eyes suddenly gleaming. "I will wait for you."

He frowned. "I hope not. Don't count on anything, on me."

"But I am," she said positively.

His face spasmed as if he had a sudden pain. He sat up and pushed both hands through his hair. "Don't do this to me!" He turned to her, his expression angry. "Let me go. I need to be free. I can only survive if I'm alone."

"I love you."

"Sh—! I don't know what love is," he snarled.

He rolled off the bed and snagged his slacks from the floor. He slipped into them and stood to pull up the zipper. "This feeling you call love, it makes me weak inside." He pulled a fist in against his bare stomach. "My gut turns to water."

He began collecting other items of clothing as his voice went on relentlessly. "The fight goes out in me when I'm with you. And that's very dangerous . . . for both of us."

He wanted so much. Wanted her, wanted the peace of lying in her arms. But he couldn't have it. It was too late for him. Long ago he had made choices he now couldn't outrun. He could only drag her down, maybe get her killed.

When he had everything he turned back to her, his arms outstretched, his face distorted by emotion. "Let me go, Michaela."

Michaela sat on the bed, her body arranged in an elegant tangle of arms and legs. "If that is what you want." She reached out to loosen the mosquito netting. Both sides drifted to the center, eclipsing her within.

"I'm sorry," she heard him say in a voice that was terrible in its gentleness.

She reached for the netting and twitched it aside as he crossed the threshold. She didn't call him back. She couldn't do that to him. She bit through the inside of her lip instead.

She had won from him exactly what she'd asked for. Yet she wondered if he realized what he'd given her in return. Did he know what he had whispered to her in the backwater silence as he lay heavy and spent upon her?

I need you.

He had whispered those words into her hair, the mutter of a man who had let down his guard. Would that need bring him back?

"It will," Michaela said to the quiet room and heard the faint tinkle of her bracelets in reply.

Tante Delphine stepped out of the shadows as Guy entered the downstairs hallway. He wasn't embarrassed or ashamed, only wished that he could stay and protect Michaela from what was certain to be the older woman's disapproval. He knew, looking into her face, that she was aware of what they'd just done.

He moved toward her unhesitatingly, his shirt and shoes in one hand and his jacket slung over his shoulder by the other. "Don't worry. I'm leaving, Tante Delphine."

Her dark eyes flickered in the gloom. "You certain you ain't running away, *mon garçon?*"

His eyes narrowed. "I'm not running. You know why I can't stay. Why I shouldn't have come in the first place. But just now, that was what Michaela wanted." His jaw flexed. "And I wanted her to have it."

Tante Delphine looked him up and down with a snort. "I see what you are better than you do."

"Perhaps." He was angry at himself and flayed by regrets, not for what he had done, but what he couldn't do. "Just don't blame Michaela. None of this is her fault."

Her silver head rocked slowly back and forth. "You know the legend of the 'Tiger in the Rain'?"

He shook his head wearily, in no mood for fairy tales.

"Ho! You should. The tiger is a fierce and beautiful animal. This creature knows his power in the world. He is afraid of nothing, not the brilliance of noon nor the dark impulses that rule the night. But even the tiger fears what he cannot explain. For instance, the thunder and lightning that come with the rain."

Intrigued, Guy asked, "What's that supposed to mean?"

She held him with her strange black eyes. "You are a tiger. You recognize the worst in men's souls, can look their weaknesses and their ugliness in the eye and not flinch. But oh, *mon beau tigre,* what you see in my 'Tite's gaze frightens you. When you are with her, you are like the tiger in the rain. One day you understand. Then you come back, *oui.*"

Guy grunted. "I made Michaela no promises."

She looked past him, up the stairway he had just descended. "You didn't have to say the words."

He winced. "Then it may be that will make it easier for her to hate me."

Tante Delphine stepped aside as he moved on toward the front of the house. "Go with God, *mon beau tigre,*" she murmured to herself. "'Cause Michaela hate you about the same you hate her."

Chapter 11

"You ready, boss?"

Guy inhaled deeply of the desert night air from the balcony of the hotel room before turning to the man who had spoken to him.

Shorter than his boss but so broad he looked like a fire plug dressed in a tux, Sam Lass stood in the opening of the sliding door. For five years Sam had been Guy's personal trainer and bodyguard.

"I've told you before, never sneak up on me, Sam."

"Sorry, boss. Only you looked to be thinking really hard. I didn't want to interrupt."

Guy's lips twitched. Sam was like a trained Doberman; excellent protection, loyal to a fault, but not so smart that he thought to challenge an order. "It's a beautiful night, Sam. There's no moon but the Milky Way seems so close it could be mist from the mountains. I've always liked the night." He turned his head away. "Did you make the arrangements?"

"Yeah, boss. Meeting's set for 3:00 a.m."

Guy nodded. He had been aware from the beginning that Pike might not have been acting strictly out of his own need for revenge. Maybe he was being paid. It had taken him two days to get an interview with the only person who might possibly know why Pike wanted him dead.

Live hard. Die young. Leave a beautiful corpse. He hadn't really thought about his life in those terms but the fatalism had always had a certain romance to it. Until now.

"Sam, do you ever get tired of your life?"

"No, boss. Living is one of the most favorite things I do."

"I meant *how* you live. *Why* you're living." Guy turned to his friend. "You ever think about that?"

"You got mortality on your mind 'cause you been shot," Sam answered seriously. "That's all, boss. Your life flashed before your eyes on account of you could've died. Only, you didn't. So don't think about it no more."

Guy was no longer listening. His thoughts had drifted, as was usual these days, back to Michaela. Where was she tonight? How was she? Was she lying in that upstairs bed remembering? Or was she cursing his memory and her stupidity?

"I sure am glad to see you, boss," Sam ventured into the silence. "You had me worried, leaving the hospital like you did. About went crazy with the cops crawling all over the place, looking for clues."

"Then it was better you didn't have anything to hide," Guy countered.

Sam perked up. "Say! I guess you're right. Only, I could have helped you. You never said who did help you."

Guy hesitated a heartbeat. "I met a woman."

"Oh yeah? Why am I not surprised?" Sam grinned so wide it bowed out his cheeks. "A real looker, right? One of those blondes you're so fond of with legs that go on for days?"

"Not blonde and not tall."

Sam frowned. "But hot enough to do damage, right?"

Guy shook his head. "How she looks doesn't really come into it."

"This sounds serious," Sam said doubtfully.

"Serious?" Guy considered the word. Michaela was the most serious thing in his life. And he had just walked away from her because he had no choice.

"She got a name, boss, or didn't you catch it?"

"Michaela. Her name is Michaela."

"Sounds foreign. Exotic. Bet she's hot."

Guy didn't reply this time. He didn't want to talk about Michaela. She was Michaela. She was beautiful yet he had the feeling that he was no longer an impartial judge of that beauty. Whatever she was, that is what he wanted.

Being a man, he had half hoped that making love to her would take the edge off his seven-year-long itch. It hadn't. It had made it worse for all the reasons he suspected it might.

The reality of Michaela was better than his superstition-driven memories of Kiki. The flesh-and-blood woman was smarter, prettier, wiser, more wonderful than anyone he had ever known. Meeting her again was like coming out of a long sleep where nothing had been quite real, or immediate, or fully potent. Well, his senses were alive now, and the overload of sensation was pumping through him like an adrenaline high. He felt he could leap a tall building, go six rounds with George Foreman, or slam his fist through a wall. He had been to college, knew the psychological term for it. Acute sexual frustration.

How simple the answer was. And yet, he had never before thought of women in esoteric terms. He'd been attracted to women's bodies ever since his hormones had kicked in. He'd never felt awkward or uneasy with women. They were tantalizingly gorgeous creatures born to pique his pleasure. Brains, personality, character; they were added, sometimes unnecessary, attractions. The emphasis had always been how they looked, how they felt, how they made him feel.

Now suddenly, because of Michaela, the equation had flipped. Everything was coming in a different order. The wiry silkiness of her thick hair, the dark depths of her chicory-coffee eyes, the warm scent of her body, the fragrance of gardenias that permeated her clothes, the musical tinkle of her silver bracelets, all of these little things made her singular and unforgettable…because of how he felt about her. He felt protective and afraid for her, afraid of himself and what he might do to her if he was not careful or if she was careless enough to allow him into her life. Those feelings had surfaced before he ever touched her, kissed her, tasted her.

But what was this feeling she had aroused in him? It made him weak, and slightly dizzy, and very very sad, as if he'd been hit with a virus that had infected his emotions as well as his body. This couldn't be love. He felt sick.

He raised a hand to massage his aching temples.

"You should go out for a while, boss," Sam suggested. "You look tense. Why not play a hand or two, for old times' sake?"

"No. I made myself a promise four years ago to never again gamble for money."

"Okay, then take in a show, see a few old friends. You don't want West to see you looking like you need something from him."

Guy nodded. Sam was right. He was tense. He did need something. He needed a future. And to get that, he was being forced to go back into his past.

He had no sentimental attachment to Vegas. The drive in from the airport had been enough to convince him that this was the very last time he would ever set foot here. He had rarely seen the town in daylight. It was a nightlife town. It looked its best in low lighting when only the bright neon, like fake jewels, hid the hard edges and the desperate faces. Once he had loved the desert that surrounded the town. Now it seemed in his eyes a metaphor for his sordid past with its regrets and mistakes. Empty. Barren. Isolating.

"You ever been in love, Sam?

"Not good enough, Mr. Wilson." Michaela slapped the kitchen tabletop with her palm. "Not nearly good enough."

The New Orleans attorney closed his briefcase as an expression of annoyance flickered across his face. "Mr. Matherson pays me to take care of his personal finances. Criminal law isn't my field."

"So I see." Michaela got up and began pacing the kitchen of Belle Isle. Guy had been gone three days but she was no closer to solving the mystery of why someone called Jackson Pike wanted him dead. "Matherson's out there hiding from a bullet. We've got find out why he won't go to the police. We know that a man named Pike was arrested in Las Vegas for murder and bound over for trial four years ago. Why can't we find out what part exactly Matherson played in Pike's case?"

"Because Mr. Matherson's testimony, if he did give any, was kept private. As I've said, my contact would confirm only that certain depositions were given and used as a bargaining tool by the prosecutor's office in order to force this Pike to cut a deal." Michaela paused in her pacing. "The deal was for manslaughter second degree," he added for clarity.

She glared at him. "I know that. What I want to know is why the DA wanted Pike to cut a deal? They had him, didn't they?"

Beau Wilson shrugged. "Does it matter?"

"I don't know that it matters. I won't know until I have the answer to the question."

"I don't think you're going to get it, at least not through my office."

"I don't know what Mr. Matherson is paying you but you aren't earning it," she snapped.

Beau Wilson offered her a look of glacial indifference. "If you think you can do better, you're welcome to try."

"More coffee, Mr. Wilson?" asked Tante Delphine who sat at the far end of the table snapping beans.

The young attorney smiled at her, a polite automatic surface smile which briefly masked his irritation. "Yes, thank you."

Tante Delphine glanced at her great-granddaughter. "The gentleman wants more coffee, 'Tite."

Michaela moved grudgingly toward the stove, feeling that her great-grandmother had just set the battle for equality back thirty years. "Who pours coffee at your office, Mr. Wilson?" she asked as she refilled his cup.

He looked uncomfortable again as he said, "I usually get my own."

To distance himself from Michaela's enmity, Beau Wilson looked around Belle Isle's kitchen as he stirred sugar into his cup. He had not really seen Belle Isle on his first trip. It seemed to be right out of the last century. The big square room at the back of the house was dominated by a long plank table. The floor was laid in flagstones, the walls whitewashed. Cooking utensils of another century hung from the walls. A huge cast-iron wood-burning stove was set into the open hearth which, he suspected, had originally been where the cooking was done. Beside the stove stood a copper boiler. He had read enough about old Louisiana architectural designs to suspect that it still provided the house with its only source for hot water. He knew half a dozen clients who would pay, well, really *pay* for a place like this.

"Beautiful house," he said when Michaela had returned the pot and sat down beside him again. "I don't suppose it's for sale?"

"It isn't." Hostility rose from her in ripples. "Now back to business. I need to know who cut the deal and why," she continued, her dark gaze trained on him. "You've got to find out."

Beau shook his head. "I can't, believe me. I don't have those kinds of connections in Nevada. I deal strictly in real estate and finance."

"Someone in your office must," she persisted.

Beau stared at her. "As should someone in your uncle's firm. Why haven't you asked him to help you?"

"Because I don't want to involve any more people than necessary."

"I suspect you'd rather not explain your unconventional connection with Mr. Matherson," he surmised neatly.

Michaela conceded the point. "Something like that. Still, you're Mr. Matherson's attorney. If the police should get wind of your actions, it would make sense to them that you were making inquiries on your client's behalf. And, more importantly, you can invoke client-attorney privilege to avoid answering certain questions."

He nodded graciously. "I appreciate the fact that you've kept my client's confidences. I doubt it was in the capacity of client-to-attorney that he told you his story."

Michaela met his inquiring gaze with a closed expression. "It might as well have been."

"He isn't under warrant for arrest," Beau reminded her. "He's simply listed as a missing person, with the suspicion that he might have involuntarily disappeared. If he was here I'd tell him what I'm telling you. Go to the police. Tell them what you know about this Jackson Pike and the shooting. Give them something to run with."

Michaela shook her head. "There must be reasons why Guy wouldn't go to the police. Until I know what they are, I can't risk making things worse for him."

Beau nodded. "If Mr. Matherson trusts you, so do I, to a point. However, I won't jeopardize my position in my firm by further unauthorized searches into the background of a client."

"Even if it could save his life?"

"We don't know that it will."

"But if it could?"

"We have no proof it even was this Mr. Pike. Mr. Matherson was only speculating."

Michaela's face changed. "You know him. Guy has a phenomenal memory for detail. If he said it was Pike, you can believe it."

Beau nodded. "You're right. So, what now? Legally, I'm not authorized to do anything until my client phones in again."

Michaela's eyes brightened. "Has he called you again?"

Beau shook his head. "Not since he called and asked me to deliver the money to you a second time. If you hadn't told me then, I would never have known he'd been here."

"You told Mr. Larroquette you thought he was here," Michaela retorted, remembering her very unpleasant conversation with Daniel yesterday. He had come to Belle Isle and pitched a very uncandidatelike fit.

Beau flinched. "I told Mr. Larroquette nothing. He called my firm and spoke to one of the senior partners who told him I'd come upriver on a client's behalf."

"How did he learn it was me you came to see?"

"Mr. Larroquette has a considerable amount of clout."

"So I hear."

"What do you suggest we do now?" Beau asked, just to be polite. He glanced at his watch. He had two hours to get back to New Orleans where he was expected at a business dinner. After a moment he realized the room had grown strangely quiet. He glanced up.

Michaela was smiling at him across the table. "I'm going to Las Vegas."

His brows lifted. "You aren't serious? You'll learn nothing there you can't learn here."

"How do you know? I bought Guy a ticket for Las Vegas. Maybe he's still there."

"Think about that, Ms. Bellegarde. Mr. Matherson wanted to disappear. Do you really think he'd tell you where he was headed? He probably traded that ticket in for one going to some other destination."

"No, he didn't," she answered confidently. "I could check because that ticket was charged on my credit card."

He smiled. "Good for you. But that doesn't imply he's still in Vegas. I'd advise you to wait a few more days. He might even come back."

Michaela breathed in carefully through her nose and out again. He might come back. She had not slept more than two hours at a time since Guy left, without anticipating that hope. She started at every sound—a snapping twig, a shifting of leaves, the creaking of old boards—anything that might be mistaken for the sound of Guy coming back. "I can't sit here and do nothing."

"How long do you plan to be gone?"

Her gaze shifted toward her great-grandmother. "I have to be back day after tomorrow. The following day is my Grand-mère's one-hundredth birthday."

Beau smiled and nodded at the elderly woman. "Happy birthday, Ms. Bellegarde. I hope you will try to convince your great-granddaughter to stay home."

"I tell her to follow her heart, *monsieur.*" She tapped the left side of her chest with a finger. "The strong listen to nothing but the heart."

Beau's mouth twisted. "I guess I know where your determination comes from." He came to his feet. "I'd like to stay longer but I must get back." He offered Michaela his hand which she shook. "Try to stay out of trouble, Ms. Bellegarde. Guy Matherson has always struck me as the kind of man who can look after himself."

"I hope you're right," Michaela said as she walked with him toward the front of the house. "I'll check in with you every day."

He paused at the front door, squinting to keep the late afternoon sun out of his eyes. "You're certain the answer lies in Vegas?"

Michaela shrugged. "I don't have many clues. I have to start somewhere."

He looked at her as if he had previously missed some striking detail of her features. "Whatever I can do to help I will. I like Mr. Matherson."

"I'm going to go up and pack," she announced as she swung back through the kitchen door.

"When you gon' leave?" Tante Delphine asked.

"First thing in the morning. I bought the ticket earlier today with some of the money Guy left me. The nice thing about money is that a person can make last-minute plans."

Michaela blushed as she felt her great-grandmother's dark gaze probing hers. "What is it, Grand-mère?"

"Troubles are gathering about you," the older woman said gravely. "You must do nothing to cause yourself grief."

Apprehension rippled along Michaela's nerve endings. "Are you saying this will end badly, for Guy?"

Tante Delphine met her great-granddaughter's apprehensive gaze. "I say the storm clouds is rolling in and the tiger got a powerful enemy who will use his weakness against him."

"You think I am Guy's weakness?" Michaela asked softly.

"Ain't you?"

"I only want to help him."

"What you want!" she scoffed. "It's a shame the wants in this world is always put ahead of the needs. What the tiger needs. That's what you should ask yourself."

"You don't think I'm it." Michaela could not disguise the resentment in her voice.

Tante Delphine lifted her frail shoulders in a huge theatrical shrug. "It's not for me to say."

Michaela pulled herself together, vexed as she had never been before with her great-grandmother's advice. "You're telling me to stay home, like a good little woman, and wait for him. I won't. We're entering the twenty-first century, Grand-mère. Women are equal to men. They take action when necessary."

"Equal ain't the same as better." Tante Delphine rose from her stool with her colander of prepared green beans. "Are you gon' 'cause you can help? Or, 'cause you think he needs your help? The tiger don't need no help in his own jungle."

Michaela's eyes burned with anger and unshed tears. "I thought you, of all people would understand. I know he doesn't need me." Her chin trembled. "That's the trouble, Grand-mère. Maybe he doesn't need me at all. But I need him."

Tante Delphine smiled. "Just so you know why you go, 'Tite. Just so you don' tell lies to your heart."

"You think I will be hurt."

"I don't think on these things," she countered. "I feel them, 'Tite. You got the understanding. What do you feel?"

"He loves me," Michaela said in defiance of her doubts.

Tante Delphine smiled. "Tell me what I don' know."

Michaela relaxed a little. "He wants to protect me from himself." She smiled shyly. "I make him crazy."

"Crazy is good for a man like that, with so much self-control. But don't scare him away, 'Tite. He needs to hunt in his own jungle and win his prizes himself."

Michaela laughed as she came back to give her great-grandmother a hug. "Grand-mère, you're so old-fashioned! I love you, anyway. But I must get busy if I'm going to leave early."

"The world don't change much as the words to describe it," Tante Delphine murmured to herself when her great-granddaughter had gone. "Since time began, courting is the same between a woman and a man." She chuckled to herself. She had a hundred years of experience to prove it.

Michaela descended the steps of the modern Las Vegas courthouse with a frown that had nothing to do with the glare of the late afternoon desert sun. Behind her very dark sunglasses her gaze was focused inward in thought.

She had learned almost nothing from a day spent combing through public records. Charged with murder, Jackson Pike had pleaded guilty to lesser charges of manslaughter and was sentenced to seven years. No one she spoke with seemed able or willing to offer more than the usual spiel as an explanation for why Pike had been released on parole at his first hearing. A model inmate. Good behavior. The man who wanted Guy Matherson dead had good manners and steady work habits.

The district attorney's office said they didn't have the time or manpower to dig into the files in order to clarify why Pike was even offered a deal. The case seemed so straightforward. Local hustler killed bystander in shoot-out with police. Neither victim nor perpetrator warranted much interest once justice was served.

"Well, somebody must know something," Michaela murmured to herself. She stared out across the boulevard and wondered if she dared look up her old boss. Would he even remember her? She was one of hundreds of young women who traipsed through this town every month of every year in hopes of finding quick and easy money. Would he remember her? If he did, would he know anything about Jackson Pike?

Several hours later she was sitting in a bar in one of the larger casinos on the Strip, nursing a cup of coffee and waiting to learn if Ted Barlow would see her. She had called his office earlier and been told to come in after 8:00 p.m. That had given her time to change from shirt and slacks into a dark, tailored suit and heels. She had even put up her hair and tucked her silver bracelets under her sleeve. At least now she looked like an attorney instead of a law student.

She glanced at her watch. Barlow had kept her waiting in the bar an hour now. She waved off the waiter angling toward her with a coffeepot in hand. There was just so much she could drink before she would need to excuse herself and find the ladies' room. Somehow, emerging from there to find Barlow waiting for her didn't seem a good strategy.

Sitting and watching the continuous carnival of nightlife that was part of Las Vegas's attraction, she again felt as if she were nineteen years old, with no experience of the world but with a great big belief in the basic decency of human nature. Maybe it was because she didn't have much choice. She had used up half the time she had allotted herself in Vegas. It was Thursday evening. She had to fly home in the morning, no ifs, ands or buts about it.

She *knew* Guy was here, could almost feel his presence in the air. Several times since arriving in town, she had suddenly looked over her shoulder, certain she had heard his deep velvet voice across a room.

She idly spun the eleven silver bracelets tucked under her cuff. Thinking about Guy was dangerous to her concentration and her determination. Inevitably thoughts of him turned to thoughts of his wide sensual mouth, the graceful lines of his face, the heat and strength in his lean long body, and how all those components had worked together to lift her off the planet. Well, there had been one other strategic part involved.

She hastily gulped her coffee. The last thing she could afford was to be fogged in by sexual longing. She needed every brain cell on alert.

Still, she had to think about Guy in some capacity. After all, she was here for his sake. If only she had been thinking clearly she wouldn't have allowed him to leave with so many questions unanswered. He had gulled her completely. What she knew about him she could fit into a thimble and still leave room for her finger inside. She didn't even know most of his vital statistics. She didn't know his birth date or place, or even how old he was. She hadn't even made him explain why her twelfth bracelet was permanently soldered to his wrist. It had never occurred to her to ask if he was married.

She wasn't a fool or easily gotten around. She was smart and prudent and self-contained. Shy, not aloof. But it seemed one and the same to people who didn't know her. Guy was the only man she'd ever known who treated her with the casual assuredness that said he knew what she was thinking and that it was mutual, and more, all right. Looking back there was only one humbling explanation for her total lack of reasonability where he was concerned. She was in love.

She had started off well. At the hospital, even on the road, and later during the first days of his recovery, she had kept her distance, asked the hard questions, noted every evasion, saw through the dodges and waited for the truth. But somewhere along the line she'd lost her perspective. The Socratic Method had bowed before the power of Eros. He had said they were attracted by electromagnetic forces.

"Bunk!" She'd let lust, pure and simple, get in the way.

Rather than getting her goat, defining the culprit eased her mind. It explained why she had accepted from Guy an explanation for his shooting that made no sense. It explained why she had gone along with his urgent desire to keep the police away from the man who had tried to kill him. But it didn't answer the question: why was Guy determined to solve this himself? Was he just that much of a loner? Or, was it egotistical male pride? Or, was it—

"Ms. Bellegarde?"

Michaela looked up into the face of the man she'd been waiting for. "Mr. Barlow." She stood and extended her hand to the man in short sleeves and wing tip shoes. He had aged. His weight hung from his tall frame the way a porch sags on a run-down house. But his face was smooth as a baby's and his fingers were full of gold rings. "Thank you for seeing me. Won't you have a seat?"

Ignoring her invitation, he checked her out in a quick up and down motion of his gaze. "Too short."

"I beg your pardon?"

He rolled his eyes. "You heard me. You're too short to work here. Can't be seen across the room. Even in four-inch platforms you'd only be what, five foot six?"

"Something like that," Michaela answered shortly. "But that's not why we're going to have a conversation." She whipped a card out of her jacket pocket. It was one from her uncle's law firm. "My name is Michaela Bellegarde. I'd like to talk to you about Jackson Pike and Guy Matherson."

He took the card as if they were conducting a drug deal, palming it. When he looked down it, he hissed a four-letter word. "I don't talk to lawyers. I have lawyers that talk to lawyers for me." He turned away.

"He's in town, Mr. Barlow."

The man swung around on her. "Who?"

Michaela smiled, uncertain of which person he would find of more interest, Pike or Matherson. When in doubt, she always ducked. "I am here to see to Mr. Matherson's best interests."

Barlow's expression radiated annoyance. "Matherson revoked his own welcome here years ago. He can't gamble here."

"Because he offered evidence against Pike."

Barlow's gaze narrowed. "I wouldn't know nothing about that. What I do know is he isn't welcome, and neither are you." He snapped a finger and two hovering waiters hustled over.

"Ms.—" Barlow glanced again at her card "—Bellegarde's coffee is on the house. Fill it once."

He turned and walked away.

The young men eyed her in wary interest. "More coffee, Ms. Bellegarde?" one of them asked.

Michaela shook her head and opened her purse. "And the rest was not on the house." She plunked down three dollars and walked out of the door.

She was fresh out of inspiration and more than a little defeated by her lack of progress. She didn't really think to look down the hotel hallway as she stepped off the elevator at her floor. Usually when she traveled alone, she stayed alert until she had turned the dead bolt and shot home the chain of her door.

The man must have been standing in the alcove where the ice and soda machines were. One moment the hall was empty. The next it was blocked by a solid body in a dark suit. She did slow her step as she approached him and it became obvious that he was intentionally barricading the hall.

He was huge. Not especially tall but so broad he effectively formed a wall between her and the rest of the hallway. He stood so still he didn't seem quite human.

Michaela's first thought was to turn and flee. The next was that she was being an idiot. A big man in the hallway did not constitute a crime, only an inconvenience.

She paused a few feet before him and said briskly, "Excuse me. I'd like to pass."

The Wall spoke. "You Ms. Bellegarde?"

The hair lifted on Michaela's nape. No one knew she was in town. She stared at the impenetrable face before her that resembled nothing so much as a closed fist capped by long, sun-streaked blond hair. Who had sent this goon to check her out? "I'm Ms. Bellegarde. Why do you ask?"

"I shoulda known." Michaela was amazed by the smile that transformed his stone face, revealing his youth. That smile made him seem more like a surfer dude on steroids. "You're the attorney, right?"

Michaela recovered quickly from her surprise. "I am. And I'm going to ask you again, what do you want?"

He was definitely smirking now. The effect made her want to close the top button of her jacket. "He wants to see you."

Michaela's quickened pulse reined in. She assumed he meant Mr. Barlow. "He wants to talk now?"

The Wall nodded his massive head and reached for her. "You shouldn't be standing around in public. You're an easy target."

The hand he wrapped about her upper arm belonged to a prize fighter, Michaela decided. His fingers were the size of frankfurters and cut off her circulation without even trying. "You've got to come with me."

She thought about struggling. She thought about screaming. She thought about the pepper spray in her purse and about a half dozen other self-protective moves. But she couldn't see the point. "I'm not going anywhere," she bluffed. The truth was, he was already pulling her down the hall.

He stopped suddenly and she collided with his shoulder. He didn't seem to notice the impact but *she* noticed. As she pushed away from him she touched his rocklike bicep. It was probably equal in girth to her waist.

Panicking at last, she dug in her heels in the hotel carpet and grabbed the knob of the nearest door. "I'm not going anywhere until you tell me who sent you!" she shouted.

The Wall looked back at her and then pointedly at the knob she was clutching. "Guy isn't going like you making a scene."

Michaela let go of the knob. "Guy Matherson sent you?"

The Wall frowned. "Yeah. Didn't I say that?"

"No," she said succinctly. "You did not!"

"Oh." He frowned. "You coming?"

"You bet!" Smiling, Michaela followed The Wall past several other doors, to the door past hers. He didn't even get a chance to knock before the door swung open.

Guy stood on the other side dressed in a tux. His pin-tucked dress shirt minus its studs gaped open on a tightly muscled chest and the upper edge of his bandage. "What the hell are you doing here?" he demanded.

Michaela eyed him, tux and all, and remained blessedly cool. "That, I believe, should be my line."

Chapter 12

"This—person is a friend of yours?" Michaela questioned once she had stepped inside the door.

Guy nodded. "He's my physical trainer."

"I suppose that's a euphemism for bodyguard." Michaela sent Sam an injured glance as she rubbed her upper arm. She was certain she'd have bruises by morning. "He should learn better manners."

Guy shrugged. "What Sam lacks in manners he makes up for in loyalty."

"How did you know I was here?"

Guy remained unsmiling. "You asked a lot of questions. Someone was bound to notice. Have a seat, Michaela."

She looked around and discarded the idea of crossing the hotel room to take a chair. That would put both Guy and Sam between her and the door. It occurred to her that she was very annoyed. She perched tentatively on the foot of the bed nearest the door and shifted her hostility to Guy. "You haven't called."

He leaned his hips against the dresser before her and

folded his arms. For several seconds he regarded her with the absolute singularity of purpose with which a cat watches its potential prey. "How would you know? How long have you been in Vegas?"

"None of your business and none of your business." She smiled but it wasn't meant to be encouraging. "Next question."

"Who have you talked to?"

"Barlow. The DA's office."

"And?"

Michaela shook her head. "Oh, no. It's your turn. I flew out here to try to save your butt." Her gaze took in his tux. "While it appears that you only came out here to have a good time."

She heard Sam snicker where he stood holding up a wall.

Guy continued to survey her with studied detachment. "I found what I came for."

"And what is that?" she rapped out impatiently, wanting to leave because he didn't look at all pleased to see her. He looked as if he wished she were a thousand miles away. He looked as if he were getting ready to go out or expecting someone. Some...one...else.

She gave the room a quick reconnoitering glance. She saw things she'd been too rattled to notice before. There was a champagne bucket complete with an iced-down bottle standing by the table and two chairs. There was a domed dish on the table. Beside it was a plate of obscenely huge and decadently red strawberries.

Her gaze came back to his face and saw he had read her mind, and her feelings, all too accurately. She didn't need a diagram or his bland expression as further clues. She had it. This was the scenario for a seduction. Her stomach dropped into her shoes. She hadn't counted on that...not that.

"I believe I asked you a question," she said coolly as she reeled in every emotion but the desire to leave here with her pride intact. "What did you find out?"

He straightened up off the dresser. "It's personal."

"Oh, thanks!" She felt her temper snapping the restraints just she'd put on it. "You had a linebacker drag me in here just so you could tell me to mind my own business? Sam could have delivered that message in the hallway."

Guy braced his foot on the bed beside her right hip and leaned in on his knee. The sexual tension in the room careened out of control as he leaned in toward her. "Michaela, don't go to pieces on me. I'm saying Pike's vendetta is personal. There's nothing behind it but his own rage."

Michaela looked up at him. Despite the fact he was planning a cozy little evening with some woman she hated without even knowing a single thing about, she suddenly wanted nothing more than to grab him by the lapels and haul him onto the bed with her. Then the legally trained part of her mind homed in on the salient facts implicit in his words.

"You mean you thought someone might have—?" she struggled for the right expression "—put a contract out on you?"

His cheeks firmed but he still wasn't exactly smiling. "Something like that."

"My God!" She compressed her lips over the gasp of horror. "If it wasn't a—a hit," she stumbled over the word, feeling as if she had just stepped into a gangster film and been given all the bad lines, "then why not go to the police?"

"I waived that right four years ago."

"I don't understand."

"I was offered the witness protection program. I refused."

"You—? Why?"

His mouth widened. "I had things I wanted to do, people I wanted to see. I didn't want to lose my past."

Michaela put up both hands in protest. "I don't understand. You're saying you deliberately left yourself open to retribution? That's pretty stupid," she finished, provoked past censoring her thoughts.

He was staring at her so hard she could almost feel his gaze stroking her face. "What was stupid was letting you get involved in the first place."

"Then why did you?" she demanded irrationally.

"I think it had something to do with this."

As he leaned down to her, Michaela half lifted off the bed to meet his kiss. *Damn him, anyway!* she thought in a last-ditch effort to control the moment. But it was much too late.

He tasted of sunshine and whiskey, of deep dark desire and the tart juice of strawberries.

She knew she'd lost her edge, her footing, perhaps even her mind before she backed away enough to see the triumph gleaming like facets in his aquamarine blue eyes. Caribbean eyes. He had tropical blue eyes! That's where he fit into her ancestral psyche. Grand-mère had said he had a touch of the Old Blood. Now she understood.

Sam's giggle sent her gaze skittering sideways. She had forgotten they had an audience.

"Get out of here, Sam." Guy said the words without even glancing up from her face, almost as if they were an after-thought. Yet Michaela noticed there was nothing casual about Sam's reaction. For such a large man, he moved with remarkable speed. Even so, he didn't slam the door behind himself. He closed it so softly that the distinct *click* of the lock could be heard.

"Now," Guy said, smiling down at her in a wicked way that nearly had her slipping out of her shoes.

But she had had two seconds to pull her scattered thoughts back together. She wasn't going down for the count just yet. She was an attorney. It was time she began acting like one. "You have rights. One of them is the right to protection. You've been shot. If you identify Pike as the gunman, you will be placed in protective custody until the police pick him up."

He looked at her with what seemed great patience. "I've heard all it before, from the district attorney's office."

"They did tell you your rights? Explain how it works?"

"You needn't worry, counselor. My rights were not violated."

"But you put yourself needlessly in . . . danger." She was certain now his eyes were smiling. "Why are you looking at me like what?"

"I'm just wondering how long it's going to take you to realize that you've behaved even less rationally than I have. This is my life. Who invited you in?"

Michaela felt herself go cold and then fill with heat. There was nothing impersonal about his gaze or the finger skimming down her cheek. That finger wasn't rock steady. It trembled ever so slightly. He wasn't in control, he was struggling to maintain that cool impartial veneer. She had once thought he was a man who never sweat, didn't worry or fear or hurt . . . or give a moment's thought for anyone else. Now she had seen him in pain and drenched in his own sweat. In walking away from her at Belle Isle, he had demonstrated his worry and fear for her. As for control, he'd been buried deep within her flush body when he'd lost complete control, and it had been the best moment of her life. He had said then what he could not or would not say now. But she remembered the words all the same. *I need you.*

"Who invited me into your life?" she repeated and met his very bright blue gaze. "You did when you took my bracelet seven years ago."

At last his smile appeared. "I did, didn't I?" His fingers wandered over the soft surface of her lower lip. "Is the bracelet steeped in voodoo or some special brand of Tante Delphine's magic?"

"I don't know," Michaela answered honestly. "She gave the twelve of them to me when I turned thirteen. Each flower represents a different wish she holds for me." She reached out and encircled his wrist with her fingers to push his cuff back and reveal the silver band strapping his wrist. "You see the floral design? Grand-mère put her wishes for my future in the language of flowers." She pointed to her own bracelets. "Roses are for love, orange blossoms for a bride, nightshade represents truth, hepatica for confidence, willow for bravery, and so on."

She saw him glance down at the etched flower on his bracelet. "What is it? A daisy?"

She laughed. "No. Daisies represent innocence. Yours is a violet." She looked up into his face without trepidation. "I'm afraid you really did yourself in with this one. Violets represent faithfulness."

His expression swamped her emotions like a wave crashing on the beach. "I've been faithful to you—after my fashion."

"That sounds like a line, Mr. Matherson."

"It does. Luckily I have proof, don't I?" His gaze dropped to the bracelet.

"Why did you do that, have it soldered on?"

"I didn't want to lose it."

"What did you say to people when they asked you about it?"

"You mean what did I tell other women?"

"Yes." It shouldn't have hurt her to think about other women in his arms. She'd had no part in his past life. But a tiny pain deep down made her wince inside.

"I told them the truth," he said simply. "It represented the luck I'd been given by a very beautiful woman whose name I didn't even know."

The tiny pain dissolved. "Now you do," she said huskily.

"Yes, Michaela." Even his eyes were smiling. "Now I do."

But she wasn't ready to capitulate. He seemed much too certain of his welcome and her feelings. She wanted to bask in his smile a little longer, to see the desire she had ignited burn steadily, for her, in his eyes. "That must have made some women jealous."

He chuckled. "You know, it made all of them very jealous. Some handled it better than others but they almost all wanted the bracelet. For luck. Their luck, because they knew you were the enemy.''

Michaela shrugged, feeling better with each word he spoke. "I wasn't a threat. I wasn't even aware of your existence most of the past seven years."

"But it doesn't work that way, Michaela." He caught her chin to lift her face up to his. "*I* knew. That was enough. They all knew that sooner or later I'd find you again."

"And you did," she whispered.

"Yes, I did," he whispered back.

"So, what now?"

"We part again for a little longer." The hand at her chin moved up to caress her cheek. "I have to finish with the past before I can consider the future. You know that."

"I know that," she repeated. "So, I should leave now." She didn't move.

She saw his expression change. He looked as if he were struggling with himself. "I keep feeling like I'm putting another black mark against my soul every time I touch you. You're in danger when you're near me. You should get up off that bed and walk out that door, and out of this hotel, and catch a cab for the airport."

"I should," she agreed pleasantly. "But I'm not going to. I haven't taken an easy breath since you left Belle Isle. I kept imagining you lying somewhere, alone, hurt, or—"

He covered her mouth with his fingers. "Don't, Michaela. You should not worry about me. I don't ever want to cause you pain. I can't be with you if I know it's hurting you."

"Not being with you hurts more."

He looked as if he wanted to kiss her but he didn't move. "You always know what to say."

She reached up and lay her hands on his shoulders. "It's just how I feel."

"I know, and that's the miracle of it." She saw him look around as if he needed something else to think about. He spied the bottle in the ice bucket. "Champagne?"

"No." Her nails dug into the shoulders of his tuxedo jacket to hold him still. "I want to finish something I began seven years ago."

He gave her a doubtful look. "What would that be?"

"This." She rose to her feet and reached up to push his jacket from his shoulders. It drifted toward the floor as she began pulling his shirt from his trousers. "The last time we were in a hotel room together you wanted me to pretend that we had been on a date and come back to your room because we wanted to be alone. Remember?"

His eyes narrowed. "I remember."

"Only you were too tired to—how did you put it? Oh yes. Jump my bones. So I was supposed to tuck you in. Remember?"

She looked up into his face when he stood stripped to the waist and saw him watching her with eyes so dark they seemed black. He didn't say a word or even try to touch her. She leaned into him and lifted up on tiptoe to bring her mouth under his. The kiss was soft and sweet and so warming her blood seemed to sing. Still, he made no move to help or hinder her.

After a few seconds she embraced him, sliding her hands up and down the long muscles strapping his back. Compared to Sam he seemed almost slender, yet he wasn't. The shoulders she traced were broad, the chest deep. His masculine leanness only added to the sense that he was a man who allowed himself very few pleasures or indulgences. He possessed the raw edginess of a man who was always a little hungry, always in need. The tight leash he kept on his emotions refined the hunger that pulsed beneath her hands.

She brushed her cheek against his chest, smooth and hard and warm, and heard the rapid pounding of his heart. The musky scent of his body intrigued her. She shut her eyes and concentrated as she dragged her open mouth across the surface of his skin, recording tastes and smells and textures. Finally she found a masculine nipple, pebble hard, under her lips. She licked it. The shiver that went through him made her smile. She tongued first one and then the other, amazed and pleased by his reactions.

When she reached for his belt his hands came up to help her but she pushed them aside. She smiled away his frown. "My game, Mr. Matherson."

She lowered his zipper then pushed trousers and briefs together off his hips, following the compact curvature of his buttocks with her hands. She chuckled at the feel of the bristling silky hair covering them. And then she reached around to the front.

He was hot and hard, and silk-skinned. She moved her hands away and reached for his wrist. "Come and lie down," she said, not quite brave enough to look him fully in the face anymore.

He did as she asked, shucking his trousers and shoes before reclining back against the pillows.

When she had removed her own jacket and shoes, she lay down beside him. She stroked his chest and belly, watching him watch her through eyes that were no more than slits of blue between thickets of black lashes. Only then did she wonder if she had nerves to match her desire. When he reached over and turned off the light over the bed she knew he understood and was grateful.

In the semidarkness, her courage redoubled. She bent over him, kissing a path down his chest as he pulled the pins from her hair and released a flood of long dark wavy hair that spilled over his arms and chest and groin.

She moved lower and encompassed as much of him as she could with her mouth. He was impressively made, might easily have hurt her if he had not remained passive, but he didn't move. He threw an arm over his eyes. His other hand was locked in the masses of her loosened hair. She touched and tasted, savoring him, absorbed in the tremors that shook him and the deep moans her actions wrung from him. She had never been intimate with a man this way before but it seemed so natural, so right, so necessary to love him in every way possible. He throbbed and pulsed under her attention, as if his whole spirit were embodied there. She couldn't seem to get enough. He was hot and firm and inviting. She could taste him and wanted more but finally he couldn't be still beneath her any longer.

"Stop, Michaela!" he whispered in a strangled sigh. He half lifted up into the sitting position to catch her by the shoulders and lift her away.

"I don't mind," she protested as he lifted her up and onto himself. "I don't," she repeated as she brushed her hair back from her face, damp with perspiration and the tears of the emotional storm she had endured.

"I know, Michaela. I mind." His smile of gratitude made her heart flip-flop. "I need you. Need to be in you. Part of you."

She smiled. "Whatever you want."

"I want you." He lifted up and kissed her. As she tasted the hunger in him she knew she had not been totally in control. He had given that control to her by clamping down on his own powerful needs. Now those needs needed expression.

They nearly fought each other as they removed her clothing. Urgency and desire made them clumsy but, at last, she was lying naked beside him. It was his turn to explore.

He kissed her everywhere, the bend in her elbows, the indentation of her waist. He licked her navel, the backs of her knees, the arches of her feet. Michaela reveled in his touch, in the need he aroused and soothed then aroused again. She was whimpering before his mouth claimed the hot moist center of her.

"Yes, sweetheart! That's it!" he whispered roughly. "Let it happen. Let me satisfy you."

She arched against his mouth, heels dug into the mattress, unable to keep still. He caught her hips, making love to her with his mouth until she shattered.

Guy held tightly on to her, drinking in the pleasure he had recreated for her, filling his senses with her taste, her little helpless cries of joy, the unique texture of her skin, learning her all over again as if it were the first time.

When he finally surged up and on her, the need within him had moved from the usual surface hunger down deeper until it was against his very bone. For her, anything. She grabbed his shoulders and buried her face in his neck. He felt the hot moisture of tears on his skin as she sobbed softly against him.

"Have I hurt you?"

She lifted her head. "No! It's—! Please, Guy. I need you!"

"Not half as much as I need you!"

He was long past thinking of technique or control or mastery. Every square inch of his skin tingled. Every muscle in his body strained toward the goal. He was all desire and need for the woman beneath him. When he found and slid into her incredibly tight honeyed warmth, he moaned like a man who had passed some arduous test.

He tried to make it last, to make amends for all that had come before, to give her what he had no words for. She had returned his caution with an openness that nearly stopped his heart. She had literally saved his life. Now it seemed she wanted to redeem his worn and battered soul.

He knew then he wouldn't make it without her, not only the momentary release of desire, but the forever of his future. He wanted her, needed her there with him, needed her to be part of everything. But most of all, in this moment, he needed her to share his triumph with her.

He reached down between them, pressing gently where she squirmed so deliciously against him. He caught her gasp of pleasant surprise as his fingers found her, rubbing and pressing in a rhythm which augmented his strokes. He felt her clamp down on him and thought he'd lose it. Then she was fluttering down deep, caressing him with her body in a hundred little ways as she cried out his name. More grateful for her pleasure than he had ever been for anything, he at last gave in to the need that surged out of him and into her, drowning desire with release.

"'A place for when the world is too much with us'?"

"That's Wordsworth," Michaela pointed out. Lying on her stomach with her elbows on the bed and her hands under her chin, she leaned over and planted a kiss on his jaw. "Now impress me by finishing that quote."

"Think I can't?" Guy grinned and stacked his arms behind his head on the pillow. "'The world is too much with us; late and soon, Getting and spending, we lay waste our powers: Little we see in Nature that is ours; We have given our hearts away, a sordid boon!'"

"'A man with poetry in him is a man I could love forever,'" she responded. "Grand-mère wrote those lines in a letter to Great-grand-père Julian when they were courting. She once showed the letter to me. She has a stack of them tied with a ribbon. He fought in France during the Great War. He sent her love letters in French. She says it's the best language for love."

Guy turned on his stomach beside her. "You want romance *and* poetry? Let's see, 'The clever man, the clever man/How wisely did he reason! But now alack, his wits are gone, His wisdom's out of season. The glances of a maiden's eye/Have turned his head to jelly; A monkey tumbled from a tree could not look half so silly.'" He gazed wryly at her. "Thomas Mann."

"'She that with poetry is won/Is but a desk to write upon,'" Michaela answered tartly. "Samuel Butler."

Guy laughed, the masculine sound at once indulgent and derisive.

Michaela's smile wavered. "What's so funny?"

"I've never known a woman who demanded poetry as part of the afterglow."

"You should broaden your horizons," she said shortly, "or raise your standards."

"I just have, haven't I?" He leaned over to kiss her, his lips tender and lingering and caressing. "You quote poetry and listen to night sounds like they were the finest orchestra on earth. Then there's the way you make love, counselor. It ought to be illegal. You aren't quite real."

"It's Belle Isle's influence," Michaela said dreamily. "There, anything and everything seems possible. It has that effect on people."

"Does it? Or is it you?" He stretched catlike under her regard. "I think you missed your century. You were born to be courted, to be wooed."

"You don't hear me disagreeing."

"You should have flowers and parties, go dancing and on moonlit walks, receive champagne and presents. You even need a stern old woman who keeps you from slipping away with your lover."

Michaela lifted a brow. "Let's not get too carried away. I rather thought you liked slipping away with me like this."

"I do." He looked at her, hoping his gaze didn't give everything away. Everything about her had taken on a new preciousness. He liked the way her ear whorled like a nautilus shell. Her full round breasts were the most erotic he'd ever touched and tasted, the dusty nipples more tempting than chocolate. Her physical beauty gilded his heart. She meant everything to him. Suddenly he was thinking in terms of years ahead, of the inconceivable, of a future.

He reached out to push the hair back from her face. "Michaela, once this business with Pike is over, I want you to come and live with me in New Orleans."

Michaela ruthlessly squashed the leap of her heart. *Take it slow!* Grand-mère had warned her. The tiger liked the hunt. She turned her face away from his and began circling his navel with her fingertip. "I may not have a duenna to guard my virtue, but you can't imagine what would happen if I even tried that. My family would march *en masse* to New Orleans and bring me back."

Guy cupped the back of her head in his broad hand. "You'd let them do that to you?"

She refused to look at him, afraid he would see how she really felt, that she would arm wrestle and defeat fifty Bellegarde relatives to be with him. "It would be difficult. Once you meet them, you'll understand why."

Guy frowned at this unexpected kink in his plans. "I don't deal well in groups. By the sound of it, you've got more relatives than most people have acquaintances."

She turned a questioning look on her tiger. "You're not afraid of them?"

He closed his eyes in exasperation. "I want it to be you and me. That's enough. Plenty. Even that scares me a little."

"What about children? I don't mean ours specifically," she added when she saw his eyes open in alarm. "I just mean as a concept. Don't you want children?"

"Sure. But I don't know if I should."

"Why not?"

He chuckled. "I'm not exactly family-oriented."

"What about your own?"

The shutter dropped before his expression. "What about it?"

Michaela went back to her task of massaging his navel. This was going to be harder than she thought. "I know nothing about you. For instance, where were you born and when?"

"In New Orleans, December twenty-fourth, 1963."

"Really? A Christmas baby!" She smiled and spread her hand across his abdomen, chasing ripples of response. "You were born practically in my backyard."

He nodded. "That's why I came back to New Orleans when I decided to settle down. I didn't live there long as a child but it was the only place that had ever even remotely felt like home."

"Where else did you live?"

He bent forward to place a kiss on her shoulder. He knew he was going to have to tell her sometime. But knowing didn't stop the sickness he felt in the pit of his stomach. "My mother had big dreams. She wanted to be a singer so she packed me up when I was about six and headed for California. We got as far as Nevada."

"You mean you grew up near Las Vegas?"

"I grew up *in* Las Vegas."

"I see. Your mother did cabaret work in the casinos?"

"Not exactly."

"What about your father?"

He looked at her. "I never knew him. I don't think he ever knew me, either. I was told I was a mistake my mother didn't intend to repeat."

Michaela heard behind those tight words all that he did not say. He was illegitimate.

His expression was poker proof. "I've shocked you."

"Don't be ridiculous." She met his daunting gaze with honesty. "Children aren't responsible for how they come into the world."

"It gets worse," he said with a warning edge to his voice.

"Tell me."

"My mother wasn't much of a singer. She wasn't much of a dealer or waitress, either. But she was young and pretty and there's always a use for young pretty foolish women in the world."

This time Michaela had to think longer before she saw in his eyes the angry truth. "That must have been awful for you."

He shrugged. His voice was flat, unemotional, detached. Now she knew where that ability to isolate himself from the world had come from. It had been a habit from an early age. "She worked at one of those places outside of town, in the desert. I don't know which one. We never really talked about it."

"What did you do?"

"I got out as soon as I could. I had a talent for school, for math in particular."

"You really were accepted at MIT."

"I was. Fat lot of good it did me. I couldn't begin to afford the only good thing that had ever happened to me." Time had not completely dimmed the bitter memory. "That's when I began to think about money as something I wanted a lot of. I settled for a local college. I sweated my butt off, hustled lots of jobs, saw it through. But I promised myself the day they put the diploma in my hand that I would never work that hard again. I felt I'd earned a life of ease. I wanted money, lots of it, and quickly. So I went back to Vegas to make that fortune."

Michaela tried to hold his pain inside herself. "Why do I feel like you're about to tell me something even worse?"

He touched her chin. "It's not so bad. While I was away in college Mom found a man who wanted her. She took off for Alaska with him."

"Is that where she is?"

"I don't know. She didn't bother to tell me she was going. I heard it on the grapevine when I got back to town one Christmas."

Michaela's throat swelled up so she could hardly breathe. She didn't know how to respond to such a loss, the emptiness of abandonment, a void like that in a child's life. She didn't really begin to comprehend it. So she thought about how fiercely he made love, as if he were trying to get inside her skin, to bury himself forever in her. She understood that need to be part of something more than herself. She'd always had that sense of shared experience with her family. Guy was looking for it, even if he didn't realize it. No wonder he wanted her exclusively for himself. He'd never had unalloyed love. That frightened her a little because she didn't want to fail him.

Guy saw the trepidation in her expression and felt as if she had punched him in the gut. He looked away from her. "So now you're ready to write me off. Right?"

"Not hardly," she managed over the lump in her throat. Everywhere they touched, his arm pressing to her side, his leg lying along hers, he had grown rigid with tension. She knew better than to touch him though she knew he needed touching and comforting, and loving as never before.

He made a sound like a bitter strangled laugh. "I'm no charity case.'"

"You don't seem so, no," she said simply.

"I don't need or want pity. Never did."

"I can understand that."

"Then why are you crying, Michaela?"

"Am I?" She reached up and smoothed a tear from her cheek. "I must have something in my eye."

He moved one of his hands from behind his head and embraced her shoulders. "Come here."

She snuggled down close to him, throwing her arm and leg across him to hold on.

For a time they said nothing. Then she heard his voice as she had never heard it, hushed, weary and a little lost. "Do you suppose the world is a matter of random chance, who your parents are, and everything that comes after that? Is what goes into making people good or bad just happenstance?"

"I don't know," she answered honestly. "I suppose some things must be. But we have choices, you know. If we live long enough we all eventually get to make choices. I think that's when the meter starts running on our humanity, when we begin making our own choices. We get to choose right or wrong. Everybody makes mistakes. As long as we're trying to do good, I think that counts for a lot."

He lifted her face so that he could look into her eyes. "And if I choose you? Do you think that can be a right choice for me but still a wrong choice for you?"

Michaela saw the trepidation in his gaze and the love he was afraid to admit. "You can't choose for me. I have to choose for myself."

His mouth curved in a reluctant smile that warmed her nonetheless. ''And?''

The predatory gleam reminded her. The tiger was a hunter. ''Come back with me to Belle Isle. I want you to meet my family. They're going to like you. Then, if you want, we'll talk again about choices.''

He gleam faded. ''I don't think so. If you come with that many strings attached I'm bound to foul up. I can't ask you to choose between your family and me. If I had what you had, nothing would make me give it up.''

Michaela refrained from saying he could have exactly what she had, if he would only allow it. Love doesn't exclude, it expands to include. But she didn't think he would understand that just yet. ''Then stop asking tough questions and kiss me again.''

He resisted her seeking mouth. ''You need to get some sleep. You have a plane to catch tomorrow.''

''I'll sleep on the plane.'' She caught his face between her hands and planted a sweet openmouthed invitation on his firm lips.

She saw the gleam come back and then she tasted the longing of a lifetime in his kiss. He didn't yet know it but she knew he had just made the decision to love.

Chapter 13

Tante Delphine's feast day dawned with a bloodred sky, the sign of good weather and good luck.

Though the party was not scheduled to begin until 2:00 p.m., laborers began streaming across the river at daybreak. Barbecuers brought with them racks of ribs and sausages and briskets, huge jars of sauce, stacks of lumber, and the oil drum grills in which they would slow-roast meat throughout the day. The Knights of Columbus brought their portable stage which they began erecting on the lawn in full view of the house where party-goers could dance. Other men brought chairs and picnic tables. Electricians brought cables and strings of colored lights. A truckload of watermelons and several kegs of beer came over soon after. The musicians, who'd driven up from New Orleans after an all-night gig in the French Quarter, arrived in time for breakfast. Charmed by Tante Delphine, they remained in the kitchen to shuck oysters and peel shrimp, grease yams for roasting and shell pecans for the last of the pies to go into the oven.

Michaela gave up after an hour trying to convince her great-grandmother that, as the honoree, she shouldn't be preparing food but resting so she could enjoy her guests when they arrived.

"No one ever set foot on Belle Isle in invitation didn't receive my hospitality. It ain't gon' begin today!" Tante Delphine had declared in a voice that brooked no argument.

Chastened, Michaela turned to people who most certainly did want and need her help and advice. There were an inordinate number of plugs and extension cords required just to meet the lights and the music and the catering requirements. By noon, there was a hot debate going between the electric bass player and an ice-cream truck driver over who had the greater need of the last available plug.

"Ice cream first, music later!" Michaela shouted, plowing in and breaking up what promised, according to most of the men, to be a rather interesting fight. The musician had youth and ranginess on his side but the ice-cream vendor was a Cajun with a wrestler's girth and twinkle in his eye.

Just before noon she went down to the dock in the Buick to pick up the first of the family members who had offered to come early and set up the food tables.

As they streamed off the ferry, she greeted each of her cousins in turn with hugs and kisses.

"Sheila! Cathy! And Fred, is that really you behind that beard? Michael! Where're the kids? Look at you, Andrea! Is that number three in the basket?"

"I declare, that Yancy gets meaner with every season," Cathy said when the man drew their attention with a roar of foul language over a snarled rope.

"'Bout snapped my head off," Andrea concurred.

Michaela accepted this news with a shrug. "You know Yancy."

"Gators wouldn't even take him," Fred said chuckling. "Still, he's making a pretty piece of change."

This got Michaela's attention. "How so?"

"He's charging folks to park on his property. Says his ferry can't take all the cars across so we have to park. Dollar a head."

"That's outrageous!" Michaela looked back toward the ferry. "You all go ahead and pile into the Buick the best you can. I'll be along in a moment."

"I'm going along," Fred volunteered. "You and Yancy going toe-to-toe? Wouldn't miss it for anything."

Michaela returned to the dock with her cousin in tow. "Morning, Yancy,"

"Hrump!" Yancy didn't bother to look up as he shouldered her aside in order to release one of the ferry ropes to the pier.

She accepted the snub as the price for their discussion the day before. She had promised him all the food and drink he could hold if he would carry passengers in a sober condition.

He hadn't shaved in nearly a week and his shirt looked suspiciously like it had been slept in for an equal amount of time. Still, his eyes were sharp with resentment instead of glassy with liquor. He had kept his promise not to drink the night before. Or, at least, he hadn't gotten stinko drunk. Though he was in a foul mood, bitter and snapping at the many passengers he had ferried across to Belle Isle, at least he was sober.

"I hear you're not allowing people to bring their cars across."

Yancy looked up at her from the deck of the ferry, a battered straw hat sitting too far back on his head to shade his eyes. "This ferry can't carry but so much weight. All them cars would weaken it. Besides, where you going to put them all?"

"I hadn't thought of that," Michaela conceded. "But charging people to park on the other side wasn't part of our agreement."

"We didn't make no deal about parking. My property. What I do there ain't your business."

Begrudgingly, she had to acknowledge that he was right. "You are coming over for the party about sunset?" she asked as he was about to cast off again.

"Think you got enough beer to last that long?"

"I'm sure we do," she answered shortly. Yancy seemed to have a one-track mind where liquor was concerned.

He grunted again and hauled in the last line. The barge caught the current and began to drift out into the stream. Suddenly he looked up. "Say! Where's your man?"

"Away!" Michaela flushed as her cousin Fred turned curious eyes on her.

She had almost forgotten Yancy knew about Guy. She wondered exactly what stories he'd told about her at the local bars. No doubt they were quite colorful and crude. Not that it mattered. She would be a lot happier if Guy was here for people to gossip about. She had left him in Vegas because she'd had little choice. He hadn't told her exactly what he was going to do. He hadn't promised to contact her before he had settled things. He hadn't even promised to come to Belle Isle again. He might not turn up for a few days, a week, or a month. All she had was the desperate belief that he needed her as much as she needed him.

"Remember!" she called after Yancy, "You'll need to stay sober enough to take the party-goers back to the mainland tonight!"

He laughed loud and rudely. "I said I'd get them across! Didn't say nothin' about gettin' them back!"

She knew he'd said that just to be spiteful but it bothered her all the same, as he knew it would.

"Why do you let him treat you like that?" Fred asked as they climbed the levee side by side.

"Yancy is one of Grand-mère's charity cases. He even wangled an invitation to her party."

"How's that?"

"He bartered it. Come on, there's lots to be done before two o'clock. You did bring a costume for the evening?"

Fred laughed. "I did. Going to be a riverboat gambler. Just like our great-great-great grandfather. Tante Delphine once told me she remembers him though she had to be a tiny girl. Said he was a fine fancy man with lace cuffs and a wide-brimmed hat, gold buttons, and a ready smile for the ladies." Fred brushed up his glossy black whiskers with the back for his fingers and waggled his eyebrows suggestively. "Andrea better be nice to me. Our gambling ancestor had five wives and each of them loved him better than the last."

"Well, gamblers aren't nearly so glamorous these days," Michaela answered drily. Immediately an image of Guy popped up in her thoughts to call her a liar.

"What's this about a new man of yours?"

Michaela jumped, startled that Fred had seemingly read her mind.

Fred grinned at her. "Come on, I haven't heard a word about you even dating since you and Larroquette broke up last winter."

"That's because there's be nothing to tell." Michaela linked her arms through his. "We better get up to the house. I saw Andrea was carrying one of her icebox cakes. Mustn't let it spoil. We got scads of people to feed today."

"Speaking of which, how are you paying for all this?"

"Yancy isn't the only one who's bartered an invitation from in return for services," Michaela said and went on to explain.

She had been astonished when she returned to Baton Rouge yesterday and learned what had taken place during her two-day absence. Grand-mère's party had taken on a life of its own. It seemed the local grapevine had been working overtime. The once-small party list had burgeoned as the Bellegarde relatives were inundated with calls from well-wishers and would-be celebrants. Suddenly, her great-grandmother's birthday had become an Event.

Tante Delphine was a legend along this section of the Mississippi yet many people had never met her. Fewer still had ever set foot on Belle Isle. From butcher to baker to barbecuers to liquor-store owners, everyone was offering deep discounts or freebies in exchange for an invitation to the party. The local TV stations had even called her uncle Leon, along with the newspapers, hoping to cover the hundredth birthday celebration.

"I wanted to refuse," Michaela said in conclusion. "After all, it is a private party. But Uncle Leon reminded me that Grand-mère likes nothing so much as attention, and this was possibly going to be her last opportunity to garner the accolades she so well deserved."

"Dad has a point," Fred answered. "So, let's get this sideshow on the road."

Michaela had lost count of how many guests they were expecting after the number topped 150. Everyone was bringing food so that feeding them all had become a nonissue. Where to put it all had replaced would there be enough, on her list of worries.

As the early afternoon wore on, Michaela realized that she probably wouldn't even know all the people who came today. To her amazement, the idea that family members should dress in costumes from any era during the last hundred years—as an homage to Tante Delphine's ten decades—had gotten passed around among many of the others guests. She passed strangers dressed as flappers, as bobbysoxers, a doughboy, lots of soldiers and sailors, hippies, yuppies, and even an elegant Edwardian couple. She was pleased that, so far, no one had chosen her part, as a thirties vamp. She had yet to change from her jeans and boots but it was impossible to work in silk and heels and she seemed to be needed in half a dozen different places at once.

Throughout the afternoon, recorded music blared from half a dozen speakers, a mixture of blues, New Orleans-style jazz, Island music and Count Basie. A few of the younger family members stuck more recent tunes in by Luther Vandross and Chaka Khan. One thing all the pieces had in common was a bone deep, foot-tapping appreciation for rhythm. While the young adults indulged in a game of vol-

leyball, children played horseshoes and lawn croquet,
chased one another around the grass and climbed trees when
their parents weren't looking. Others milled about the island, sightseeing and marveling that such a place existed
under their noses without them ever realizing it. Still others
sat in the shade of moss-draped oaks, eating and sipping
drinks and chatting with acquaintances.

Amid the music and food and laughter and conversation, Tante Delphine drifted among her guests like an elegant butterfly, looking more petite and regal than usual in
a shimmering saffron yellow silk caftan and her signature
crown of sterling silver braids.

Each time Michaela glimpsed her, a deep satisfaction
flooded her anew. The party was a success, more so than she
had dared hope for. Grand-mère was more than happy, she
was radiant.

After a while, though, it became obvious to all that the
excitement and exertions were taking their toll on Tante
Delphine. One of the peacock chairs was brought out from
the porch and placed in the shade of an ancient live oak.
From that venue, the Bellegarde Decagenarian held court
for her admirers.

Michaela made certain her duties carried her regularly
past her great-grandmother's circle. Yet she was halfway
across the lawn slicing watermelons when a cry suddenly
went up from the crowd around the live oak.

"Help! We need a doctor!"

The knife that Michaela had been using slipped from her
hand into the grass. She was halfway across the lawn before she realize that she was running. She knew long before
she reached the shady spot that the cause of the distur-
bance was Grand-mère. The crowd parted to let her
through.

"Seth's fetching Dr. Pritchet," someone said beside her
but Michaela didn't even glance at the speaker.

Tante Delphine had slipped sideways in the chair. Dwarfed by its size, she looked like a child who had fallen asleep sitting up. But she was unearthly still.

Her heart knocking jerkily against her ribs, Michaela knelt down beside her and grasped her hand. "Grand-mère?" she said in a stifled voice. "Can you hear me, Grand-mère?"

The elderly lady's eyes popped open. "What you don' squatting in the grass, 'Tite?"

Michaela's breath caught for an instant in her throat. "Are you all right, Grand-mère?"

"Course, I'm fine," she grumbled, but her eyes looked cloudy, her expression uncertain. "Just stealing forty winks."

"Where's Dr. Pritchet?" Michaela called out anxiously over her shoulder.

"Don' fret over me, 'Tite." Tante Delphine admonished, her face as pouty as a disgruntled child. "I am fine."

With Michaela's help she pushed herself upright in her chair and then looked around the ring of concerned faces. "Won't somebody bring an old woman a glass of lemonade?"

"Sure thing, Tante Delphine!" Half a dozen people took off at a trot.

A moment later Dr. Pritchet arrived wearing Bermuda shorts and an LSU T-shirt with a smudge of barbecue sauce down the front. "What's this I hear about the birthday girl dozing off on her guests? Seems like a perfect afternoon for a nap."

"That what I say!" Tante Delphine turned an injured look on Michaela. "I don' need no doctor."

"Well, since I'm here, you will indulge me, won't you?" Dr. Pritchet asked as he reached for the elderly woman's wrist to take her pulse but she snatched her hand back.

Dr. Pritchet scowled but his eyes were smiling. "I have a lot of patients here today, Tante Delphine. How will it look if you send me away without even a pulse? I appeal to you as one professional to another, let me look good.''

Tante Delphine sniffed but then heaved a great sigh. ''I tell you, ain't nothing the matter with me.''

''Then let me confirm that,'' Dr. Pritchet replied and reached for the medical bag his son had just hurried over with.

Michaela stood anxiously by as the physician listened to her great-grandmother's heart then took her pulse. Suddenly the party seemed the worst miscalculation she'd ever made. She knew her great-grandmother was frail. Anyone a hundred years old was bound to be frail. Feeling worse with every second, she castigated herself with guilt, thinking of all that she had put Grand-mère through this past week. Hiding a man who had been shot, who might have died, who was being hunted. The stress had nearly brought her to her knees. How much more it must have affected Grand-mère. She had let things get entirely out of hand, had not stopped to think of the effect her actions might be having on the one person she loved as much as it was possible to love.

After a moment, Dr. Pritchet straightened up and patted the elderly lady on the shoulder. ''Now then, Tante Delphine. Why did you disturb my fine meal? There's nothing wrong with you, and you know it.''

Tante Delphine smiled up at him with childish delight. ''Don' I tell Michaela this? Maybe I just feel the need of the attentions of a handsome man, *oui?*''

Dr. Pritchet chuckled and then smiled reassuringly at Michaela. ''Her pulse is a bit rapid but her heart sounds fine. She fell asleep. It's the excitement. That's all.''

''Don' I tell you, 'Tite?'' Tante Delphine said smugly. ''I am fine. *Tiens!* Never better. *Jamais de ma vie!*''

Never in her life. Michaela's gaze moved worriedly between the doctor's confident smile and her great-grandmother's smiling black eyes. ''Maybe you should go in and lie down on your own bed for a while, Grand-mère.''

"Maybe you should stop worrying," Tante Delphine snapped. "Ah, my lemonade." She took a small sip and closed her eyes for a moment. When she opened them, a frown appeared on her face. "You still here, 'Tite? Don' I got lots of guests for to keep me company? Go, dance, flirt with the young men. Leave an old woman to her simple pleasures."

Chagrined, Michaela backed away. "I'll be back," she promised. But she doubted her great-grandmother heard her. She was, truly, surrounded by admirers.

In fact, it was Michaela who felt a little left out of the party raging around her. Everyone was having a wonderful time. Everyone was smiling and laughing, talking and enjoying the pleasures of this perfect day. It wasn't too warm for comfort but balmy enough to be spent out-of-doors. But perhaps it was too much, too many people, too many things, too much noise, things seemed on the verge of becoming out of control.

A man in a trench coat bumped her shoulder, bumped her hard.

"Oh, excuse me," she said automatically even though she knew he was the one at fault.

He muttered under his breath but kept moving. She stared after him, amazed by his rudeness. From the back she did not recognize him. He appeared to be middle-aged. His light brown hair had thinned out at the crown. The trench coat surprised her. It was near eighty degrees without a cloud in the sky. Belatedly, she remembered that many of the guests were in costume. Maybe he thought he was Rick from *Casablanca*. Then she noticed he wore sneakers. The incongruence nagged at her.

"Who was that?"

Michaela looked around to see Andrea who had come up beside her. "I don't know him."

"He spoke to me a little earlier, wanted to know who you were. I remember the trench coat because he was sweating.

Not local," Andrea added. "Had a nasally sound like a Midwesterner."

"Maybe he's with the liquor store or one of the other groups who more or less invited themselves."

Andrea shrugged then gasped and touched her distended stomach. "Whoa, Junior. Your opinion doesn't count just yet."

Michaela smiled at her pregnant cousin. "When are you due?"

"In late December. Fred hopes it's before Christmas. I hope it's after. The girls are counting on a big Christmas and a new baby would make that a little more difficult."

"But all the merrier," Michaela suggested.

Andrea nodded. "What I am saying? I'm a sucker for babies. So, when are you going to find a man and start your own family?"

Michaela blushed. "Oh, I don't know. Maybe sooner than you think."

Andrea's eyes lit up. "You've found a man?" She looked around eagerly. "Who? Where? Point him out!"

Michaela laughed. "He not here today."

"Are you serious? Where is he?"

"Working," Michaela said in a more subdued voice. "He's from New Orleans, owns a computer firm down there."

"Sounds solid, dependable."

Michaela nodded. Talking about Guy, even if he wasn't here, made her feel better, more like the rest of the people gathered on the island. She was connected, he just wasn't here today for everyone to see. "Next time he's in the area, I'll try to drop by with him."

Andrea grinned. "You do that. He might as well get accustomed to the Bellegarde brood early. As an in-law myself, I can sort of show him the ropes, help ease him into things. At least he'll have a head start when he meets Tante Delphine."

"He's already met her," Michaela answered then wondered if that had been wise.

"Really?" Andrea's eyes widened. "Since you're not frowning he must have gotten her blessing. That's a first. She never liked Larroquette. So, when's the wedding?"

Michaela shook her head. "It's not that serious yet."

"Liar!" Andrea gazed at Michaela with a wisenheimer expression. "You should see your face. The man has you heart and soul. He must be quite something."

Michaela decided there was no point in arguing. "Just don't tell anybody else yet. Okay?"

Andrea nodded. "Like I said, this family takes a bit of getting use to. We'll break him in gently, I promise."

The afternoon continued smoothly. Though her great-grandmother shooed her away every time she came near, Michaela kept a constant eye on Grand-mère.

After a hefty number of pounds of ribs and brisket and sausage had been consumed; after gallons of potato salad and red beans and rice had disappeared; after hundreds of scoops of slaw, gelatin salads, and deviled eggs had been served; after quarts of pickles and peppers, sacks of sliced onions and tomatoes, and dozens of loaves of bread had been distributed; after plates of bourbon, icebox, and homemade pound cake and pans of sweet potato and pecan pies were emptied; after uncounted pralines and slices of watermelon had been consumed, the company settled down for the main event of the evening, toasting the birthday lady with whatever libation came to hand.

Michaela lingered in the background while Uncle Leon made the formal declaration to Tante Delphine.

"Michaela! There you are!"

Michaela turned without surprise toward the speaker who had strolled up. "Daniel. This is a surprise."

"We just arrived," answered the woman at his side. "The traffic coming up from *Nawlins* was so-oo awful," she continued. "We just about thought we wouldn't make it at all, which would have been a shame. Because Daniel has something very important to present to Tante Delphine.''

Michaela recognized the statuesque woman with a mane of streaked blond hair from Daniel's most recent campaign photos but she resented the pair's assumption that she would. ''I'm Michaela Bellegarde, your hostess. You must be?'' Michaela questioned.

''Oh, sorry,'' Daniel jumped in. ''This is Morgan Fouquet, of the sugarcane Fouquets. Morgan, Michaela.''

Michaela nodded and offered the woman her hand. ''Welcome to Belle Isle, Morgan.''

Morgan smiled a contest winner's toothy smile. ''Thanks. It's just so, well, amazing, isn't it? That in this day and age, anyone actually owns a *whole* island.''

''I suppose it is unusual,'' Michaela answered reservedly, too polite to ask how Morgan had come to be at her great-grandmother's party. She turned her focus on Daniel. ''I didn't expect you, Daniel, especially after our last conversation.''

Ever the politician, he didn't miss a beat in embarrassment or hesitation. ''I've been sent as an emissary.''

''Whose emissary?'' she challenged.

He smiled self-confidently. ''You'll find out when Tante Delphine does.'' He looked past her toward the food tables. ''I hope there's some food left. We didn't have time for lunch before we left town.''

''I'm certain we can scrape together something,'' Michaela replied without much enthusiasm.

''Not now, of course, after we've paid our respects,'' Daniel said. ''Come on, Morgan, honey, let's get in line to greet the birthday lady.''

Michaela watched the pair stroll away arm in arm. Morgan was tall and slim with enough curves to give the clinging jersey knit dress she wore a real workout as she tiptoed across the yard. She would definitely be an asset on the campaign trail. Begrudgingly curious about Daniel's surprise for Grand-mère, she followed at a slower pace.

Daniel's surprise turned out to be a framed certificate from the governor declaring Delphine Bijou Bellegarde to be a state treasure. Daniel read it at the mike podium that had been set up for impromptu tributes with all the pomp and circumstance of a candidate who needed every photo op possible.

Michaela wanted to commend him for the gesture, which obviously touched her great-grandmother, but she couldn't ignore the TV and newspaper crews scrambling around the two of them to record the moment.

"Daniel couldn't have known about the coverage," she murmured to herself and then, contrarily, wondered if he had been the one to tip the media off in the first place.

Daniel's tribute broke the ice. After the fanfare subsided, other guests came up to the mike to offer their congratulations. And then, as was usual when river people get together, they began swapping stories. It all began with Mr. Thorpe, who ran the local pharmacy.

Mr. Thorpe, a tall, thin, balding man from the state survey office in Baton Rouge, stepped up to the mike and grinned in satisfaction. "Was a time in these parts when nearly everybody went to seek Tante Delphine's advice. I once sought her out myself. I was a young man then."

He touched his thinning scalp and grinned. "My wife was having a terrible time with her first pregnancy. The doctors expected her to lose the baby. Now, I wasn't the kind of man to take to superstition. But I was desperate. I went to see Tante Delphine for her advice because my own grandmother swore by her. Tell you what she said. She told me there was no need to worry about Annie or the baby. The boy would be fine. That was my Jack she was talking about." He beckoned to his son. "Step up here, Jack, and let folks see you."

A man in his midthirties stepped out and waved to the crowd. He was a remarkable younger version of his father.

"Don't care what doubters say about fakers and charlatans," Mr. Thorpe went on. "Tante Delphine has the genuine gift of sight. She knew Jack was a boy before the doctor.''

He lifted his plastic cup of beer in a curiously touching gesture. ''To Tante Delphine, good health, good times, and a hundred years more!''

The crowd cheered and clapped their approval. No sooner had it died down than another person stepped forward to relate a personal tale, one handed down in his family from nearly a century ago. What began as a series of toasts, quickly became a round of story-telling as guest after guest related their own family's story of Tante Delphine.

As the afternoon slipped steadily toward dusk, Michaela was amazed to learn how many people, still living, her great-grandmother had delivered into the world. Many others claimed they had been cured by her of dreaded diseases that conventional physicians had thrown their hands up in despair over. Still others were certain she had lifted curses from them, altered runs of bad luck, brought business to them, or helped them find their mates.

Michaela was certain the tales had grown as they were passed down through the families. No one person could have done so much for so many. Yet, as she watched her great-grandmother smile and nod, clap her hands and laugh like a young girl in response to the tributes, she began to believe that just maybe the legends weren't so distorted after all.

In preparation for the party she had done a little research. Grand-mère had been born the year Edison gave the first public demonstration of a moving picture camera. She had been alive before radio, telephone, airplanes, television and microwaves. She had lived through epidemics in a time before penicillin. She had been a child during the Spanish-American War; married before the first world war, reared seven children through Prohibition, the Roaring Twenties, and the Great Depression; cared for grandchildren during the second world war, McCarthyism and Vietnam; understood complexities of human nature in ways the Sexual

Revolution, the Me Generation, and Feminism could not resolve. She had even lived to see the rise and fall of communism, a philosophy of which she had calmly said seventy years ago, "This, it ain't gon' last." So many changes, so many upheavals, so many good and bad times, and through it all Tante Delphine had survived.

Finally, about dark, the colored lights and chinese lanterns that had been strung above the dance floor were turned on. As the live band tuned up to replace recorded music, Michaela slipped away to dress for the evening.

The house was dark, except for the light in the rear hall that marked the location of the bathroom. Now at the end of the day, when couples were preparing to pair off for an evening of dancing, Michaela allowed herself to think again about Guy.

He had said he wouldn't be back until things were settled with Pike. He wouldn't elaborate on what he meant by 'settled' but her imagination had supplied enough scenarios to keep her awake half the last two nights.

She was glad she had told Andrea about him. It made him seem more real, more solid, more substantial in her life. Andrea was right to wonder how he would adjust to the Bellegarde brood. Guy was a loner. He didn't like crowds. He would find their boisterous enthusiasm for life a bit overwhelming. Yet she had no doubt that he would more than hold his own, if he chose to be part of it.

After a quick shower to remove the perspiration and grime of her day-long activities, she wrapped herself in a towel and hurried upstairs where she had placed her things so that she could have complete privacy in which to change.

After closing the door she dropped her towel onto a nearby chair and scooped up her panties and stepped into them. The gown she had chosen to wear was a thirties Jean Harlow style. Cut on the bias to drape seductively over a body, it was little more than an ankle-length slip of gold silk with a deep scoop in the back. Having tried it on earlier in the week, she knew a pair of silk panties was the only garment she could get away with wearing under it.

She reached for the slinky dress edged in black lace at the neckline and slipped it over her head. It was like diving into a pool. She sighed as the cool silk slipped over her skin. Her nipples puckered in response and her arms firmed with goose bumps. She tugged it down over the thrust of her breasts and smoothed it over her hips, feeling sensuous and sexy and every inch female.

"Very nice."

Michaela's head snapped around at the sound of a masculine voice. She had deliberately not lit a kerosene lamp in order not to draw curious eyes to her open window while she dressed. Now she realized that she couldn't see into the deep gloom where the mosquito-netted bed stood while she was back-lit by the dying sunset. But she was not afraid of her Peeping Tom.

"I hope you got an eyeful," she said defiantly as she approached the bed.

Chapter 14

Guy had counted on the fact that sooner or later Michaela would come up to this room. He had found her things laid out on the chair. All he had to do was wait.

He had promised himself he wouldn't come to Belle Isle again, at least not until he was free to do so. But he hadn't counted on the fact that everything he encountered after she left Las Vegas reminded him of her. Whether it was the bright beauty of dawn, the way another woman turned her head on the street, the brim of a hat he spied in an antique store window, or the memory of the scent of gardenias, he couldn't take two breaths without some inconsequential thing recalling her to mind. He had come here just to tell her that—no more, no less.

From everything he'd been able to learn, Pike had disappeared. None of his former connections, or Pike's, had seen or heard from the man in four years. If he was out there waiting, he was lying very low. Like a gator in the swamp, he must have waited for Guy to make a splash that would catch his eye. Guy was lying low himself, so low his belly was getting calluses from scraping the ground, but he had to see Michaela.

Getting onto the island had been a snap. He had not known how large the party would be until he saw the cars lined up on the mainland side. This was some birthday! He had joined the guests waiting their turn to cross, smiled and nodded, pretended that he was a business associate of Michaela's. Despite her fears to the contrary, no one had looked at him in startled recognition, or even with the usual female interest he was accustomed to drawing. Or maybe, he just wasn't paying attention anymore. He didn't need to. He didn't want to.

When Michaela stepped into the room covered only by a towel that left her legs bare from the top of her thighs down, he wanted to make himself known at once. When she discarded the towel, he felt the urge to jump out and snatch her lovely naked body, flush from her bath, and haul her into the bed with him. He fought the impulse. Instead, he waited while acknowledging deep inside himself that when he looked at Michaela Bellegarde, he knew had found something worth gambling the rest of his life on.

Now she was standing before him, like a dream come true, and all he could think about was that he didn't deserve her. He felt like an interloper, a cheat and a fake. The realization had an unexpected effect on him. He was suddenly shy.

"Well?" she demanded. "Are you planning to hide in there the rest of the evening?"

He reached out and twitched the netting aside. "Hi, Michaela."

He sat cross-legged on Great-great-aunt Indigo's hand-crocheted coverlet. *Guy was here! Sis boom ba! Rah rah rah!*

Michaela shoved aside the giggling cheerleader delight cartwheeling through her. Even in shadow he looked like a man who hadn't slept well in weeks. Though he was dressed in a navy pinstriped suit complete with tie, she reminded herself that he was still recovering from a serious injury. She hadn't been particularly thoughtful in sparing him additional physical strain during their last two encounters. Not that he had complained. But she cared, and worried about him more than he would want her to.

"You look like dog's dinner," she said carelessly.

"You look good enough to eat," he replied. He patted the coverlet beside himself. "Want to come over here so I can take a bite?"

She backed up a step. "When was the last time you had a decent meal?"

He smiled. "With you."

She frowned. "We didn't eat."

"But I got my fill. Now I'm ready for more. Come here."

She knew better than to approach him. The pull between them had her trembling already. But this was not the time or place. If they were going to have a future, their relationship would have to have a life of its own outside the bedroom.

She turned toward the door. "Come downstairs with me. I'll fix a plate for you and we can talk."

He watched her walk away and smiled at the way she shimmered in her silk covering. Light sluiced over every graceful undulation of her body. His hands itched to do the same. Anybody who saw her would know what he knew firsthand, she had on damned little underneath! "That dress should be illegal."

She tossed a provocative glance over her shoulder, her loose dark hair brushing the top of her hips as her head moved. "I didn't think you liked moldy relics from the attic."

"I like everything about you, or hadn't you noticed?"

"I noticed." She paused to lay a hand on the doorframe. She was turned in profile, her hair spilling forward to veil her bare shoulder. Her physical beauty gilded his heart. "Are you coming?"

"Oh, sweetheart!" Loud ribald laughter burst from him.

Michaela's cheeks flooded with color. "Men!" she muttered as she moved on.

Guy grabbed the fedora he'd taken down from the attic and caught up with her in a matter of seconds, falling into step beside her in the hallway. Perfectly content to simply share her space, he inhaled the fragrance of gardenias from her skin as if it were pure oxygen. Some day soon he was going to buy dozens of gardenias for her to wear in her hair. And then he was going to lay her down in some secluded spot and tuck more gardenias into his favorite places on her body, *à la Lady Chatterly's Lover*.

He had read D. H. Lawrence in college and been underwhelmed with his dated overheated paeans to the purifying aspects of sexual love. But with Michaela he couldn't think of her without wanting to touch her, to hold on, to make certain she was as real as his feelings. It wasn't just sexual but it was primitive. He needed to just *be* with her. Did she feel that way, too, or was he going crazy alone?

Without looking at him she reached down and took his hand, squeezing it hard. Just maybe, he had his answer.

They made a striking couple as they appeared under the archway of the front door. As if someone had called particular attention them, a hush came over the guests nearby as dozens of faces turned their way.

"Oh, I forgot. Larroquette is here!" Michaela whispered quickly under her breath.

"Good." Guy smiled and the recklessness in it surprised her. "About time he got the message you're taken. By me." He placed the fedora on his head and gave the brim a small downward jerk to secure it. He winked at her. "Let's raise a few eyebrows, Ms. Bellegarde."

They crossed the veranda with her hand securely tucked inside his. The attention of the company should have made her happy. Instead it made her very uneasy. Whatever their thoughts, and she received everything from wide smiles of approval to raised eyebrows to outright stares, her guests weren't indifferent to the picture she and Guy presented. She met the various reactions with a polite smile or a nod but her grip got tighter and tighter on Guy's hand. She really didn't want him out in the open, even on Belle Isle, not when she wasn't perfectly certain he was out of danger. She was beginning to think she'd made a mistake by not taking him up on his offer to join him in the upstairs bed. At least she would then have known that he was perfectly safe and hidden.

Fred and Andrea caught her eye with big fat grins of approval.

When Guy turned away, Andrea pointed to him and gestured in question. Michaela nodded. Andrea pantomimed touching something really hot and rolled her eyes. Michaela laughed, feeling a little more at ease. She was among family and friends. No one had come to Belle Isle today without knowing someone else connected to the family.

So why couldn't she shake the unease that had been encroaching little by little on her happiness all afternoon? Was it a reaction to Grand-mère's minor upset earlier in the day, or was it more? She felt as she had the night she'd gone to visit Guy in the hospital in New Orleans.

She clasped Guy's hand tighter and felt his squeeze of response. He was with her. She should be elated, reveling in the opportunity to show him off, eager to show her family off to him. She was. But, irrationally, it wasn't enough.

"The twenties, right?" asked a fifteen-year-old as she passed them standing in the food line. The girl looked them over while her head bobbed in time to the music blaring around them. "Hot dress! Hot guy!"

Michaela started in surprise then she realized that the girl had referred to *guy* with a small *g*.

"I take it you don't bring many men home," Guy said a few minutes later when he had polished off a few of the beef ribs piled on his plate. They sat at a picnic table under a tree.

Michaela looked up at him in surprise, not about to be drawn into a discussion of her former boyfriends, or lack thereof. "You've got barbecue sauce on your lip."

He grinned and leaned toward her. "Lick it off."

Michaela hesitated only a moment before rising from her side of the table to lean across and wipe his upper lip with the tip of her tongue.

When she moved back, she was smiling. Guy's smile was broader and then she realized why. He was looking down the front of her dress where the gold silk gaped away from her unrestrained breasts.

"All the way to China?" she suggested primly when she'd subsided onto her bench.

The aquamarine gaze that met hers was tenderness smoked with desire. "Clear to Paradise, sweetheart. And don't do that again."

She smiled in spite of embarrassment. "Why not?"

"Because I'm not as housebroken as you think."

Her smile wobbled. She believed him. He dared what most men just thought about. That reckless nature had brought him into the open tonight, to be with her. She wanted to go along for the ride, but she wasn't yet certain she was emotionally equipped to handle Matherson on a high-stakes winner-take-all spree.

Guy had never been possessive about women. In fact, he had been downright careless. But as they resumed their stroll among the guests, he couldn't stop noticing the way other men were staring at Michaela. It wasn't just the dress she wore—and that was enough to elicit any man's attention—it was the *way* she wore it. The dress seemed to release in her some hidden talent for flirtation. It wasn't that she was out to charm everything in pants. She just seemed more at ease, more certain of her appeal as a woman. She was blooming before his eyes and he didn't like the way other men were admiring the blossom—his blossom.

Guy glared them down. He didn't have to say a word. He let his expression do the talking for him. It shouted *Keep off! Private property! Scram!*

Perhaps he hadn't yet gotten around to explaining to Michaela that they were exclusive, that as far as he was concerned they belonged to one another, but he would before he left again.

Finally, they reached the place where Tante Delphine still sat chatting with Leon and Corrine Bellegarde. But before Michaela could draw their attention, Daniel Larroquette jumped in front of them.

"Matherson! What the hell are you doing here?"

Guy met his arrested expression with a bland look. "Larroquette. What are you doing here?"

"I'm a friend of the family." Daniel glanced at Michaela, an accusation in his eyes. "I thought you didn't know where Matherson was?"

Michaela's gaze narrowed in response to his tone. "I didn't until about an hour ago."

Daniel's jaw tightened as he looked back at Guy. "I suppose you're aware that the state police are looking for you? They've even brought the FBI in on it."

"It's nice to be wanted," Guy replied. "You can tell them you've seen me and I'm fine."

"I can—?"

"Aren't you going to say hi, Guy?"

Guy shifted his attention to the statuesque blonde who had laid a hand possessively on his arm. "Hello, Morgan. How's the campaign trail?"

She rolled her eyes and tossed her golden mane. "Simply atrocious! As usual. Haven't had a manicure or massage in a week. But what about you?" Her eyes ran down his shirt-front and her hand followed, pausing at his belt buckle rather than his left side. "Are you all right?"

"Fine." Guy lifted her hand four inches while Michaela struggled to keep from pushing it away altogether. "I was shot up here, Morgan, or were you just shopping around?"

Proclaiming herself to be a genuine blonde, Morgan blushed face, throat, and bosom. "Oh, you men! Always trying to embarrass us ladies with references to sex."

Michaela made a sound very much like a growl.

Guy glanced down at her, provoked to a smile. She was jealous. That was the best news he'd had all day.

Unwilling to be forgotten, Larroquette pushed forward. "I need to talk to you, Matherson. Now."

Guy met his furious gaze with a flat stare. "Not now. This is Tante Delphine's hundredth birthday party. I don't suggest you do anything that would interfere with that." He took Michaela's hand. "Are you ready?"

Michaela saw Morgan glance uncertainly at her fiancé's angry face before she and Guy moved away. "Isn't that just like a man," she heard Morgan say, "always putting his pleasure before business?"

Michaela didn't hear Daniel's reply but she didn't care. Guy was more than a match for Daniel. So that meant Daniel wouldn't do anything foolish like tip the remaining media people off as to Guy's identity. That didn't mean, however, that they might not figure it out for themselves. She wanted him to offer his congratulations to Grand-mère and then she'd take him back to the house and make certain he stayed there until the party was over and everyone else was gone.

Tante Delphine hadn't moved from the peacock chair. She sat in a little ring of light provided by oil lanterns brought out from the house. A little farther away citronella torches smoked to chase away gnats and mosquitos as darkness gathered in on the island.

Despite her trepidation over what her reaction might be, Michaela stepped up before her great-grandmother and said,

"Look who's come to wish you happy birthday, Grand-mère."

Tante Delphine looked up with a smile of welcome for Guy. "Ah, *mon beau garçon.* I knew you could not keep away."

Her gaze moved to Michaela and she searched the younger woman's face. "Still, you make my 'Tite happy," she said when she again looked at Guy. She reached for his left hand and touched the silver bracelet hidden under his cuff. "You promise it will always be so?"

Guy smiled ruefully. "It will be my first priority from now on."

A frisson of surprise raced through Michaela. Did Guy understand what he had said, how her great-grandmother, and therefore all her family, would interpret his promise? Oh lord, she dearly hoped so!

The older woman nodded slowly but she didn't smile. "You got yet to deal with the snake in your jungle. Only I tell you this much, *mon tigre.* He gon' find no welcome here. Long as you stay on Belle Isle, you safe."

"Thank you for the blessing, Tante Delphine." As Guy bent to place a kiss on the back of her purple-veined hand, he reached into his jacket pocket and produced a small box tied with a saffron yellow ribbon. As he straightened he pressed the box into her hand. "For you, Tante Delphine. Happy Birthday."

Her eyes lit up like two black opals in the sunlight. "I do love presents!" Her audience laughed, sharing her pleasure as she untied the ribbon and lifted the lid.

"Mon Dieu!" Shaking her head in disbelief she lifted out a jeweled pin and held it up to Michaela. "Look, a tiger!"

Michaela bent closer for a better look. It was indeed a tiger, a black-enameled gold tiger studded with diamonds that shot sparks of reflected light into the crowd who oohed and aahed their response. There were two emeralds for eyes, a sapphire in the center of its forehead, and a collar of rubies. It wasn't a dainty piece but bold and exotic, and quite obviously expensive.

Tante Delphine rolled her black eyes at Guy. "This is how you see me, so gaudy and bold?"

Far from taking offense, Guy laughed. "This is how I see you. Your size doesn't fool me. In your heart you are strong and proud and fearless as any tigress."

Her silver brows rose as she smacked her lips. "This is how you see me?" she repeated.

He nodded.

She held the pin up to her saffron silk caftan just over her heart and then she nodded once. "*Oui*. This is how I want to be remembered. The tigress of Belle Isle."

Amid the applause, she reached up and pulled him down by the lapel so that she could plant a kiss on his cheek. "You a very smart devil," she whispered in his ear. "But like sees into the heart of like. You gon' give me great-great-grandbébés real soon!" She patted his cheek before letting him go.

Michaela couldn't hear the exchange but she saw the flush that crept up Guy's cheeks as he straightened. The fact that he refused to meet her questioning gaze when he again stood beside her made her even more curious about what had been said.

"Now I got some gifts of my own to give." Tante Delphine looked around in the gathering gloom, frowning slightly. "Where is my little Leon?"

"Right here, Tante Delphine." Looking every inch the distinguished counselor in a navy blazer and pale gray slacks, Leon Bellegarde offered her an large manila envelope. "I believe this is what you're asking for, my dear."

Tante Delphine took it and nodded. "This is it." She looked up and waved her hand. "I need some room and some light."

The crowd around her receded like a wave from the shore. "Good. Now, where is my 'Tite?"

"Right here, Grand-mère." Michaela moved forward into the ring of light, reluctantly letting go of Guy's hand.

"You come sit here, at my feet," Tante Delphine directed, drawing Michaela down beside her chair. "Leon, stop the music. I got something to say everybody needs to hear."

Within minutes her audience had swelled to include nearly every person on the island as the news ran through the crowd that Tante Delphine was about to make a presentation. One of the band members thoughtfully provided a microphone for her.

"I know some of you haven't yet noticed but I am getting old." She paused to allow the expected chuckles and laughter to subside. "I am," she added in the backwash of amusement. "After one hundred years a person begins to think on her future."

"You mean the next hundred years?" someone in the dark called out.

"Something like this," she answered with a deep chuckle. "Only I ain't the Mississippi River. I don' expect to flow on forever in this old bag of bones. But it's not a sadness, this thought of mine. It's a gladness and a relief, I tell you true."

She reached out to stroke Michaela's hair. "It's been a good life, this one of mine. Good and hard and long and sometimes sad but most often I thank the *Bon Dieu* I live to see it all. Four fine sons, three beautiful daughters, thirty grandchildren and about forty-five great-grands, so far."

"Forty-six come Christmas," Fred shouted.

"Forty-six, you think? It's gon' be forty-seven!"

More laughter and hoots.

"Anyhow, I expecting some great-great-grands real soon. No! I don' say who or how."

She paused and sighed deeply, revealing the fatigue behind her happiness. "So, who gon' look after things when I'm gone? I ask myself this question every time the river floods, the roof leaks, or the poachers come around. Never before does the answer come. But this last time I ask the question I got the answer.''

''Who? Who? Who?'' chanted the crowd.

She held up a hand for silence. ''My family knows I love them all but I can't see Belle Isle divided, not by my hand. It comes down the centuries through one Bellegarde. It came to me from my grandfather. That's all that saves it. This time, it goes from my hand to Michaela's.''

''No!'' Michaela turned a horrified glance on her great-grandmother who was holding out the manila envelop to her. She shook her head wildly but Tante Delphine continued.

''In here is the deed signed by me this very day to make Michaela the sole owner of Belle Isle.'' She smiled down into Michaela's suddenly pale face and cupped her cheek in her bony hand. ''You love this place better than anyone but me, 'Tite. It is now for you to love for your own.''

Michaela looked away from her great-grandmother's smiling face and threw a pleading glance back over her shoulder to where Guy stood regarding her in silence. She couldn't read his expression. She wondered if she saw calculation in his gaze or was he, too, remembering what he'd said to her less than a week ago. If she continued to play her cards right, Belle Isle would one day belong to her, he'd predicted. But she hadn't played any cards or any game at all in hopes of inheriting Belle Isle. It had never occurred to her that she might own the island. She had expected her Uncle Leon, or even her father to inherit the land. Anyone but herself.

She rose to her feet, needing to get away, to find a moment to collect her thoughts. But she was inundated with good wishes. People rushed her, smiling and talking and patting her shoulders and arms. The noise level was rising and washing over her in an enormous wave of sound that made no sense to her benumbed mind.

"I tried to warn you!" Uncle Leon shouted by her ear. "Last week, at my office. But we were interrupted by a call. I was going to warn you then what Tante Delphine had in mind."

"What?" Michaela turned blindly toward him. "You knew?"

He smiled. "Of course I knew. I had already drawn up the papers. In fact, I thought you suspected as much, the way you kept asking if I was coming out here today."

"No, I never suspected," Michaela answered, wondering where Guy was, and why he didn't come and rescue her.

"It's a big responsibility. You come into the office in a few days and I'll go over it all with you. Of course, as a member of the firm, you'll receive professional courtesy services."

Michaela nodded and reeled away from him. But when she looked at the spot where Guy had been standing, he was gone.

Guy had backed out of the way of the flock of well-wishers. He suspected that even in the best of families, there was bound to be dissention. For Michaela's sake, he wanted to know how much and how bad.

He moved toward the place where the grumbling was loudest.

"I know she's been good to Tante Delphine," wailed a woman in her early thirties to the man who might be her husband. "But Michaela's had the time! She isn't married and she doesn't have a real job. It's been easy for her to shine in Tante Delphine's eyes while the rest of us are tied to the mainland with other responsibilities."

"Hush, Sarah. Someone's going to hear you."

"I don't care! It's not fair, her getting the property entirely for her own. I'm just as much a great-granddaughter as Michaela is!"

The man with her tried to put his arms about her. "We'll talk about it when we get home. Think on it some. There's

lots of blood kin may feel the way you do. Maybe there's
something can be done.''

''I'm not saying I want to take it away from her. It's just
not fair, that's all,'' the woman whined.

Guy heard the complaint without any compassion for the
complainer. In his experience, the world had never been fair.
Sometimes it just stepped on more of your dreams than at
others. But, no one was going to step on Michaela's dream,
not if he could prevent it.

Suddenly he cared very much about not catching a bullet
in the dark, not for his own selfish reasons but because Michaela needed him. She didn't know how to fight dirty and
he'd seldom fought any other way. In one short week he had
come to understand what Belle Isle represented to the two
women who lived here. Separated by nearly eight decades,
Michaela hadn't yet developed her great-grandmother's tigress instincts but he would be there to protect her until she
had. If she would let him.

He turned back in search of her but she was no longer
standing beside Tante Delphine. As his gaze ranged over the
darkening lawn, he realized that her golden silk gown had
disappeared from view. At first he wasn't worried, thinking that she had probably been dragged off by relatives who
had swallowed their disappointment enough to want to toast
her envious good luck. But after fifteen minutes of stopping and asking strangers about her, he began to have a very
uneasy feeling.

He entered the house with a quiet stride, straining for
sounds on the floor above. The music had begun again and
it was useless to try to determine if there was anyone on the
second floor. He began a detailed search of every room,
beginning on the first floor. He surprised two teenagers
necking in the pantry. He intercepted two less fluttered
adults coming out of the bathroom. The kitchen was filled
with women washing dishes and chatting. Men who had
drunk a lot of whiskey and beer sat on the back veranda

swapping lewd jokes. He nodded to Yancy and moved on, bumping shoulders with a man in a trench coat.

At last he headed up the rear stairs to the second floor. The fragrance of her perfume hung in the air at the top of the stairway. He smiled.

He should have guessed. Perhaps she was even waiting for him. He hoped she hadn't slipped out of that gold dress. He wanted very badly to peel her out of it a little at a time, stopping to kiss and lick every place he uncovered.

He heard it before he reached the doorway, the soft sounds of weeping. "Michaela?"

The room was dark with black shadows where the bed stood. Those black shadows were where the weeping came from. He reached automatically for the light switch that would have been just inside the doorway in any other house.

Muttering, he made his way across the void of darkness toward the bed. He found an oil lamp, used his lighter to ignite it, and turned it up. Even as the light wavered and filled the room Michaela stirred. She turned and lifted herself off the bed to launch herself into his arms. "Oh, Guy! Thank goodness!"

A moment later she was sobbing in his arms, crying so hard he didn't know how he would stand it if she didn't stop soon.

He stroked her hair with one hand while he held her tightly with the other. He felt so useless with nothing to give her but the comfort of his arms. "What's wrong? Did someone say something to you? Did someone hurt you, sweetheart?"

He was certain now she had been accosted by one of her jealous relatives. Damn jerks! He'd get even with every one of the greedy selfish bastards, exact revenge for every tear she shed.

He pulled her down with him onto the mattress, intending to kiss away her tears but she clung to him so tightly he couldn't even breathe easily. She seemed to be dissolving in his embrace, losing all sense of herself, and it shook him far more than he had expected.

Then, overriding his rationale, came an irrational resentment toward her. How could a grown woman be so defenseless? And over what? She had stood up to him not once but twice when he'd had her backed to the wall. She'd taken on his enemy when she didn't even know who or what she was fighting. She had helped him when he'd been incapable of helping himself. She had looked after him, worried about him, been his nurse and his guardian angel. And never once through all that had she looked like she'd wanted to shed a tear. Only that ridiculous hat in the attic had made her eyes well up in maudlin sentiment.

But this, this complete demoralization made no sense. Had she really been wounded by an ugly remark? Or was she only defenseless when it came to her family? Did she really believe they were all saints? The sound of her weeping was making him crazy. He wanted to black the eye of the world for making her cry.

"You can tell me, Michaela. You can tell me anything. I'll make them pay. I swear I will!"

Michaela looked up uncomprehendingly into his face, stunned by the anger burning in his eyes. He looked like a stranger, a hard livid stranger capable of snapping bones and pulverizing flesh. "What are you talking about?"

She stared up at him, her eyes a sea of dark tears and her lower lip quivering so badly Guy wanted to catch it in his teeth just to stop the provocation. "Your enemies. I'll help you hold Belle Isle, I swear it!" he whispered in fierce determination.

She shook her head. "No! I don't want Belle Isle."

Guy felt as if she had poured ice water of him. Then he hooted with laughter. "Of course you do. You love this old place. You hit the jackpot, sweetheart!"

"No," she said in a reasonable tone so at odds with her distress. "Loving something is not the same thing as wanting it for one's own. I'm not ready for such responsibility."

He made a gesture of denial. "It's just nerves talking. Sometimes a big win affects a gambler like that. Cold sweats. Some even toss their cookies. You're a winner!"

She twisted angrily away from him. "I can't think of it right now. I won't!"

He had made several sharp turns in logic in the past few seconds. Now she was asking him to make a few more. She didn't want Belle Isle. Even he knew that couldn't be right. It came to him in a flash, the look on her face when Tante Delphine had mentioned not going on forever like the river. Michaela had looked stricken.

He pulled her hard in against his body, trying to hug all the pain out of her and absorb it into himself. "Is it that you don't want Belle Isle," he whispered harshly into her ear, "or is it that you don't want to think about what your inheritance actually means?"

She lifted her head back, her eyes wide and startled. "What do you mean?"

He offered her his gentlest voice. "That Tante Delphine is very old, that she can't live much longer."

She leaned forward, laying her cheek on his. "You do understand!"

"I'm trying, Michaela," he said roughly. "I am trying."

"You're wonderful."

He choked.

She rubbed her cheek on his, enjoying the pull of his stubble against her softer skin. She kissed him just below the ear. "It's why I love you."

Guy closed his eyes and swallowed hard. He hadn't wanted her to say that again. No! Yes! He hadn't dared hope.

"Michaela," he began reluctantly but she reached up and covered his lips with her hand, her bracelets tinkling in his ears.

"Don't say anything, Guy. Just kiss me. Kiss me like you mean it."

That was the easiest thing he'd ever done.

Chapter 15

Michaela wasn't frightened anymore. Lying in the darkness in Guy's arms she felt safe and serene and completely satisfied with the world. The guests had long since departed. She hadn't bothered to bid them farewell. She knew they must be talking about her, gossiping more likely. But, after all, it wasn't strictly speaking her party. She wasn't the guest of honor.

The fact that she had spent the last few hours lying naked in the arms of her lover within the hearing of nearly every member of her family should have shocked her. The idea of it might still, when she gave it calm and reasonable thought.

She had been anything but calm and reasonable in Guy's arms. He had made love to her twice. The first time had been so hard and swift that she had never really caught up with him but had been swept along by his demanding need.

The second time she had soared and touched the stars. She had done swan dives of desire, arabesques of longing, somersaulted off cliffs of passion, delved into secret desires, and floated away on streams of pleasure. And all because of the man lying beside her. Even when he was pushing her beyond herself, demanding and seeking things she didn't know she was capable of, she had felt absolutely certain and safe with him. The trust he so desperately needed to believe in she gave to him freely.

He was sleeping now, his slumber so deep and complete he didn't even twitch when she bent and kissed his ear. She rested her chin a moment on his shoulder. He had earned his peace.

She would never forget how ferociously he had defended her. He'd been ready to take on her entire family in order to protect what he thought she wanted most in the world, Belle Isle. She would always love him for that. She knew how difficult a journey that had been for him, to come to the moment when he was thinking strictly in terms of the desires of someone else. He had recently ridiculed her ethics, had made her feel small and provincial and gauche for believing in selfless acts. But tonight he had proved that he was capable of making such gestures himself. He might be too chagrined to own up to it in the morning. Or may not be. Maybe tomorrow he would begin thinking about their future, together. Maybe he would accept her words of love.

She sat up and pushed the hair from her eyes. Her long mane flowed over her back and onto Guy's bare shoulder. He was exhausted, and not only from their lovemaking. She suspected he hadn't spent a completely relaxed night since he'd left Belle Isle. Now he was back and the tension had flowed out of him and out of her and with it the fear of closing his eyes.

Suddenly she was hungry. She hadn't realized before but she hadn't really eaten all day. She had been much too busy helping set things up and then keeping things replenished. Even when Guy served himself, she had been too full of love and happiness to think of eating. But now her stomach was making noises like a dishwasher. She was certain she would find a leftover slice of cake or pie, or even a wedge of watermelon in the kitchen.

She slipped out of bed and reached for Guy's dress shirt that lay on the floor by the bed. It covered the basic necessities and she didn't expect to meet anyone but Grand-mère in the house this time of night.

After all the laughter and music and murmurs of dozens of voices during the day, the house seemed inordinately quiet. There was only one lantern burning at the foot of the stairway. She turned and looked down the hall but there was no light under her great-grandmother's door. It had been an exhausting day for all. Only she was too wired to sleep just yet.

She didn't bother to carry the light with her. She knew this old house—her old house!—like the back of her hand. She owned Belle Isle. There were signed papers somewhere that attested to her ownership. Her home. Her house.

She tested the thoughts and found her mind shying away from them. Belle Isle belonged to Grand-mère, had done so for eighty years. Until that much beloved lady left this earth, Belle Isle would belong to her. But Michaela didn't mind thinking of herself as a caretaker. The responsibility didn't frighten her. The bills might, especially if she didn't start drawing a paycheck soon. Then she remembered Guy's gift. One hundred-thousand dollars, if invested prudently, could mean she should never have a financial crisis again.

The kitchen was still warm from the oven's day-long use. The trapped smells of sweet and spicy vied for dominance as she reached for the lantern that hung by the door. To her surprise, the hook was empty.

"Strange," she murmured to herself. One of their guests must have moved it and forgotten to put it back. She padded in bare feet across the stone floor.

The figure that detached itself from the rear door was nothing like the nightmare phantoms that had stalked her dreams as a child. Reality never was like a dream. That was the first thing she thought. The second was that she knew who it was even before the light from the hallway behind her struck the metal in his hand.

Michaela was glad she didn't scream this time. It would have awakened Grand-mère and she didn't want her dragged into this. She heard a click and light flooded into the room from a high-beam flashlight.

"Ms. Bellegarde."

The raspy voice made the hair on her arms lift. "Mr. Pike," she replied.

"That's right." He sounded pleased she guessed his identity. "Where the hell are the lights?"

Michaela could no longer see even his silhouette. He was just a disembodied voice behind a blue-white blade of light.

She thought about running but he had every advantage. She didn't want to die, not after tonight. "If you'll give me a moment I'll light the chandelier over the table."

She moved slowly, not wanting to the give him any reason to lose his nerve and begin firing. But it was hard. She broke two wooden matches before she struck a light from the third. The wick didn't want to catch. One of the three kerosene lamps was out of oil. But gradually the room filled with light. Only then she did look down.

She saw a balding man in a trench coat standing on the other side of the table pointing a gun at her. She knew nothing about weapons but she knew what it was. A 9 mm semiautomatic, this was the weapon that had wounded Guy.

She saw him staring at her and realized he was looking at her bare legs. She dropped her arms to lower the hem of Guy's shirt. "What do you want?"

The man looked up at her and she saw he had a thin narrow face with a two-day stubble and eyes that were either bloodshot from lack of sleep or too much alcohol. She hoped it was sleep deprivation. She noted with a start that she had seen him before, that he had been on Belle Isle all afternoon. Andrea had commented about him. He might have shot Guy any time. If he had seen him.

"Where is Matherson?"

She decided not to deny that he had been here but she wouldn't confirm that he was still here. "He left hours ago."

The man stared at her shirt, Guy's shirt, then mouthed a curse. "Thought I might have missed him." His hand flexed on the butt. "So I've come back for you."

Michaela hoped she didn't look as frightened as his words made her feel. "Me?"

He smirked. "You're the woman whose bed Matherson's keeping warm. If he hears you're missing, it might encourage him to come out of hiding."

Michaela tried her best to stay in control, to think like an attorney interviewing a prospective client. "So you can shoot him?"

"Yeah." The smile that spread across Pike's face turned him from an ordinary nondescript stranger into a cold-blooded killer. "So I can kill him."

Michaela looked down at her hands clenched over the back of a wooden chair and wondered how she was supposed to warn Guy, how she was supposed to protect her great-grandmother, and still survive the next few minutes. "I don't suppose it's going to do any good to point out the fact that the police suspect you're the one who shot Mr. Matherson the first time."

No reply.

She looked up again, realizing she was more frightened when she couldn't see his face and read his expression. "If Matherson should die, you'll be the first one they look for. In fact, they're already looking for you."

He eyed her with a lopsided grin. "You think I don't know that? You think it makes a difference?"

"Why doesn't it?" she asked in frank curiosity. He was talking. That was something. "You're out of jail. You're free to go on with your life."

"What life?"

Suddenly Michaela knew why she had been so uneasy hours earlier. Grand-mère was right, some people projected anger, hatred and pain. She could feel Pike's rage like radiant heat from a stove. Bad vibes, was the modern phrase. Pike gave off very bad vibes.

She thought she heard the creak of a stair and stumbled into speech to cover the sound. "You—ah, can begin again. Build another life."

"With what?" Pike was sweating now. The trench coat was too warm for the balmy night. Nerves were doing the rest. Maybe that was good, Michaela thought without daring to hope. Or, maybe it was going to make things worse.

"Matherson took my life, took my money, took my chance to be somebody!" His voice went up sharply on the last word. Would Guy or Grand-mère hear him? Sneak away and find help? "What's the life of an ex-con worth? I'll tell you. It ain't worth spit!"

She didn't make the mistake of contradicting him. She hadn't had much experience with stressed-out desperate criminals but she knew better than to push. "So you just want revenge," she said quietly.

"That, and maybe the money. My share."

Michaela's hope meter soared. "You think Mr. Matherson is going to go to the bank for you before you shoot him?"

His expression turned ugly. "You talk too much."

"So I've been told." She looked away, not wanting him to see the panic in her eyes. He wasn't the only one sweating now. "But I'm an attorney, Mr. Pike. It's my job to talk reasonably to criminals."

He laughed. "So Guy's doing a lawyer! That's good. Maybe I'll ransom you to him. My money for your sweet ass."

Michaela looked up at him again, this time to steady her nerves. She saw the look in his eyes gradually change from little interest to pointed interest. She was part of Guy. He hated Guy. It didn't take any great leap of imagination to guess where his thoughts were heading. B movies and plot-by-number books aside, she had just become more vulnerable than before.

She moved quietly across the room and reached for the raincoat she kept on a peg by the kitchen door.

"Hey! What are you doing?"

She calmly put the coat on. "I'm saving myself a few dozen insect bites." She glanced back at him. "I presume we're going into the swamp to hide."

He looked disconcerted. "Hell, no! We're going back to the shore."

She just stared at him. "How you do propose to get across the river at this time of night?"

"Ferry," he said, clearly annoyed.

"Yancy will have gone to bed by now. He was drinking pretty heavily about dark. Nothing short of a direct hit by a lightning bolt will wake him before dawn."

She heard him hiss a vulgarity. "Then looks like we got time for a few other things." He came toward her, a slick smile on his narrow mouth. "I haven't seen a woman like you in four years." He waved his gun at her coat. "Want to show me what kind of woman my money is buying Guy these days?"

"No, she doesn't."

Michaela and Pike whipped around at the same time. Guy stood in the hall doorway in his trousers. His feet and chest were bare and his hands were empty.

"Matherson!" Pike's gun came up and Michaela wondered for one irrational second why Guy didn't have a gun. But this wasn't the wild west. He shouldn't have the need, or the temptation.

"Let her go, Pike." Guy's voice was flat, almost business-like. "You've got what you came for. I'm here."

Michaela groaned in frustration. Why hadn't he stayed back, kept out of the way until he'd found the moment to get the better of Pike? But she saw by his expression that he had heard everything, knew everything. He hadn't waited because he didn't want Pike to touch her. That realization made her irrationally giddy, then more angry than she'd ever been in her life. She would have let Pike cop a feel or possibly more if it had meant it would have given Guy the advantage.

Pike was grinning as he turned away from Michaela and aimed his gun at Guy. "I didn't think you'd make it this easy."

Guy didn't move. "I thought you wanted the money."

Pike hesitated. "You think I believe you'd get it?"

"If you shoot me, you'll never get it."

Michaela saw Pike's face twitch. "You set me up, you son of a bitch!"

"You set yourself up," Guy said in cold castigation. "You were cheating me. I don't like being cheated."

"You were getting plenty."

"You could have gotten us killed."

Michaela saw a drop of sweat drip off Pike's chin and make a dark circle on the front of his khaki-colored coat. "Why aren't you dead? What did you do? Who did you rat on in order to stay alive?"

Guy shrugged, never looking once at Michaela who stood to one side between the two men. "Some of the same people you did."

Pike snorted. "Then why did you walk while I had four years rotting in prison to think about pulling this trigger and blowing you away?" His eyes narrowed. "Nothing else is going to satisfy me."

It was at that moment that Michaela knew Pike was mad, or at least beyond reasoning with. He had been talking to her just to pass the time. But he'd had only one purpose in mind since he had walked out of that prison. He had gone to a crowded house to take his first shot. Had dared enter a fully staffed hospital on his second attempt. She believed him when he said he wanted Guy dead and nothing less was going to satisfy him.

She heard the faint sound of a gun safety being released. "Be a man, Matherson," Pike said impatiently. "Give me a clear shot and I'll make it easy. One bullet to the brain. You won't hardly feel a thing."

"Right." Guy's voice remained calm, void of any feeling as he moved from the doorway into the kitchen. "Move back, Michaela."

Suicide! Guy was going to commit the next thing to suicide.

"No! Don't!" Michaela stepped between Pike and Guy.

She saw the look of surprise on Pike's face, heard Guy's shout of warning, and then the room exploded with the sound of gunfire. She felt herself being thrust forward by the force of Guy's body as he tackled her. Even as she hit the stone floor with an impact that knocked the breath out of her, she saw Pike, unaccountably, sprawled out before her.

The air went out of her in a hard push. She gasped and gasped again, tears trickling from her eyes as she fought to get oxygen back into her lungs. She heard voices, opened her eyes, tried to speak but didn't have the breath. But she could see.

Standing in the doorway that led to the kitchen garden was Tante Delphine, the barrel of her ancient shotgun smoking.

"Been killing vermin all my life," she said with an odd catch in her voice. "You think I let some snake murder the father of my great-great-grandbébés?"

"What did you use?" Sheriff Proctor asked as he watched the paramedics swab the oozing wounds that had once been Jackson Pike's right profile and shoulder.

"Salt shot," Tante Delphine replied in a tight voice. "It makes powerful mess and stings like hellfire. But it don' kill him."

"Perhaps not," the sheriff remarked with a reflexive twinge of sympathy for the whimpering bloody mess that was her victim. "He gonna live?"

One of the paramedics looked up and nodded. "It's mostly superficial."

"Ain't nothing superficial about the mess it's made of his face," Yancy offered with a snicker.

Yancy, it seemed, hadn't gone to bed after all. He had sneaked back onto the island after his last haul to 'borrow' the half-full beer keg he had made certain had been left behind. The sound of gunfire had brought him out of hiding. The results had sent him to the mainland for the sheriff.

"Hoowee!" he continued in appreciation. "Tante Delphine sure can handle the business end of a shotgun!"

The sheriff turned back to the shooter with an expression of admiration and exasperation. "I'd be most pleased if you'd put that shotgun away for good now, Tante Delphine. You could have killed yourself."

Tante Delphine looked up from the protective embrace of her great-granddaughter's arms, looking for the first time like what she was: a tiny, frail, elderly woman. "I'm gon' be some sore in the shoulder," she said wearily.

"Grand-mère?" Michaela questioned in suspicion. "You're hurt, aren't you?"

Tante Delphine started to shrug but grimaced instead. "I think maybe the gun's kick done dislocated my shoulder."

That was all that was required to transfer one of the paramedics' attention from Pike to the woman who'd brought him down.

While they took care of the two patients, Sheriff Proctor turned his attention to Guy Matherson. He stood apart from the others, dressed in a suit with his hands in his trouser pockets. His expression was blank but his eyes were the most alive of any man's he'd ever encountered. Right now that bright blue gaze was watching Michaela as if he expected her to hatch, or fall apart.

Sheriff Proctor approached him. Matherson had been strangely quiet since his initial explanation of events when he and the paramedics first arrived. This was the man the entire state of Louisiana had been searching for for more than a week. The fact that he was on Belle Isle and with Michaela Bellegarde was going to make an interesting story, he had no doubt.

"This was a hell of a way to introduce yourself around here, son."

Guy lifted his head with a jerk, as if he were coming out of deep reverie. "I'm sorry for the trouble, Sheriff. I had hoped to avoid..." he shrugged "...this."

"You know you're going to have to come with me, make a statement. There's a whole lot of folks wanting to ask you questions."

Guy nodded. "At your convenience."

Sheriff Proctor frowned. The man sounded so polite, so calm for someone who had nearly lost his life. Maybe too calm. He glanced from Matherson to Michaela who was kneeling beside the stretcher on which the paramedics had placed Tante Delphine. Yup! There was definitely a story there.

Fifteen minutes later the ambulance was carrying two passengers toward the dock and the waiting ferry.

Because there was no room for passengers in the ambulance, Sheriff Proctor offered Michaela a ride to the hospital before he took Guy in to the Baton Rouge police department.

Michaela sat beside Guy on the back seat of the sheriff's car. He hadn't said more than five words to her since the shooting but now he held on to her hand so tightly she wondered if he thought she might disappear.

She stared at his profile but the elegantly chiseled features offered her no clue to his thoughts or feelings. It was a poker face, Guy Matherson's professional face.

"Guy," she said softly as the sheriff's car sped through the deep night. "Are you angry with me?"

"Yes!"

The hiss of sound expressed enough feelings to squeeze her heart. She leaned her head against his shoulder and closed her eyes. "Because I tried to stop you from offering yourself up as a martyr?"

"Because you could have been killed. Because it would have been my fault. Because I can't stop—!" She felt him tremble as the emotion in his voice defeated the iron grip he'd had on himself.

He turned toward her on the seat but his back was pressed up against the door as if he were ready to bolt. "What is it with you people!" He sounded like a man lost in the dark. "You hardly know me! You owe me nothing. I'm not worth what you were prepared to offer. Good God! Your great-grandmother shot a man for me! Are you all crazy?"

She nodded, choking on happiness and leftover fear and, most of all, the reassurance that he cared enough to realize exactly the kind of sacrifices that had been made and were ready to be made for his sake in the name of love. "We love you."

"Oh, God!"

His shoulders curved forward and he doubled over as if he'd taken a punch in the gut. She reached up and brushed a curl off his forehead. He flinched as she stroked his cheek and she felt the dampness of tears. But she wasn't going to let him get away this time. "I love you, Guy. It's a gift. Take it with you, no strings attached."

Guy's hand shot out to hold her hand to his face. He didn't know how to say what was in his too full heart. He'd never had to put into words these feelings he had never before felt. He felt lost, confused, frightened by things he . . . could . . . not . . . explain. *Like a tiger in the rain.*

Laughter burst from him, all the more explosive for its unexpectedness. He was in love!

That's what Tante Delphine had meant by her story. With her generous heart and wisdom, she accepted him as a part of her family long before he understood how much he wanted that. Twice she saved his life. She knew better than he how things would turn out.

"I love you." The words popped out at the back of his subsiding laughter.

Michaela strained forward. "What? What did you say?"

Guy took her face in his hands. He wished it was light so that he could see her expression but it didn't really matter. He'd have tomorrow and the day after and the day after that to see her face as he told her and showed her how he felt about her.

He brushed his thumbs cross the fullness of her lips. "I love you, Michaela Bellegarde."

He hadn't known, even after all they had shared, that a kiss could taste so good, that it could make him feel that all his life the real world had been hidden behind a cloud and now it was blazing full on his face—because of Michaela.

An hour later as she lay curled against him on the hard uncomfortable seat of the squad car while they rolled through the streets of Baton Rouge, Michaela suddenly remembered where she was headed.

"I know Tante Delphine can't live forever," she said softly, her hand tucked inside Guy's shirt front. "I think she has only one regret, that she may not live to see her first great-great-grandchild."

"Oh, I wouldn't underestimate her," Guy replied. "I think she takes care of things in her own unique way." He reached into the breast pocket of his jacket and produced a note.

"What is it?" Michaela asked.

"I don't know exactly. Tante Delphine slipped it into my hand before they put her into the ambulance. Looks like she's been carrying it around awhile."

"Let me see." Michaela sat up and unfolded the paper then held it up so that the street lights could shine on it. She gasped in astonishment and then laughed.

"What it is?"

She looked at Guy with tears above her smile. "It's a list of quote, 'good names for great-great-grandchildren.' There's an astrological explanation for each."

Guy felt as if he'd been touched by the sun. "Is that all?"

Michaela offered him her heart. "I think it's enough. There are twelve names on the list!"

Over the course of twenty-some-odd years as a law enforcement officer in East Baton Rouge Parish, Sheriff Proctor had witnessed many unexpected sights through his rearview mirror. Still, he'd never thought he'd see Michaela Bellegarde necking for all she was worth with one of his detainees.

* * * * *

COMING NEXT MONTH

#667 HER SECRET, HIS CHILD—Paula Detmer Riggs
Intimate Moments Extra

For sixteen years Carly Alderson had lived with a secret, embodied by her daughter. Yet Carly had never dreamed the past would catch up with her, or that Mitch Scanlon would remember.... He'd changed her life one long-ago night—and now held her very future in his hands.

#668 HIDING JESSICA—Alicia Scott
Romantic Traditions/The Guiness Gang

Mitch Guiness knew how to re-create a person from head to toe, but Jessica Gavornee was one tough lady to change. A federally protected witness, she refused to trust Mitch with her innermost fears—and secrets—allowing him access that went only skin-deep. But Mitch found himself wanting much more....

#669 UNDERCOVER MAN—Merline Lovelace
Code Name: Danger

Sweet, demure Paige Lawrence's engagement had gone bust. Though David Jensen still owned her heart, she sensed that he had other things on his mind. Then she learned the truth behind his lies—and found herself risking everything for her undercover lover.

#670 DEFENDING HIS OWN—Beverly Barton
The Protectors

He was the best. Deborah Vaughn knew there were worse things than being guarded by Ashe McLaughlin. Getting killed, to name just one. But she couldn't shake her response to his remembered touch—or the fear that he would discover their child born of deception....

#671 OUR CHILD?—Sally Tyler Hayes

Ten years ago her sister's kidnapping had wrenched Carolyn McKay and Drew Delaney apart. Now Drew had returned, a missing-children expert intent on breaking that case and a new one with frightening similarities. But Carolyn wondered if Drew could handle reopening the past...and finding the child he never knew he had.

#672 ONE FORGOTTEN NIGHT—Suzanne Sanders
Premiere

Detective Mike Novalis had sworn never to compromise himself again. He'd been burned once by a beautiful prime suspect, and he feared Nina Dennison was no different. But Nina remembered nothing of her past—let alone whether she was guilty or innocent. And the only man she trusted was the one she should have feared most.

Take 4 bestselling love stories FREE

Plus get a FREE surprise gift!

Special Limited-time Offer

Mail to Silhouette Reader Service™

3010 Walden Avenue
P.O. Box 1867
Buffalo, N.Y. 14269-1867

YES! Please send me 4 free Silhouette Intimate Moments® novels and my free surprise gift. Then send me 6 brand-new novels every month, which I will receive months before they appear in bookstores. Bill me at the low price of $2.89 each plus 25¢ delivery and applicable sales tax, if any.* That's the complete price and a savings of over 10% off the cover prices—quite a bargain! I understand that accepting the books and gift places me under no obligation ever to buy any books. I can always return a shipment and cancel at any time. Even if I never buy another book from Silhouette, the 4 free books and the surprise gift are mine to keep forever.

245 BPA ANRR

Name	(PLEASE PRINT)	
Address	Apt. No.	
City	State	Zip

This offer is limited to one order per household and not valid to present Silhouette Intimate Moments® subscribers. *Terms and prices are subject to change without notice. Sales tax applicable in N.Y.

UMOM-295   ©1990 Harlequin Enterprises Limited

It's our 1000th Special Edition and we're celebrating!

Join us these coming months for some wonderful stories in a special celebration of our 1000th book with some of your favorite authors!

Diana Palmer **Nora Roberts**
Debbie Macomber **Christine Flynn**
Phyllis Halldorson **Lisa Jackson**

mini-series by:

Lindsay McKenna, Marie Ferrarella, Sherryl Woods, Gina Ferris Wilkins.

And many more books by special writers.

And as a special bonus, all Silhouette Special Edition titles published during Celebration 1000! Will have **double** Pages & Privileges proofs of purchase!

Silhouette Special Edition...heartwarming stories packed with emotion, just for you! You'll fall in love with our next 1000 special stories!

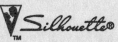